Portal to Murder

Alison Lingwood

For John with love and thanks

Portal to Murder

Anger lent him strength, power to do what had to be done. He was concerned that the remote car park, often a trysting place for lovers by dark, would be occupied, but in the shroud of the early hours he found it deserted as he cruised in using just side-lights. Quietly he closed the car door and opening the boot, unloaded its contents. Wheelbarrow first, then the spade. Finally the resisting bulk that was the body.

He knew nothing of the onset and progress of rigor mortis but it seemed to him that she was slightly stiffer, more rigid somehow. He had anticipated folding her into the barrow, a supplicant rag doll as she had been earlier, but now her arms stuck out and her head overhung at a strange angle, rhythmically banging against the wheel as he slowly heaved the burden across the car park. Even in the pre-dawn February cold, the effort of manoeuvring the barrow over the low stile posts made him sweat. He knew that it was necessary to work quickly, the sun would rise in just a few hours and there was much to do.

It was difficult to negotiate the path in the darkness, but looking over to his right he could just make out a faint glow from buildings in the distance and segments of lights from the motorway snaking between the hills.

After a quarter of a mile he came across the large gorse bush, then the finger post he was looking for and he turned right down the hill. He plodded down the woodland path with his bundle before plunging into the trees on the left. Pushing the barrow became more difficult over the ridged ground but he was close now. This place was well known from his childhood and his memory had not played him false.

Trees had grown, some had fallen, but the chosen place was easy enough to find. Already the sky was lightening and fingers of brightness began to peep over the Woodpecker Woods, but it was very near now, the darkest hollow beyond the brambles. Stopping to wipe the sweat from his forehead he remembered his grandfather telling him about the planting of this wood after the pit closed in the thirties. The rows of saplings had been planted on ridges of soil to stop their roots standing in sodden clay in the winter. The whole area was criss-crossed with drainage ditches and it was to the largest of these, deep in the woods that he pushed the barrow. This ditch was deeper than the others, formed to take water from a culvert beneath the bridle path. Ideal.

Reaching his destination he used the spade to clear some undergrowth and leaf mould from the ditch, rolling the body into the shallow grave. He pulled closed the pink coat but left it unfastened. Having part-covered her with the spoil from his digging he leaned on the spade and took the handful of jewellery from his pocket. He looked thoughtfully at the few pieces and debated whether to throw them in with the body, wanting only to be rid of all connection with this debacle.

A slow smile spread across his face as on reflection he carefully replaced them, patting the pocket as if to keep them safe. The placing of the jewellery would have been a nice conceit but he thought better of it; an idea had come to him.

He looked down on his handiwork and saw that it was good. Loading the spade into the barrow he retraced his steps, noting thankfully that the dry ground showed no signs of his passing.

But the anger remained.

Chapter 1

'Hello. How are you?' Susannah entered the kitchen with a laden laundry basket as Angela unfastened her coat and changed outdoor shoes for a pair of slippers.

'What have you been doing this weekend?' She caught the slight aroma of body odour as Angela walked past her, and wrinkled her nose.

'Not a great deal actually,' said Angela wondering how much to share. She took the laundry from the dryer and started to fold it. 'Did I tell you that I'd signed up to that website you told me about – *findyourmates.com*, to see if anyone got in touch.' She well knew that although this was old news she had not yet mentioned it to her employer.

'And did they?' Susannah looked anxious. Perhaps no one would care enough about Angela to bother. Certainly she was not the sort of person to attract attention. Maybe no-one would even remember her.

'Actually yes and no,' said Angela, pausing for effect. She waited till she had Susannah's full attention before continuing. 'Funnily enough no-one from the secondary school, but a boy who was in my class in primary school. He uploaded some photos of our class at various ages but I could hardly recall any of the faces, never mind link them to a name. He remembered me well enough though. So we've had a bit of a chat back and forth remembering the other kids and the teachers – wondering what happened to them all, and of course the rocking horse.'

'The rocking horse!' Susannah exclaimed, pausing as she put clothes in the washing machine, 'What kind of school did you go to?'

Angela laughed. 'Actually it sounds bizarre I know. It was in the corridor outside the head's office. I think it had been donated by some long-ago local bigwig or something, one of those big wooden horses suspended on a frame. Anyway, when it was your birthday you could spend one playtime on it, with a friend on each end, mainly for ballast I think now. It was amazing how many new best friends you had in the run-up to your birthday.'

Susannah laughed too.

'Health and Safety people would have a field day now: it's a wonder you didn't all lose your fingers.' Putting powder in the machine and slamming the door she said on impulse,

'Look, I'm having some friends in on Saturday week, Giles will be away in Dubai, for the racing you know, and I'm taking the opportunity of repaying some social invitations that won't interest him. I don't suppose you could come in and serve nibbles, help clear up and so on. I'd pay you extra?' Aware that this sounded crass she hurried on, 'If you're not doing anything that is.'

Angela's pause was a fraction too long.

'Oh I would have done of course,' she said, 'but funnily enough I shall be away that weekend.'

Thinking of the tale she had told Kevin on the internet the previous evening, and aware that Susannah would never believe the coincidence that she was off to Dubai, she modified the fiction accordingly.

'Actually I'm going to a family wedding in

York on the Saturday. I've never been there before, but this invitation came out of the blue so I'm grabbing the opportunity. I'm going on the Friday afternoon, then the wedding is on Saturday with the reception at the racecourse. Funnily enough they are big into horseracing too, I haven't had much to do with them.' Her voice tailed away as she lowered her eyes and took towels out of the laundry basket.

'Of course,' she went on a little too hurriedly, 'I shall be home on the Sunday, so I'll be here as usual the following week.' She was not willing to risk losing out on any income this close to Christmas, nor on the present that Susannah had bought her, and which she had already found in the bottom of one of the wardrobes.

Susannah finished stowing laundry and watching Angela carefully, she put on her smart jacket and checked her appearance in the mirror. She noticed that Angela had turned an unbecoming pink, and she changed the subject to chores she wanted her cleaner to carry out that morning whilst she was out.

The conversation petered out as Angela finished folding the laundry, Susannah looked at her watch and exclaimed at the time then, after promising to hear all about the York trip after the event, she grabbed her bag and left to go shopping in Nantwich, tottering down the drive to the car in stiletto heels five inches high.

She was glad to get away from Angela, whom she found particularly hard to chat to when she was obviously lying, and today she was positively furtive. Susannah felt little sympathy for her. She may not have any money to speak of, but really! There was no need to dress like a bag lady, and she could do with a good wash and a haircut, and going out with no make-up – the limit. Susannah would not have kept her on, only she was a very proficient cleaner.

She was not at all sure she believed in the York trip, wondering vaguely what relation of Angela's could possibly have connections with the racing world. Really, she convinced herself, glancing at her reflection in her car window as she approached, their worlds had very little in common. With a rare flash of insight Susannah wondered if their chats were sometimes as much of a chore for Angela as they were for her.

*   *   *

Susannah knew herself to be a hedonist, finding it difficult to pass a mirror without checking her appearance, or a clothes store without going in. She was an avid reader of the Sunday supplements and bought for herself and Giles the latest designer clothes that she found promoted there. She told herself that she and Giles worked hard for their money, they had earned the luxury it afforded them.

Up at seven each morning she reached the gym before half past and completed a vigorous workout, swim and shower before most people she knew started their day. Not old enough to remember the song, she would nevertheless laughingly describe herself a 'dedicated follower of fashion', and often jokingly asked Giles to save her from herself. She would have been horrified if he had tried.

Angela watched her out of sight before continuing her work. As she washed down the kitchen floor she reflected that she and Susannah had an unlikely and precarious relationship. She was aware that to her employer and her coterie of smart friends, her own life would seem empty and sad; no husband or children, not even a pet for company, only the style of life to be afforded on a cleaner's wage if she avoided extravagant socialising.

Sighing to herself she filled the bucket, looking at herself in the mirror over the sink. She knew hers was an unprepossessing face. Her dark hair could not be described as auburn and lay in thin, lifeless waves about her ears. Her features lacked shape and definition. As an adolescent, when such things mattered, she had overheard a conversation that had remained with her. Being dressed as a bridesmaid in her early teens, the edge had been taken off the enjoyment of the occasion when she heard the dressmaker in the next room laughing with her mother.

'I saw a cartoon yesterday and a cat was hit in the face with a frying pan. Your poor Angela looks a bit like that.' Instead of defending her, Angela's mother had joined in the derision, for which she had never been forgiven. Later that day, taking advantage of the triptych mirror on her mother's dressing table, Angela saw that it was true. One of the first things she did after her mother died was to destroy that mirror, but the image had remained with her and she knew that that face look back at her still.

Over the years it had acquired no more definition: she was small and slim, but had disproportionately well-developed shoulders and upper arms from her physical work; her limbs had become stringier and her throat wrinkled with lines. There were now perpetual shadows beneath her eyes.

Her complexion was ruddy with fine red lines from cycling unprotected in all weathers.

Recently she had developed a problem in her left eye so that she always frowned and turned her head slightly in conversation, the better to focus on whoever she was talking to. She was unaware that this gave her a vague and uninterested look that people found off-putting.

She glanced at herself in the mirror one more time before turning away, and smiled at the thought of the secret life she had made for herself, unknown to Susannah; unknown to anyone except Kevin.

*   *   *

Angela had been impressed by Kevin getting in touch. She was surprised herself at how keenly she looked forward to his messages. He had told her that he was married with a grown up son and daughter. He spoke about his wife and daughter a lot, less so about his son, and the only photos he posted initially were the old school ones. Angela hadn't been able to reciprocate. She wondered what it said about her relationship with her own parents that she was unable to find a single school-age photo of herself that they had thought worth keeping.

The correspondence had been going on for several weeks. Angela could barely remember Kevin from primary school, and without the photo would not have been sure of matching the correct face to the name. She had been disappointed when her own submission to *findyourmates.com* had yielded no replies, but undaunted, she had replied to Kevin's message and he had promptly responded. Now they wrote regularly and she had come to depend upon their shared reminiscences, eagerly checking her computer each evening, hoping for the next instalment.

* * *

But now she was running out of things to tell him. Six weeks into the correspondence her memories of primary school had been exhausted. Opening a message the previous week she had been alarmed to find a change of subject mirroring her own thoughts. Kevin had written that he was unable to remember anything else about school so he was going to bring her more up to date. He told her about his job as an accountant, twenty-eight years with the same Canadian company in Thunder Bay. He told her that his wife had died, and he loved to spend time with his grandchildren. There were even rather fuzzy photos of two golden haired boys on swings. He told her he spent most of the school holidays with his daughter and the boys.

Angela had left it for four days before she replied. She had some thinking to do. Looking back at all the emails she had sent, Angela couldn't think of a single interesting thing to tell. She found herself feeling desperately sad. Her whole life could be told in five minutes and would be of no interest to this well-travelled, educated man. This would be the end of the friendship, she would send no more emails and receive none.

Waking on the fourth day she realised that she could create for herself a new life. She would never meet Kevin again anyway, he was thousands of miles away in Canada, so she could say what she liked.

Bit by bit she created a persona she felt worthy of sharing.

This was Angela's first mistake.

Chapter 2

As soon as she turned the car in front of Miner's Cottage Maxine saw something of the damage. The small window down the side path to the garage had been boarded up, she could see a glazier's details stencilled on the hardboard panel, and as she got out of the car her neighbour Anne was hurrying up the path to meet her.

'Oh Maxine,' she said, 'How awful for you to come back to find this. It happened last night; I didn't know what to do.' Maxine stood stunned for a moment in the roadway surrounded by her bags.

'Do you want to come and have a drink in mine or do you want to see it straightaway?' Anne entreated.

'I think I'd better see it,' said Maxine. 'Have the police been?'

'Oh yes, about half an hour after I rang them. Such a mess they made,' Anne's Welsh accent strengthened with the emotion. 'Everything is all covered in fingerprint powder and they wouldn't let me clear up properly. They said you had to see it so you could be sure what had been taken. I've just put drawers back in and such, but it'll be a shock, cariad. It's such a mess, and we never heard a thing.'

Carefully Maxine opened the front door. Glass had been swept up into a couple of black bin bags in the corner of the hall, and the window frames and furniture surfaces were covered with the remnants of aluminium fingerprint powder.

'They said I mustn't throw anything away. I

said surely I could dispose of the broken glass, but they gave me such a look.'

'Anne you are the best friend ever. This must have been so hard for you. I'm sure you've done everything you could to make it easier for me. Have you any milk? I could do with a cup of tea.'

Maxine hoped that Anne would go home for milk. She just wanted to sit down on her own and cry. But Anne had stashed milk in the fridge and she led the way into the kitchen. Maxine had only ever seen such a sight on television dramas. There were even pictures hanging skewed on the walls, which made her want to laugh; as if she would have anything hidden behind pictures. Would anyone?

Still clutching her bag and case she moved through to the tiny living room. In here the carnage was worse. There were more bin bags piled in the corner: two, no three of them that would have to be sorted through. There was a blank space on the wall where her favourite painting had hung. A limited edition print by William Russell Flint that had special sentimental value, as well as being the nearest she had to a genuine work of art. Maxine suddenly slumped on to the sofa, feeling drained. She had been looking forward to a restful holiday with Pippa and now all this had to be faced.

She looked up as Anne followed her into the room, and gratefully took the proffered cup of tea.

'What's the bedroom like?' she asked. Anne raised her eyebrows in reply.

'Come and stay at mine tonight cariad' she offered, 'You won't be able to sleep here.'

'I doubt I'll sleep anywhere,' said Maxine putting her head into her hands. 'What a bloody awful start to the holiday.' Maxine considered for a moment talking to Anne about Pippa and Clyde but managed to focus on the matter in hand, pushing thoughts of an unhappy Pippa and her partner to one side. Sipping tea she asked, 'When did you say it happened?'

'We don't know exactly. As I said, we heard nothing. I came yesterday afternoon to push the Sentinel through. Everything was fine then. I came in this morning at about eleven to see if there was any post on show, and I found all this. It's as if someone was waiting till you had gone away. I rang the police straight away. They thought someone must have known.'

'What a horrible thought, someone waiting, perhaps watching.' 'Oh sorry Anne, I can't drink this.' Putting down the cup Maxine stood up. 'I need to see upstairs.'

Anne followed her up. Maxine's own bedroom had been turned over in the same way as the living room. Pippa's room seemed untouched, perhaps because there was so little in it.

'I just closed the wardrobe and the drawers in here,' Anne said, 'Nothing seemed to have been messed with, certainly not things tipped all over like in your room.'

Maxine went straight to the desk. Her papers seemed to be undisturbed. The children's books she was in the process of translating seemed not to have been touched.

'Thank goodness all the work I've done on these was in my laptop,' she sighed, 'There wasn't really anything else in here,' she wandered to the window. 'Only spare bedding and stuff.'

She smiled sadly to herself. All the treasures that Pippa had accumulated over the years had gone now. Much of her childhood possessions had been ruthlessly culled because of the lack of the room in her flat, and Maxine had felt the amputation keenly.

Having surveyed the extent of the upstairs damage they returned to the living room and the now-cold tea. Maxine sipped and grimaced. 'This is going down the sink,' she said, and came back into the living room with two glasses and a bottle of Chardonnay. Pouring wine she flopped again into the sofa and smiled weakly.

'Good job the sun goes over the yardarm so early in the winter.' Anne's thoughts were following a different tack.

'I suppose,' she said, always one to look for a silver lining, 'It's something to be thankful for that they didn't spread muck everywhere. When my aunt was burgled ...' she began, then on seeing the distraught look on Maxine's face, she stopped.

'Come on, let's see what impression we can make on this mess. You'll feel better once we've made a start.' They worked on for an hour setting the place to rights. Suddenly Maxine sat back on her heels.

'Shit, the safe.'

'I didn't know you had a safe?' Anne poured the last of the wine into their two glasses.

'Yes, upstairs,' said Maxine, fumbling through her keys and heading for the stairs. As soon as she pulled Pippa's bedside table away from the wall she knew. The safe was not sophisticated, just a cavity in the wall shielded by an imitation electrical socket. Close examination of the plastic by anyone in the know clearly revealed a keyhole. The whole thing had been prised off the wall and the cavity was empty.

'Oh God,' said Anne following Maxine into the room. 'What was in it?' Maxine sat down on the edge of the bed, hand on her forehead.

'I'll have to think. There wasn't so very much really. It sounds grand having a safe, but it was one of those things that seemed more useful than it actually was. Anyone could easily see the hole for the key. Rather like those false burglar alarm boxes I thought, but there were a few bits in there. My will and insurance papers, passport, car documents, those will all have to be replaced. There were a few bits of jewellery. I took the stuff I wear regularly with me to Pippa's, but there was some stuff of my mum's. Oh, I can't think what else.'

She drained the glass and glanced at her watch.

'It's nearly four o'clock. If I give them a quick call I can collect the dogs from the kennels before five. I'll feel better once I've got them back here, and I'll have an early night. I didn't sleep well at Pippa's. All this will look better after a night's sleep.' Anne looked hard at her friend, but was tactful enough not to ask why Maxine had not been sleeping.

'Of course you will,' she said, swooping up the wine glasses and taking them downstairs. On the way down she remembered,

'Oh, and the police are calling again later.

They wanted to know what was missing and who would know you were away. I wasn't much help I'm afraid.' Reaching the kitchen she said, 'There's a casserole in your fridge. I'd made a batch up yesterday and brought one round here when I found this lot, in case you couldn't be bothered cooking. Shall I put it in the oven for you?'

'No thanks. You are good to me, but I think I'll leave it till later when the police have been. You have been a big help.' Anne was surprised to see Maxine crumple into tears. Maxine was such a confident person who rarely let her guard slip. Still, such areas of weakness made her seem more human and this must have been a shock. Anne put her arms around her friend, and eventually Maxine confided her fears for Pippa.

'I know you can't do anything Anne,' she said, 'but I have to tell someone. I'm worried sick. Pippa is pregnant, and she's talking about staying on at work, while that lout Clyde looks after the baby. I wouldn't trust him to look after a goldfish. The idea scares me to death. How come she has such terrible taste in men? Is it my fault for leaving her father? '

'Do you want me to stay over tonight? Tom won't mind.' Anne asked as she rinsed mugs and glasses.

'No. Thanks, but you need some rest too. I might need you bright and alert tomorrow morning.'

Maxine saw her out and bolted the back door. She checked all the windows and double-locked the front door, then set off to walk down the hill to the kennels.

On her return with the ecstatic dogs, and armed with a cup of strong coffee, Maxine started her list of what was missing. In the living room the DVD player and the radio had gone. The television remained, presumably either too big to move, or not sufficiently cutting edge to warrant the effort.

All the drawers had been rifled and Maxine cried again when she realised that her father's medals had gone. The loss of the painting distressed her greatly. Some cash had been taken from a tin in the kitchen, and the bathroom cupboard had been trashed, although as far as she could see only a few painkillers and a repeat prescription form had been taken. She felt totally violated.

*   *   *

Maxine had had mixed feelings about her daughter's invitation to stay over Christmas. Whilst she dearly loved Pippa, she had not been impressed by her few meetings with Pippa's partner Clyde. Laden with presents and wine she had locked up carefully and headed up the M6 towards Manchester a few days before the holiday.

Her first thought when Pippa opened the door was how tired her daughter looked, eyes smudged with dark shadows and her hair uncharacteristically lank. Following her into the living room she smiled at Clyde who was lounging on the sofa in front of a television programme, but she was immediately aware of a coolness between him and her daughter. Clyde took his time turning off the television and smiling at Maxine.

'At last,' he drawled, though Maxine had arrived at the appointed time. 'Now we can eat. I'm starving.' With a quick movement he leapt to his feet and looked meaningfully at Pippa.

'Lovely,' she said, tucking a stray lock of hair behind her left ear. 'It's all ready.'

She went through to the tiny kitchen. Maxine left her bags by the sofa where Clyde ignored them, and followed.

'What can I do to help?' she asked, more brightly than she felt. Pippa paused in lifting a casserole dish from the oven.

'Oh,' she said, 'there's wine in the fridge and some beer for Clyde.'

Maxine ventured, 'Are you okay, Pippa? You seem tired.'

'I'm fine, Mum, just busy at work you know, it's our busiest time, the run-up to Christmas.' She spoke sharply and Maxine smoothly changed the conversation to Christmas plans. Pippa took the casserole to the table and sat back in her chair.

'I finished work today though, so now I can relax.' She gave her mother a strained smile.

The atmosphere was palpable throughout the meal, and Maxine worked hard to keep the conversation going. Clyde was even more taciturn than usual, and she noticed that her daughter ate very little and drank hardly anything.

After the table was cleared away, Maxine helped wash up and was just hanging up the tea towel when Clyde appeared in the doorway.

'I'm off to the pub, are you coming girls?'

Maxine took her cue from her daughter who was shaking her head.

'I think I'll stay and chat to Pippa,' she told him, 'We don't get chance very often.'

Pippa looked relieved, and the two settled

down in the small living room but Maxine found it difficult to say any of the things she really wanted to. As the conversation dwindled to nothing the younger woman dozed off on the sofa and Maxine took the opportunity to take her bags into the spare room. Waking Pippa gently with a cup of coffee at ten o'clock she seized her chance before Clyde returned.

'Pippa. Coffee,' she said. As her daughter rubbed her neck and stretched, she ploughed on, 'Darling I don't want to interfere, but is everything really all right? You look so tired tonight.' The younger woman gathered her thoughts for a minute, then, 'No, I told you Mum, everything's fine. I've just been busy that's all.'

Before Maxine had a chance to press further, the door banged and Clyde came in on a waft of beer and cigarette smoke.

'Well, girls,' he said, more expansive and red-cheeked through drink. 'Have you put the world to rights?'

When Pippa made no reply he went and leaned over her to give her a kiss. She flinched from the beer breath and Clyde turned away impatiently.

'Have you told your Mum our news?' he said, head on one side, his tone saying more than his words. Pippa exhaled deeply.

'No,' she said sharply, 'We said we weren't telling anyone just yet.'

'Oh but your Mum? Surely you've told your Mum?' He turned his back so that he was facing Maxine. 'How do you fancy being a granny?' he asked, 'Pippa has got herself pregnant.'

Maxine glanced across at her daughter, who was looking at her in some trepidation.

'It's true, Mum,' she said in a bright, false voice. 'We just found out, and it's very early days. We weren't going to tell anyone just yet, but' she reached for Clyde's reluctant hand, 'you're different. Clyde's right. You should know straight away. Of course we're delighted,' she finished lamely.

Maxine looked from one to the other. Clyde looked anything but delighted, and Pippa was watching her anxiously.

'Well, congratulations to you both,' she said, hoping she sounded more enthusiastic than she felt. 'By next Christmas you'll have a family of your own. Of course I see now why you went easy on the wine.'

'We should celebrate now,' said Clyde, heading for the fridge, 'Wine, Maxine?' as he got himself another beer.

'Oh, no thanks, Clyde, I won't be able to sleep if I have more to drink now. I'll just rinse these mugs and then head to bed if that's okay. We have plenty of time to celebrate over the next few days.'

Pippa looked at her gratefully. 'I'm heading for bed too. Goodnight Mum.'

*   *   *

Later, unable to sleep for all the thoughts crowding into her head, Maxine could not avoid hearing the conversation from the next room. These were not the intimate sounds of endearment, but rather harsh words spoken low so as not to disturb her. She heard Clyde say, in response to a comment from Pippa,

'She'd have wormed it out of you, mothers are like that.'

'Well, will we? Get married I mean.'

Maxine wanted to be privy to none of this. She tried to ignore it and compose herself for sleep, but through the thin walls she could not shut it out, just as she could not fail to notice the negative tone to Clyde's responses. She lay wakeful long after the voices had silenced, hearing a clock somewhere nearby striking three.

*   *   *

The next day conversation was difficult with Clyde there. There was so much Maxine wanted to ask Pippa, but since Clyde came in from the pub the previous evening there had been no opportunity. Now that her daughter had finished work for the holiday she hoped that they would be able to have a proper talk. As the time progressed however, it seemed more and more unlikely. Pippa was very evidently avoiding a heart-to-heart, and seemed to find Clyde's conversation over-funny and very clever.

Maxine tried to think of the best outcome to the present situation and failed to come up with anything that seemed acceptable. She toyed with giving up her job and offering to mind the child, but what would Clyde be doing meantime. He showed no signs of looking for work, and seemed content to live off his girlfriend's earnings.

During the morning Maxine desperately fished around for a topic to talk about, which wouldn't involve families, parenthood or jobs and income. In the end she partially succeeded. To her daughter she said, 'I've brought you the Magic Decorations.'

'The What?'

Despite herself Maxine smiled. 'Well, the Magic Decorations. I brought them for Pippa.' The pause was momentary, 'and you of course.'

Seeing his quizzical expression she sat back to tell the tale.

'It's a sort of family tradition now. When I was little my Nan took me each December to Manchester to see Father Christmas, usually in Lewis's, or Kendal's in more affluent times. Eventually of course every garden centre had a Santa. Anyway we always went out for lunch afterwards and I was allowed to choose a tree decoration each year. Unbeknown to me, each year Nan made a note of the year, a description of what I had chosen, where it had come from, and so on. Then later she added a few more points about that Christmas itself – what presents I had received and other things that may help me remember it specifically. Richard and I married in December, and that year Nan handed over the whole lot to me. The decorations and the information.

'I kept on the tradition with Pippa, it seemed such a nice idea. Once she set up a home of her own I decided to pass them on to her at this visit. The time seemed right, and now you tell me that by this time next year you will have a youngster of your own.

Pippa's eyes were teary.

'That's lovely.'

'Yeah,' Clyde echoed without expression, 'Lovely. Look I'm going out for a pint. Got to meet a mate. I'll be back soon.'

Maxine took the opportunity of Clyde's absence to have a chat. She tried to make it as casual as possible, but was aware that her questions were making Pippa uncomfortable. Clyde had no work, she had said, and no real prospect of work. Whilst admitting that she suspected that he was not trying very hard, Pippa was defensive.

'I know you don't feel positive towards Clyde, Mum, but you don't understand him. It's not been easy, the last proper job he had was when he helped with your porch and that's what – back in April. With the recession and everything he was made redundant in May, and you watch the news, you know that there're no jobs in the building industry. The recession wasn't Clyde's fault.' Pippa was clearly upset.

'Of course, darling,' soothed Maxine, who felt that she understood Clyde only too well. She privately wondered whether they weren't actually ideally suited. Pippa was always a champion of the underdog, and Clyde could no doubt be an underdog when it suited him.

'Anyway,' Pippa went on, as she herself had a good job they would have enough money coming in. They were lucky really, she had prattled on. They were used to coping on one income and benefits and so it wouldn't be so much of a hardship as if they had been used to two wages.

'But what do you plan to do about childcare?' Maxine chose her words carefully, and tried to keep the dismay out of her voice. She realised that on many levels this was really not her business, but Pippa was her only child and she could not distance herself from her daughter's pain.

'Well Clyde will be at home with the baby of course.'

Maxine focused on the least of her objections

to this.

'But you'll miss out on so many things.' Maxine remembered the excitement of her little girl's first smile, her first tooth, her first words.

Pippa became brusque. 'There may be some things I don't see, but that's hardly the end of the world. Many mothers aren't around when those things happen.' She broke off, surprised, as Clyde returned, and with him he had a woman of about Maxine's age.

'Look what the wind blew in.' he said without originality, 'I'll go to the pub later.' He returned to his place on the sofa and turned on the television. Introductions were left to Pippa, who told Maxine that this was Clyde's mother. The woman made a comment that disturbed Maxine. Whilst she seemed very pleasant, she took the opportunity, as Maxine helped her carry presents in from the car, to say in a low voice.

'Do you know? I have two sons, one of them is a giver, and one a taker.' She raised her eyebrows and glanced in the direction of Clyde, who once again was reclining in his natural habitat on the sofa.

Before Maxine could reply, the telephone rang with the call from Maxine's neighbour that was to change all their Christmas plans.

Chapter 3

Simon Napier was a coward and a claustrophobe. The former had been established twenty years before at the age of seven. His father, on catching him taking money from his mother's purse, had beaten him soundly. Kevin Napier was greatly disappointed in his only son.

Simon had taken after his mother's family in looks, and was scarcely five foot four. His hair was thin and gingery, and his complexion the opaque white with freckles, which often befalls the true redhead. His eyes were of the kind described in novels as *piggy*, being small and pink-rimmed. His appearance had not been enhanced by the need to wear glasses since he was eight years old.

His father had been a supporter of the return of National Service, on the 'it never did me any harm' principle. It did his family however, a great deal of harm, both psychological and physical.

Their greatest mistake was in letting him see the terror he caused. Thriving on the power it gave him, he would persecute them all the more, and took to telling them of some misdemeanour that they had committed, and that he was thinking about how he should respond.

Throughout the ensuing hours he would refer back to the incident over and over, musing about suitable punishments until, by the time the punishment came, both wife and son were almost hysterical with fear.

His diminutive wife, once a compact woman

with beautiful auburn hair, was now cowed and frightened from frequently suffered beatings. The timid son felt the brunt of his father's anger time and again. Astute enough to be aware that physical violence against his son would be recognised as such at school, and realising the extent of the terror it caused, this sadist took to locking Simon in the coal shed in the dark for the least transgression.

This continued into his teens, when Simon began to research his terrors on the internet. It was then that Simon realised for the first time that the claustrophobia he suffered was a genuine illness. Violence continued to be a familiar pattern in Simon's life and he became more and more terrified as the years passed. Outwardly respectable, his father insisted on good manners and paid for expensive elocution lessons for his only son.

When Simon changed schools aged eleven, the other children, envious of the way he spoke and of his intelligence, had teased him. They ridiculed his short stature and his appearance, calling him geek and nerd, mocking his unusual appearance. Determined not to suffer in the way that he did at home he sought out ways to get his classmates' support.

Eventually he turned his brain to his advantage, writing absence notes for other boys, impressing one of the leaders sufficiently to be accepted at the periphery of a gang, with the protection that afforded.

At the age of eighteen on a school field trip, Simon and a group of other youngsters were briefly trapped in a lift. For Simon this was the worst moment of his life, it led to fear of suffocation and panic attacks, and it was during this incarceration that the full extent of his claustrophobia was realised. It was not just a fear of being confined, but a real terror of ever repeating the experience of being shut in, which had left him with recurrent nightmares long after his release. He never entered lifts or tunnels, and his fear became so severe that he avoided tight-necked clothing, and would always have his car windows open when possible.

On leaving school, he had turned his not inconsiderable brain to ways to supplement the income afforded him by the state. His *career* was how he saw it, and he explained to Gary Lewis that he worked as hard at his schemes as other people did in a legitimate job.

Gary, not sure what he meant, and with no likelihood of ever finding and keeping a legitimate job, nodded and agreed with him. With Simon's help he enjoyed a reasonable income, without him there would just be the dole, or whatever they called it these days.

*   *   *

Gary had met Simon the previous autumn when, leaving the off-licence in Knutton, he had reversed into the older man's cabriolet as he tried to light a cigarette and simultaneously park the van. Already over the drink-drive limit he was relieved when Simon seemed to laugh off the incident.

'Christ,' he had said running his fingers through his ginger hair, 'Watch what you're doing old thing. The motor's only just been cleaned.'

There was no noticeable damage, and Simon had stood peering at the wing as Gary got out of his car. Simon replaced his glasses.

'No harm done, old thing, no need to worry about insurance and all that. Come and have a drink to show no hard feelings.' He put out his hand. 'Simon, Simon Napier.'

For two seconds Gary, nonplussed and having no insurance anyway, thought of giving a false name, but the guy seemed okay.

'Gary,' he responded. 'Gary Lewis.' He squinted at the other man carefully through exhaled cigarette smoke, ready with his fists should this be needed.

The two had met regularly since that first fateful occasion, and had come to develop a cautious mutual trust, each recognising complementary strengths in the other. Never one to hold his drink well, Simon had confided his current financial difficulties, but Gary, looking at the car and the smart clothes had scoffed, prompting Simon to give more detail than was wise about his past.

*   *   *

Simon was fascinated by Gary's experiences inside the Werrington Young Offenders' Institution. He sat transfixed as Gary described the situation.

'Twenty three hours most days we was shut in the cell. Nearly go out of your mind you do, pacing and pacing and never on your own.'

'Never? What about when you er ....' Simon indicated his lower regions. Gary shook his head,

'Nope, just a bog in the corner of the cell, so if your cell-mate weren't well, God it was awful. Just a bit of a wall so you couldn't actually see his bum from your bed, but that's it.'

Simon could think of nothing worse.

'How big were the rooms?'

Gary gave a sharp laugh. 'That's funny that is, rooms. Everyone's supposed to call them rooms, but don't kid yourself. They're cells.'

'How big?' Simon persisted.

'About,' Gary screwed up his eyes, thinking. 'About nine by six.'

'Nine by six *feet*?' Simon was appalled.

'Yup, just bunk beds and the bog.'

'Bloody hell.' Simon covered his eyes. He felt physically sick at the prospect of being confined in so small a space, 'Bloody hell.'

*   *   *

Simon had realized aged thirteen, that an income could be made from the system banks used in replacing cards when they expired. For some reason now forgotten he had spotted that, of the long number, only the last four digits changed. Using this information he tried an experiment.

He stole his uncle's credit card and waited for the replacement card to be issued. He had worked out that by the simple but unpleasant expedient of delving in rubbish bins for discarded old receipts that the number could be reconstructed. The situation was one he had continued to exploit for several years.

Working during the evenings in a pub from the earliest legal age, he had relieved many a drunken customer of their card, and, living in a small community he could easily, if unhappily, gain access to their rubbish.

The problems when they arose were twofold. Banks started to use three digit security codes on cards from 2005, and people were becoming more conscious about security, shredding bills, or at least ripping or soaking them, before throwing them away.

The problem was solved for him by the death of his father. At the time he met Gary Lewis, he had been living on the proceeds of his father's life assurance for four years, and funds were beginning to run low. Meeting Gary was a Godsend. Here was someone he could use to take the risks he could not undertake himself.

He had to look elsewhere for income, and it was to that ubiquitous form of technology, the computer, that he next turned his attention. This new scam was perfect, and one he had stumbled across accidentally in October when, bored one evening, he had signed up to *findyourmates.com*.

Simon adjusted his glasses and opened his homepage to find a request from a girl wanting to be his *mate*. He clicked on the name, although it was not familiar to him. Pretty girl! Emma Francis. The photograph was clearly a holiday snap on the beach. The swimsuit she wore showed off a lovely figure, only partially concealed by long blonde hair.

He clicked on their mutual friends and found that she was a local girl, who drank sometimes in the pub he frequented. He pressed the button which agreed to friendship. She must have been online because almost immediately he had access to her home page. There were two photographs of her obviously on holiday, and one with a man, so similar in appearance that he must be a relative.

He glanced through her personal information,

eighty-five friends. He ran his fingers through his thin hair.

'Nobody has that many friends,' he muttered aloud. 'How many of those do you know personally, my love? And of the rest, I wonder how many are honest in everything they post on here. If you can count five friends – five true friends you are a very lucky person.'

He stopped, his hands poised over the keys, momentarily remembering that it was his father who had told him that. He scrolled through the posts she had made during the last few days, and then stopped suddenly. *Looking forward to Saturday,* he read. *Going to stay with my sister in Switzerland. I'll be there for a week, and we have loads of things planned. I can't wait.*

'You fool, Emma,' he muttered aloud, half to the screen and half to himself. 'You've just told all those people, most of whom you've never met, that your place is going to be empty for a week. Do you really think it's wise to share that sort of information with everyone, including the village idiot?

But you have given me an idea, I think perhaps you need Simon in your life to look after you.' and he quickly typed and posted his message.

Two days later, he met Emma in the beer garden at the pub. 'Crumbs, it's cold,' were her first words, 'can't we sit inside?'

She was a stunner, better than she had looked on the photograph. A short, plump girl, with a well-endowed bust: Simon soon found himself enthralled.

'Do you know old thing, how risky it is to share information like you're going to Switzerland. Honestly, even if I didn't fancy you like mad, old thing, I'd have had to at least put you straight on this.' He looked at her earnestly through his thick lenses.

She was amazed.

'I'd never thought,' she said, sounding worried, 'I was thinking I was just keeping in touch with friends, but you're right. You and me'd never met before.' She leaned on him provocatively, 'for all I know you could be a really naughty boy.'

He leered at her as she expected, 'Oh, I am,' he told her. She liked him, she liked him a lot. She had always been attracted to clever men, but she made a mental note to wrap up warm when she went out with him, as it seemed this was a man who liked the fresh air.

In appearance Gary and Simon could hardly have contrasted more. Gary topped six foot two and tended to stoop a little. He was dark, swarthy skinned in a Byronic way and slim, with shoulders so narrow that sleeves always began a couple of inches down his biceps. The acne and greasy hair of his adolescence long gone, he was proud of his black hair, which he wore unfashionably long, but which shone with health. Surprisingly he often covered it with a knitted woollen hat, of which he had several.

Heavy browed, his hooded eyes were deep and close set aside a narrow patrician nose. His chin was strongly pointed, his Adam's apple prominent. A gawky and angular adolescent, maturity had done little to change his body, but his voice had deepened to a sonorous boom.

In contrast Simon was a good ten inches shorter with the looks of a baroque putto. His voice had the adenoidal twang often found in people of snub nose and his eyes, though of a startling blue, were small. Simon's placatory tendencies and cheerful character compensated for the lack of regular good looks, and his gingery hair and sprinkling of freckles seemed to appeal to the ladies.

He had kept in contact with Gary after that fateful meeting in Knutton. Simon felt his own superiority, rightly suspecting Gary's literary inadequacies, but recognising in his partner a sense of adventure and daring that he lacked. He knew that he could mastermind ideas, but had not the personal courage to carry out the crimes himself.

He was constantly vigilant about small spaces, so their meetings were often held in the beer garden, or at the table next to the pub door. Gary was very suggestible, and had happily accepted the practical element of their crimes, bringing the spoils back to Simon to be disposed of. He received in exchange what Simon, pandering to his arrogance, called his salary. He explained to Gary that they needed to be able to keep separate the two parts of each operation. *Brains and Brawn* he thought to himself, *Planning and Execution* he called it to Gary.

Simon was a good enough psychologist to praise Gary for his achievements as he saw himself as a Mr Big figure of the future – probably running a whole team of '*Garys*' working on his behalf. Had he been able to see into the future, he would have immediately and irrevocably broken his connection with the other man.

'You, Gary have a great gift. Sounds like you've been breaking in places since you were small. How come you're driving around in that battered old van?'

He didn't wait for an answer. 'I've got some

work coming up for someone like you. Proceeds split fifty-fifty, what do you say?'

'I say I'm bloody freezing. I can't think in this cold, why don't we sit inside the pub?'

'Gary, you have just lit up your third cigarette of the evening. You can't smoke in there, can you? That's why we're outside here.'

Gary was warmed by Simon's thoughtfulness. He admired Simon greatly. He liked the posh way he talked, and stood in awe of his quick wit and his planning ability.

He felt encouraged by the praise he received, and was willing to commit more and more to Simon's projects. He could see a life of ease stretching in front of him, where he was called upon only to do things well within his capabilities and under clear instructions.

In exchange he would be protected by Simon's brain from DSS, employment, tax, sickness benefits and all those other aspects of life that made it difficult for him to cope.

Chapter 4

Simon now had his new plan, and he was ready to put it into action. He had thought through the whole thing very carefully. His father had died nearly four years ago leaving a boxful of old school photographs, and it was going through these that had gradually spawned the idea.

He bought a notebook and jotted down in it as he remembered them, all the salient points from his solitary father's life, that could be useful. His father had never owned a computer and he was sure had kept in touch with none of his old school friends or workmates.

There was no giveaway correspondence, no Christmas cards from unknown names – very few Christmas cards at all in fact – throughout his father's adult life. His mother had spotted an opportunity to escape from life with this bully, and in Simon's early teens she had left. He found he could hardly remember her now, but he knew she hadn't been local. She had moved from Surrey with her family when she was fifteen, and had met his father a couple of years later.

His father had described her as flighty, which seemed to mean an unwillingness to stick around to look after a dour, sadistic old man and her unlovely son. She had gone off to pastures new and the last Simon had heard she was in New Zealand.

As the information in his notebook grew, so did Simon's confidence to pull this off, and the beauty of it was that his plan could work again and again. The time was ripe; carefully he pushed his glasses up his nose and typed the message on *findyourmates.com:* the name of the primary school, relevant dates and the brief message:

Hi, Kevin here. Just found this old school photo. Would love to get in touch with anyone who remembers me

Add the photo and send. Simon sat back in his chair and gazed through the permanently open window, pleased with himself.

Thank God he had decided it was not worth announcing his father's death in a newspaper. He flipped over the photo and gazed at the names written on the back in his ten-year-old father's hand. All but two of the names were clearly decipherable. He wondered who would contact him if anyone, and taking out his notebook, turned his mind to questions he would want to ask.

Early for his date with Emma one night shortly before Christmas, Simon arrived at the Railway to find Clyde sitting staring into an empty pint glass. He had been at school with Clyde and they met occasionally, mostly by accident, over a pint.

'Hey, Clyde,' he slapped his old friend on his shoulder, 'I need to sit near the door so I don't miss Emma. Not seen you for ages. What's up?'

'Bloody everything,' said Clyde, obligingly shifting tables and pushing his empty glass towards his old schoolmate, 'Bloody everything.' He was obviously already on the outside of several drinks, and Simon brought him a scotch. His glass primed he expanded.

'Been living with this girl a few months in Manchester, nice girl, good job, she's got a lovely flat – meant I didn't have to bother too much, you know mate.' He gave the ghost of a smile as he downed half his whisky and belched loudly.

'Now the bloody bitch is pregnant. Talking about marriage and all that stuff.' He caught the barman's eye, raising his glass, 'and she's invited her blasted mother to stay for Christmas, can you believe it. I'll have two of the buggers trying to bloody pin me down. The flaming old bat's coming this afternoon. Two blasted yakking women. Thought I'd come back to Stoke and spend some time on my old patch.

'You might know my bird Pippa actually. She comes from round here. Moved out a while ago 'cos her job's in Manchester. That's where we're living now; at least I'm living in Manchester at the moment.' Clyde had forgotten Simon's presence and continued muttering into his glass.

'I met her last spring when I was delivering timber and stuff for a job we were doing. Put a new porch on the front of her Ma's cottage – one of them by the old railway tracks,' He looked up and seemed to notice Simon again, 'off the A500 and turn left, near Tim Riley's place, you know. Got ideas above herself I reckon, it's only a pokey little place. Nice though, she's got some nice stuff.'

Simon shook his head in denial at Clyde's first comment. He knew nobody who lived at that side of the village. He tousled his hair, and pushed his glasses more firmly into place. The barman replaced their empty glasses with full ones.

'Then I did that job for you, on your Dad's old place. Got back to the yard and was told I wasn't needed any more. Bloody laid me off the end of that week.'

'What are you going to do? About the kid I mean.' Simon's brain was already whirring.

'I'll tell you what I'm not going to do. I'm not going to bloody get hitched – that's what. Nobody's going to pin me down, and with a damn kid as well.' He took another swig and wiped his mouth on the back of his hand. 'I'll have to find another doss though, living in her flat these last few months. Last two nights I've been on Tony's couch, but I'm sick o' that. Need to get something sorted.'

The conversation was interrupted by Emma's arrival. Clyde drained his glass and once more burped loudly. Emma giggled. He glared and then ignored her, getting unsteadily to his feet.

'Let us know won't you, if you hear of somewhere I can doss down?'

'Oh, I might know somewhere you can stay.' Emma said, 'My brother's lodger moved out last week from a house in Fenton. Got his girlfriend up the duff and now he's got a shotgun to his head.' She giggled again.

'Phone him,' snarled Clyde. 'Please. Your brother – phone him will you?' He sat down again, but Emma was shaking her head as she looked at her watch.

'Can't get him yet.' She said, 'He'll be at the football.' She scribbled on a beer mat and handed it to Clyde. 'Call me after ten. I'll have chance to talk to him by then.' Glancing at the number, Clyde put the mat in his pocket and left them.

He had bent the truth more than a little in his account of why he had been laid off. The job done at Simon's home had been substantial, knocking through two rooms to make the whole open-plan, and adding patio doors to the back and side of the living room. Simon had also wanted the wall next to the narrow staircase opening up to give it a much lighter, airier feel, and a bigger window putting in the main bedroom. He had told Clyde that his father had died, leaving him the house and a reasonable sum from an insurance policy – hence he had money to spend on these changes.

Clyde saw no reason why his employer should see any of this money, and arranged a good price for Simon. Using materials largely stolen from the yard, and with the help of one of the labourers over a couple of weekends, he made a very nice profit. He reckoned however, without his boss's surveillance system, which recorded the theft of steel joists, timber and plaster that were not accounted for on any of the invoices. Deciding that Clyde was not somebody he wanted as an enemy his boss took the easy way out by simply laying him off.   Only if Clyde had seriously challenged him did he plan to produce the surveillance footage.

Having more money in his pocket than he had seen for a while, and just having met a new lady who lived out of the area in Manchester, Clyde was not disposed to make waves.

*   *   *

On his return from Emma's in the early hours of the next morning, Simon took a detour along the A500, and followed the route Clyde had described. The cottage was easily identifiable by its new porch. When he arrived home as usual he opened the windows then scanned through his messages to find one from a woman he had been cultivating. She was one of the thirty two faces on his father's school photograph, and after several weeks of correspondence she had now given him the information he needed to take the next step.

Another woman had also replied, giving her personal email details and offering a lot more besides, but she lived in New Zealand, which was of no use for his purposes. This Angela Davies however was a woman who lived locally. He looked again at the original of the photograph he had posted. Thirty two names written on the back of it – who knew how many times he would be able to return to this particular pot of gold.

Simon adjusted his glasses, and checked his computer screen, considering his next move. He now had two potential victims in his sights. He needed to do further research on the Angela woman, but Clyde's old bird was ready to fly. After a moment's thought he swung his chair round to face the telephone, hit one on the speed-dial and waited. As the receiver was lifted he tried to keep the excitement out of his voice.

Gary listened carefully and then grunted.

'Okay. What happens now?'

'You.' said Simon, 'You, old thing, go and pay her place a visit while she's away, and have a look at the nice goods she's left behind.' Gary smiled slowly and began to nod.

'Go tonight and check the place is empty. Then back again tomorrow night's probably best, once it's dark. I'll leave the details to you, but make sure you wear gloves and don't get caught.'

Gary was affronted. A lifetime of petty theft,

burglary and break-ins had left him confident in his ability and technique. He may not be able to read so well, but he knew he had more nerve than Simon, who could never have carried out the practical role in their partnership.

Chapter 5

'I'm not sure that's everything,' Maxine told the police constable who had called round that evening, 'I remember a neighbour being broken into when I was a child. Months later they would be looking for something and realise it was gone.'

'We do find that people tend to think pretty soon of the most important stuff, mobiles, laptops, jewellery, and obvious stuff like ornaments and pictures. You can always let us know and we'll update the list if you think of anything else.'

'Yes,' Maxine said thoughtfully, 'my passport's gone, but I can get the car papers replaced easily enough. My daughter has a copy of my will anyway. My good jewellery I had with me. I don't have much, but I was wearing my rings and had my watch and gold bracelet with me. They broke into the safe of course...'

'Safe?' the police officer looked up, interested.

'Oh, nothing sophisticated. Just one of those mock plug sockets – simple enough to break into I suppose.'

'Well, there's not much that a really determined thief won't get into, if they have the time, and it seems he had plenty of that. Your neighbours were in bed, and you're not overlooked are you?'

Maxine considered, moving to the window and looking out over the blackened countryside at the lights of the motorway and of Crewe in the distance.

'No, I chose this house for its solitude. The orchard next door is seldom visited and Mildred in the bungalow opposite is about ninety and something of a recluse. Her curtains are mostly closed even in the daytime. I can see now that peace can have its disadvantages.'

'Anything in the safe gone missing?' the constable poised his pen.

'Yes, that's where the paperwork was. Oh, and there are some medals that belonged to my father gone from the drawer downstairs. They weren't anything special, just standard World War Two issue I think, but I had kept them as a memento. I have very little of his, so it was really upsetting.

I had my laptop and phone with me so they haven't gone, it's just so…' she hesitated, 'intrusive, and my picture – she indicated the gap on the wall, that was a wedding present, and one I really loved. I feel that the whole place has been defiled. I've put all the clothes in the wash – even the clean stuff. I don't like the idea of someone pawing through it. I may throw the underwear away, it feels so dirty.' she shuddered and then sighed.

The list completed, the constable moved on. Who had known that Maxine would be away?

'Not many people really, I'm very careful about that. Anne next door obviously, and my daughter and her partner. I don't even cancel papers at the newsagents because you never know who might overhear. Anne pushes papers and post through for me when I'm away. The kennels of course but I've used them for years.'

'Facebook, Twitter, *findyourmates.com*?' queried the constable.

'Oh no, I'm not on any of those sites, and if I were I wouldn't share any information like that,' said Maxine, horrified. 'I've always been nervous of on-line banking and so on. I'm a bit of a Luddite, I'm afraid. I really only use the internet to look things up.' She smiled, as the constable prepared to leave, reassuring her that everything possible would be done.

When he had gone Maxine closed the front door and leaned her back against it. She felt exhausted. There seemed an insurmountable number of tasks she ought to be doing.

She should tackle the insurance company, sort out the glaziers and look at what documents needed replacing but she felt unable to face any of it. Going upstairs she was grateful that Anne had helped her clean the bedroom and put on clean bedding. When she was rested she would be in a different frame of mind.

As she settled into bed the telephone rang and she had a moment's apprehension about answering it. The call however was from Pippa. She wanted to know the details, and Maxine told her of the burglary and everything that had been taken. Having established that Pippa would come down to stay with her for Christmas, instead of vice versa, she tentatively enquired whether Clyde would be joining them.

'I doubt it Mum,' said Pippa, 'but I'll ask him when he comes in. He's not here at the moment.' She paused and Maxine waited, but nothing more was shared.

Maxine felt that her daughter had been on the verge of saying more, but she simply wished her mother goodnight. As she walked the dogs and settled for the night Maxine wondered whether Clyde was actually out, or whether Clyde had gone.

Hopefully the latter.

*　　*　　*

That same day, Simon received the expected phone call from Gary in the early afternoon and they arranged to meet at The Railway at nine that evening.

With a drink in front of him, Gary glanced around so furtively that Simon aimed a kick at his shin and told him not to be so bloody melodramatic. Gary had no idea what that meant, but the kick was painful enough to distract him and he silently pushed a piece of paper across to Simon, then bent to rub his bruised leg.

The paper contained a badly spelt list of the things taken from Miner's Cottage the previous night, and Simon, pushing his glasses higher on his nose with a knuckle, scanned the list. He saw that it was not extensive, but there were some quality pieces – a limited edition print; a gold watch, some bits of jewellery. He finished his pint. He wanted to spend as little time in public with Gary as possible. In fact he wanted to spend as little time as possible with Gary full stop, but recognised his usefulness in distancing Simon himself from the victims of his crimes.

'Should be a fair bit there I imagine,' Gary said steadily, his eyes not leaving Simon's face, 'The watch, I think, is solid gold. No cash but a whole load of jewellery and that picture. Some of it is definitely good stuff, not sure about all of it.'

'I'll go through it,' Simon told him, pocketing the list, and smoothing his ginger hair. 'There's not much, old thing. I'd expected more than this, maybe she took a load of stuff away with her. These old girls tart themselves up to the nines when they go away. Especially at Christmas' He grinned.

'We'll need to wait now till after Christmas, but I know someone who can move it on for us, then we'll split the money fifty-fifty. Now I'll get us another drink, and I want to talk to you about another job. Shift to that table over there will you,' he indicated one nearer the door. 'We can talk more privately there.'

Gary obligingly moved tables then sat back, well pleased. Breaking into the cottage had been so easy. He recognized that he was in Simon's hands in terms of the goods he was handing over, having no idea of their value, but he had already pocketed over a hundred pounds in cash and some euro he found in a drawer, as well as some old medals that may be valuable, and a second gent's gold watch. He felt sure that as long as he kept the goods for long enough before he moved them on, he had already made a reasonable killing for a couple of hours' work.

'Christ,' he said, zipping up his jacket when Simon approached, 'Why do we always have to sit in a howling gale.' Simon ignored the question.

'This next one is a bigger fish altogether, big posh house near Scot Hay, but we have to move quickly.' Simon reviewed in his notebook the information from snippets Angela had supplied on the internet to *Kevin*. The size of the house, its approximate location and details such as conifer trees that would need pruning again shortly. Believing him to be thousands of miles away in Canada she had naively furnished him with an accurate description of her home and its environs. She had even posted a photograph.

After searching map websites Simon had been pretty sure that he had found the house. It took just a twenty minute car journey to be positive. Even the car was shown to the world on the internet, its registration number pixilated out, but as he cruised slowly past, there it was parked in affirmation on the driveway.

To be absolutely sure he had taken a couple of photographs and noted makes and models of neighbouring cars in the lane. Back at home he had checked these on the satellite maps from websites and found that they tallied.

'You'll need to check the place tonight, and then go in tomorrow.' He produced a Stoke A-Z with the house marked in pencil, and handed it and the two photographs over to Gary.

'Thanks, old thing,' said Simon, getting to his feet as Emma entered the pub and, glancing at his appearance in the blacked out window, he combed his fingers through the gingery hair. He gathered up the bags Gary had brought in and which were under the table.

'Ring me when you've done the next one. Now I'm off to get laid.' He leered at Gary's blank expression over his glasses. 'My lovely girlfriend. The delectable Emma.'

Gary turned to look at *the delectable Emma,* to be faced with a girl he knew from school. Emma Francis had had a reputation as a bit of a goer, although Gary had never had any success. By the look of the short skirt and plunging neckline nothing much had changed.

'Hello Emma,' he said, but she affected not to recognise him, only acknowledging him when Simon had said, 'This is my friend, Gary.' Then she looked him straight in the eye and said,

'Pleased to meet you, Gary.'

Gary played the game.

'And do you work, Emma? What do you do?'

'Boring really,' she said, 'I work in computers. That big office block near Festival Heights? Still it pays the rent,' she smiled up at Simon as he placed a glass of red wine in front of her.

'I'd have thought an actress or a model with your lovely figure.' Gary said, watching her preen.

'What do you do Gary?'

Gary glanced quickly at Simon, who said, 'Gary works with me, old thing. Business stuff. We have some good ideas we're trying to get off the ground at the moment. But now he has to dash off.' He signalled to Gary to leave them alone together. 'Bye Gary, speak to you Sunday.'

Gary turned away, furious. Bloody dismissing him like some servant. And that bloody snob Emma not letting on that she knew him. Up until the previous July he and Emma had sat just two seats apart in their classroom, all the time that he actually attended school that was. What was she playing at?

Still, he liked the idea of working *with* Simon, rather than *for* him. That was progress.

Chapter 6

Gary had never had a girlfriend. He was full of bravado of course, and could spin yarns about his escapades, but in fact until the autumn he had been a virgin; always more gauche and more aware of his limitations in the company of girls. He had been plagued with acne through adolescence, and his greasy hair and skin had been off-putting. He did though have a girl friend.

Unlike Simon, Gary never experienced violence during his childhood. His parents had doted on him in infancy, and with his father working abroad most of the time, his mother focused her whole attention on her son. Bereft of her husband, Mrs Lewis clung to Gary, deferring to his opinion and keeping him away from school with a variety of hypothetical illnesses, to ensure his near-constant companionship.

Gary was of barely average intelligence, and his inability to keep up with schoolmates during the brief times he was at school, gave him an ever stronger motivation to stay away.

He began to be more and more embarrassed about his inability to read. During one period when he was in regular attendance, truant officers having been unusually zealous, an incident occurred that changed the way he viewed violence. He was thirteen years old.

During a history lesson the teacher had called for pupils to read aloud in turn. Gary became increasingly more concerned as he struggled to follow the words. His hands were sweating and he itched to hit out and stop the inevitability of his discomfort. As his turn approached he suddenly fled from the room, taking refuge behind the sports hall, where he immediately lit a prohibited cigarette. Here, a fellow pupil found him ten minutes later, having been sent in pursuit.

'You've got to come back in straight away,' he parroted, making to manhandle Gary by his jacket. Gary felt a tumult of rage overpower him, and what followed was a brief and bloody skirmish that earned Gary, if not respect, then at least wariness from his classmates. The other boy returned with bleeding nose and ripped jacket to the classroom, but claimed he had fallen. Nobody broke ranks, and Gary remained unpunished and unrepentant.

The teacher whose ill-conceived idea it was to have the youngsters read aloud, was not to go unpunished however. Several distraught anonymous telephone calls were made from a callbox close to the school; to the head teacher, to the teacher's wife, and to the education department, accusing him of inappropriately touching several of the younger boys. These accusations had to be taken seriously and an investigation was launched before the man was totally vindicated. There were though, some amongst the parents, who insisted that there is no smoke without fire, and the teacher's anticipated promotion never occurred.

Gary learned two valuable lessons from this incident; that power could be had without recourse to the written word, and that power brought enjoyment. He fell in with a gang at school, who rather admired his bravado. In time he followed the gang into petty theft, then into more serious crime, and eventually, at the age of fifteen, into a Young Offenders' Institution.

When he left school at the earliest legal age, he was able to read and print his name and address, and pick out a few printed words, but little more. On his first visit to the Job Centre he was faced with forms to complete and began to realise for the first time how his lack of education could prove to be an impediment.

A girl from his class at school, also signing on that first day, unwittingly came to his rescue. Having collected up her own forms she suggested that they work through them together, and this they did, Janice reading out each question with Gary sitting beside her.

'What have you been doing till now?'

'Oh, just knocking around – bits and pieces to help my Dad.' Gary's father would have been amazed at this had he still been alive, never knowingly having been helped by Gary in his life.

Having made what he felt was a reasonable stab at the forms he remembered to thank her.

'S'okay,' she said, 'Reading those things is a nightmare. I don't mind helping you out. In return you can take me for a drink.' She rested a skinny hand on Gary's arm, and it occurred to him that this might be a useful relationship to cultivate.

Janice had sown the seeds of an idea in Gary's head, and he phoned and asked her out the next evening. Having done nothing since he left school except to continue the petty pilfering he was used to, he had a few items to dispose of. He was sure that if he waited long enough he could sell them without fear of them being traced.

'Janice,' he said finally plucking up the

courage. 'Where would you sell a camera?'

'Camera! You? Where's this camera come from Gary? Do tell me, I'm all ears.'

'My mum gave it me. It used to belong to my Dad' He showed her the modern Pentax. He had stolen it eighteen months before and reckoned that sufficient time had passed to offload it now. 'He only used it a couple of times before he died.' Gary warmed to his fiction.

'More fool your mum, I'd have kept it.' Janice had said, 'Can't you take it back to where it was bought? Get your money back maybe. It looks new.'

Gary thought quickly.

'Ah, not really. You see, she couldn't find the box or the papers, you know, just the camera and an extra lens thing, and it's probably been too long now. I thought maybe you might know someone?'

'No,' said Janice, thinking. 'Most of the people I know haven't got the money for anything like that, not even second-hand. Why don't you sell it on the internet?'

Gary flushed. 'I don't know how. It's a bit difficult...'

'Oh yeah, sure.' Janice paused, then 'I could help you with that if you wanted.'

Over the next few months the two met fairly regularly, and there was a tacit understanding that Janice would help Gary with the written word. Several times Gary took her out for a drink and he began to think of her as his girl.

Janice's perspective would have enraged Gary had he been aware of it. Her boyfriend Ken, was to be away for a further six months' tour of duty and she was lonely. There is only so much solace to be taken from letters and photographs and she was bored. Janice was after all, she convinced herself, a normal young woman. She wanted to go out and about for a drink and have a laugh.

In her own way she was no more honest with Gary than he was with her. She had no intention of regarding their relationship as permanent. She was quite happy with Ken, but he was in the forces, currently serving in the Middle East. Gary was just a diversion against boredom in his absence; company for an evening, and a purchaser of the occasional meal.

Gary had taken her out a few times in the run up to Christmas, mostly when he wanted help with writing. It was Janice who had helped him put together the Miner's Cottage list for Simon, and although her spelling was not good, it was much more legible than Gary's.

'So,' she had said the previous evening, pouting cheekily, 'What's in it for me Gary?'

'Well,' he said, smiling engagingly at her and stroking her forearm with his finger until the fine hairs stood on end. 'I've got a little pressy for Janice.' Immediately she drew back.

'Oh, I bet you have,' she said.

'No', Gary was embarrassed at her reaction, 'I didn't mean,' he coloured, 'I meant this.' He passed across a cheap cardboard box, approximately three inches square. Inside was bundled a gold-coloured chain with a small pretty pendant in the form of three smoky stones in a filigree setting.

'Gary, it's beautiful.' Janice was amazed that Gary would have bought her such a pretty gift for helping him out. She looked up at him. 'Is it really for me?'

''Course it is, don't you help me loads? It's just to say ta. It's not real,' he hurried on, in case she misunderstood his motivation, 'but it's pretty.'

'It's lovely, Gary.' Janice told him. She covered his hand with her own. She looked at Gary with new eyes; this was a side to him that she had not expected. His dark, brooding looks appealed to her. After another drink Janice had decided that what Ken was unaware of would not hurt him. 'Why don't we go back to mine for a coffee?' she smiled at him provocatively.

At home later on her own, Janice took out the little box Gary had handed her in the pub. Sitting in front of her dressing table mirror she tried the pendant against her throat. She could identify what Gary had not, the gold hallmark hidden in the filigree design. That made it perhaps more valuable than he had realised. It was a pretty thing – one she would love to have kept but she could foresee all kinds of difficulties when Ken came home. He was not one to understand gifts from another man.

Chapter 7

The morning after the burglary Maxine found she was very hungry. The casserole Anne left for her the previous day had seemed unappealing last night and was still in the fridge for later, but she enjoyed a hearty breakfast, and after walking the dogs, finished the cleaning up task. Walking the dogs in the woods was always the best therapy for putting the world to rights, but today she turned in the opposite direction and walked through the fields instead. She felt her spirits lift as she went to change to meet her friend Harriet. It was then that Maxine missed the pearl pendant.

She looked through her jewellery box and realized that it had been in the safe. Head in hands she sat on the side of the bed and burst into tears. She felt so guilty not to have noticed its loss immediately. It had no great intrinsic value, but Pippa had bought it for her from her first month's salary. She remembered her daughter's delight at the gift, having noticed her admire it in Vine Gold's shop window in Hanley.

Somehow its loss affected her more than anything else that had been taken. It was so very personal and she felt the violation all over again. Wiping her eyes, she went to the bathroom and retouched her make-up. Selecting another necklace, she glared in the mirror at the effect and decided that it would have to do, although it didn't look nearly so good. Glancing at her watch she saw that it was time to leave.

The antiques emporium at Walgherton was a favourite meeting place, and she arrived half an hour before the time she was to meet Harriet, the better to stroll through the barns and browse.

An eclectic mix of goods was always on offer at the various craft and antique stalls, and this was supplemented now by a range of seasonal goods, hopefully marked up as last minute Christmas presents. Maxine paused before Staffordshire pottery and ceramics, and feeling the passing of this fine local industry, found herself sighing as she had so many times in the last few days.

She looked briefly at some of the jewellery on offer, but had not the heart to seriously search for a replacement pendant. Glancing at her watch she headed for the cafe to meet her friend. If not renowned for culinary excellence, Dagfields served strong hot coffee and first class sandwiches, all that Maxine felt she could manage today.

Maxine was as dark as Harriet was fair. Harriet was a confident business woman, self-assured and always beautifully dressed. For fourteen years she had owned and run her speciality knitwear business, which thrived in the Cheshire town of Nantwich. She had recently expanded the business, opening a second outlet in Alderley Edge, home to many moneyed footballers and their families.

Maxine watched as Harriet made her way elegantly between the antiques laid out in the large barn. At nearly six feet tall Harriet would have been an imposing woman regardless of her looks, but her figure and features were striking and today she looked like a model in tailored beige trousers and jacket of her own design, knitted in various subtle shades of browns and greens. Maxine always felt somewhat underdressed beside her friend. Constantly battling excess weight, and with unruly dark hair Maxine knew her looks to be inferior, but the affection between the two was genuine, with no jealousy. Maxine had pretty features. Her skin was beautiful, a true peaches and cream complexion, in which flashed dark eyes her ex-husband had, in the early heady days of their relationship, described as *limpid pools in which he could drown.*

The two had been inseparable throughout secondary school and the friendship had continued and mellowed in their young adult lives, despite their differences in direction. Maxine had married early, aged just nineteen and Pippa, her only child, was born the following year. Only after she and her husband separated and Pippa was at school, had she turned her thoughts to her own career, developed her passion for languages, and set up her own freelance translation business for businesses across the UK, Germany and France. She also taught part time at a local school.

Harriet had left school at sixteen, determined, despite the admonishments of her parents, to take the earliest opportunity to develop in her chosen field of fashion and design. Her mother bowed to the inevitable. Being on first name terms with many of the fashion buyers in stores across the region and in Manchester and Birmingham, she had secured an introduction to a design studio. Harriet had started as the junior to learn the business and, an apt student, she had quickly become one of their top fashion designers, only leaving to set up her own company just before her thirtieth birthday.

She was blessed with family money and as a

single person could afford holidays abroad and a privileged lifestyle. Maxine, bringing up her daughter alone, struggled financially in the early years but enjoyed the blessings that motherhood brings. The friendship had changed as they do when lives take such divergent paths, but Harriet took her role as Pippa's Godmother seriously, and the two continued to meet regularly for lunch.

'What on earth happened?' Harriet asked as they waited for a free table, 'I know you were going to Pippa's for Christmas, because I called up there last weekend with her Christmas present. Then she rang to say you had been burgled. I was so shocked, I can't tell you.' Well-tended hands fluttered at her throat in a characteristic gesture.

'Did you meet the Boy Wonder?'

'Yes,' Harriet hesitated, not sure how much to divulge about the row she had interrupted. 'I can't say my first impression was favourable.'

Despite herself Maxine smiled. 'You are the master, or is it mistress of understatement? He is a total...'

Maxine had to break off as they spotted a table being vacated and hurried to take possession. The cafe was packed and Maxine was pleased to see them doing so much business.

Later, as they sat nursing their coffees Harriet commented, 'Pretty necklace, I don't remember seeing that before.'

'No,' said Maxine, 'normally I wouldn't wear it with this top; it's too heavy and chunky somehow. I normally wear the pearl drop Pippa gave me, but I realized today that it's just another thing Sonny-boy nicked.' She smiled bravely and took a sip of coffee.

Harriet put her hand on Maxine's arm, 'Oh no! That was so special. Does Pippa know?'

Maxine shook her head. 'I only just realized myself as I was getting ready to come out. That's what's so awful about being burgled – little things that must seem trivial to the thief, are tied up with so many personal memories. It's all so mindless. I gave a list to the police, but there are already a couple of things I've realized since have also gone.'

'You should replace it,' said Harriet, smiling as she took the bill from the waiter. 'You can't replace your dad's medals, but you could get yourself another pendant. Not something identical, but with something to suit you, that you like and that you can regard as Pippa's gift. It won't be quite the same of course, but it would do you good to treat yourself.'

'I think perhaps I will, but I'll wait a while. The Inspector said there's a chance I might get some of the stuff back.'

Glancing at her watch she said, 'I may go and get some work done this afternoon, if I can concentrate. Perhaps for once I can be well ahead of my deadline instead of down to the wire.'

Chapter 8

Gary waited until midnight. The house had a long sweeping drive and the windows were out of view from the lane, beyond vast gardens and what looked in the gloom like a tennis court. He entered the drive using side-lights alone and was faced with a large circular bed of flowers and shrubs, in the centre of which played a fountain. All this was surrounded by a gravel drive. Keeping to the right of the bed, he was able to park the car out of sight of both the house and the lane. He had waited until lights in the nearest properties had been turned off, and had ventured on foot down the lane beyond to ensure that all was in darkness.

At the chosen house there had been no movement of curtains, no lights going on or off, and no car could be seen through the frosted glass of the double garage doors. Nor had he expected any. To himself he called the woman *the bitch,* on the basis of a gangster film he had seen, and he knew that *the bitch* was on holiday.

This was Gary's second visit to the house in as many days, and he knew that this large detached house had extensive and overgrown outbuildings. On his last visit he had gingerly explored, opening doors to what was clearly a wood store and a dairy. Outdoor steps led to an upper storey, over stabling containing three looseboxes, but he quickly established in torchlight that the doors were so covered in cobwebs and rust that they could not have been used for years.

He was targeting the small hall window beside the garage door, partly hidden beneath a wooden pergola draped with the winter remnants of some climbing plant, ghostly in the moonlight. This window had the advantage of being set right back from the lane and hidden from any street lights' glow by dense shrubbery. Gary placed his bag quietly on the floor and took out sticky tape, his torch and a towel.

Taping across the window took some time, but meant that when he wrapped his torch in the towel and hit the glass there was little noise and he was able carefully to reach through and open the window from the inside. He waited, sweating, to hear the raucous sound of a burglar alarm, but there was nothing. Aware that some of the more sophisticated alarm systems alerted the police or a private organisation, which would then check, Gary got back in his car and drove back down the lane, parking in a lay-by from which he could see in both directions.

Confidence increasing with each passing minute, Gary waiting for almost half an hour, then, with no sign of any response to his summons, he returned to the house. Getting through the window was harder than he expected but he managed to get a purchase with his shoe on the side of the garage wall and heave himself up and over the sill.

Once inside the house, he put on the torch and cautiously looked around. He was in a small hallway that opened onto the first of several living rooms. Passing through the first of these he entered a magnificent hall with an oak staircase up to the bedroom level, and a tessellated tile floor. At the back of the room was an open arch-shaped doorway, through which he could see the huge modern kitchen. Keeping the beam on the floor, Gary checked the ground floor for an exit route and opened slightly one of several sets of patio doors onto the back garden. On a side table he spotted a laptop plugged into the mains.

Placing it and its lead by the open patio door, he peered out. He could see a wide expanse of lawns with the tennis court now to his right. The back perimeter fence was high and fronted with shrubbery, but Gary reckoned that he could penetrate that if necessary.

He looked quickly through the drawers in this first living room then, finding nothing but papers, went upstairs and into the first of the bedrooms at the front of the house. This was clearly the largest of the four bedrooms on this floor, with opulent furniture, massive wardrobes and a modern en suite bathroom. He began a systematic searching of the drawers and cupboards, and had just emptied the contents of a pale green leather jewellery box into his pocket when he saw car headlights strobe across the walls and heard a car engine being switched off.

His hands sweating and his heart beating wildly in his chest, he moved across to the side window and peered down from behind the curtain. There was now a car on the drive in front of the garage, with a lone woman in a pink coat getting out of the driver's door. She locked it and, keys in hand, approached the front door. In a panic Gary looked around. His planned way out was downstairs and with dry mouth and sweaty palms he stood for what seemed like minutes frozen with fear as he heard a key in the lock and the front door open.

'Oh my God,' he heard from downstairs, 'who's there? Where are you? I'm calling the police.' followed by the sound of footsteps running lightly up the stairs.

Driven by panic, Gary charged at the stairs, meeting the startled woman who was nearing the top. As she stepped onto the landing and tried to grab his jacket, he fought himself free in a panic and hit her with the torch. The blow caught her off balance and she fell backwards down the full flight of stairs. Gary grabbed the banister rail to stop himself falling after her. He closed his eyes but heard the sickening crunch as her head struck the tiled floor and for ten full seconds he couldn't look. He covered his face with his hands.

'Oh God, Oh God, Oh God,' his mantra repeated, his brain numb with fright. Finally he stirred himself, knew he must move, get past her before she got up and called the neighbours or the police. He charged down the stairs and, when she didn't move, he shone his torch on her.

He could see at once that she was dead. It was the angle of her head and the blood already beginning to show in her nostrils. Gary thought he would faint. He could barely manage to step over her and down the final two steps. Shaking hands dropped the torch as he switched it off and he couldn't bear to look at her. Dashing to the kitchen, he wretched drily into the sink.

Terrified that he was wrong and that she would, even now, be getting up, he forced himself back through the archway and to the bottom of the stairs. Equally terrified that he wasn't wrong, he again illuminated her face with torchlight. She hadn't moved; wouldn't move and he noticed that there was congealing blood sliding from her left ear and staining the fabric of the pink coat.

Taking a deep breath he realised that several minutes had passed. For a further ten whole minutes he waited, expecting police, neighbours, someone who had heard her challenge but nothing happened, no-one came, and gradually he began to realise that no-one would. There was no-one in the house, or they would have heard the furore, she had come home alone and no-one would be around until at least morning.

Shit, why wasn't she on holiday? But there was no time for thinking about that now, he had to move her; get away from here. Gradually he formulated a plan of sorts. Her keys were where she had dropped them on a small table by the door. Tentatively he opened the patio doors fully, grabbed the laptop and stepped out. The lane was silent, all was still in darkness.

Gary reasoned that the longer it took to find her the more he could cover his tracks, and quietly he opened the boot of her car. The position of the garage meant that he was hidden from the neighbouring windows. Going back into the house he braced himself to pick up the still figure. She was very slight – very likely she didn't weigh more than eight stones, and he was easily able to carry out this sickening task. He could see in the gloom the glistening of rings on her finger and a gold choker around her neck, but he lacked the stomach to remove them.

Looking round the living room he picked up the handbag from the floor and threw it in with her, then quietly closed the boot. For a split second he panicked that he had locked the car keys in the boot, but found to his relief that he had automatically put them in his pocket. He closed and locked the front door before getting into the driver's seat, adjusting it for his longer legs. His hands continued to shake spasmodically and he had to wait before he could get the key to engage. The engine turned over quietly and he drew round the central fountain, back into the road, glancing again at the silent and darkened neighbouring houses as he eased forward to the end of the lane, only putting on the lights as he had turned onto the main road.

Heading towards home he began to congratulate himself on his calm thinking and level-headedness. There were others he knew who would have gone to pieces in a crisis but not he, not Gary Lewis. Realising he was still wearing the thin gloves he had used to avoid leaving fingerprints he even began to laugh out loud at his cleverness, before the enormity of the situation hit him once again and he had to pull over until his hands stopped shaking.

Gary drove first to the allotments in Silverdale. Tucked away behind the primary school it was the remotest spot he could think of to acquire what he needed. The first shed he tried was securely padlocked, displaying a sign indicating that an alarm was fitted. Using only his torch he moved deeper into the plots until he came to a more dilapidated and rickety affair. This time the padlock was insubstantial and the hasp broke easily with a couple of sharp whacks of the torch head. Glancing around the shed interior he selected a spade and retreated to the car. He threw the spade into the boot, careful not to look at the figure crumpled there.

Noticing a wheelbarrow in the corner, he piled this too into the boot. Closing the lid quietly, he exhaled deeply and climbed into the driving seat. Slipping the car into gear he crept off the allotment track and took the Black Bank road towards Audley and Podmore Lane. Now for the big step.

*   *   *

Calmer once his exhausting work was complete, Gary drove first to the truckers' stop on the A500 where he took off his jacket, he was sweating so much. Then, lighting a cigarette, he headed towards Manchester. He left the motorway before reaching the airport, and headed for an area he had visited once before as a child. He cruised slowly along Simonsway looking for the turning, then took a left into Fleming Road.

A couple of minutes and he found what he had expected, a row of public recycling bins flanked by a couple of skips full of general rubbish at the back of the car park. Turning off his lights, he cruised up quietly and parked beside one of them. Checking for CCTV cameras and noting that the only one nearby was trained on adjacent shop fronts, he pulled up his hood and opened the car boot.

Keeping his face well down and away from the camera he thrust the spade as deeply as he could beneath the rubbish. It was immediately evident that he could not heave the barrow high enough to drop that in the skip, so he pulled it out of the car and jammed it as far as possible between two of the recycling containers. Hopefully someone would steal it – if not the council would no doubt clear it away.

He retraced his route to the main road and continued to the airport car park. Selecting the long stay park he pocketed the entry ticket and drove the car to one of the furthest areas, where he parked in the darkest space he could find. Quickly he searched the inside of the car for anything he could use, and recovered the Givenchy handbag from the boot.

Reluctant to waste time, he opened the purse inside and removed the cash, pushing it down into his pocket. Cards were of no use to him, but he also took the mobile phone, tucking the bag out of sight under the passenger seat. Not wanting to look round overtly for cameras as he left the car he struggled with his coat before getting out, and again he put up his hood. He added a scarf from his rucksack and headed for the station. He revelled in his cleverness – the coldness of the night was playing into his hands. If he was caught on CCTV, the gloves, hood and scarf were unremarkable on a night cold enough to freeze his breath.

Slumping in the corner seat, Gary looked triumphantly around the carriage. The woman's jewellery and mobile phone were tucked carefully in his rucksack with her laptop. On the journey back to Stoke he occasionally patted the rucksack like a talisman, his confidence growing all the time.

Only one other couple shared the carriage with him, clearly returning holidaymakers, more intent in keeping a wary if bleary eye on their luggage than looking at him.

Concealed from them by the seat in front, Gary allowed himself to relax. He suddenly realised how tired he felt, but euphoric too. He started to repeat to himself in time to the clackety clack of the train, 'I've committed a murder, I've committed a murder.' Aware that he was muttering aloud he checked on his travelling companions and found that they were both asleep. Too wired to sleep himself, he left the train at Stoke station and caught the first bus heading in the right direction. He had a mile or so to walk back to where he had left his van, again delighted that he had had the foresight to leave it in a lay-by several hundred yards from the dead woman's house.

All the time commending himself on his cool head, Gary called in at a newsagent for a morning paper, and was apparently casually scanning this as he rounded the corner and approached the van. Half expecting it to be swarming with police he found that he was holding his breath, and exhaled slowly as he found it was as he had left it, standing in isolation.

'I've got away with murder,' he chanted again under his breath. Even so, his hands were shaking again as he tried the ignition and it took him several attempts before the engine fired. Carefully he drove home – drawing attention to himself now would be disastrous.

Realising as he parked outside his own home that he had been awake for twenty four hours he yawned massively and headed into the house to his bedroom. Gary spread out the jewellery he had taken from the dead woman's house onto his bed. He picked through the items without enthusiasm.

There was a watch, a charm bracelet, three rings with stones that may have been diamonds, and a pendant with some sort of cloudy stones. Dejected, Gary scooped the jewellery into his top bedside drawer. He stowed the mobile phone and laptop, as yet unexplored, into the bottom of his wardrobe and threw himself on the bed to consider his next move. That bastard Simon had set him up, it was his fault that this had happened. Him and that bitch who had come home instead of being on holiday.

Well he had dealt with her. He would also deal with Simon.

Chapter 9

As Angela cleaned Susannah's house, her mind wandered to the next post she planned to send to Kevin. She quickly worked out timings. Today was Monday, so he would not expect her to be back from Dubai until at least tomorrow, she'd write on Wednesday evening. It was Susannah's husband Giles who had unwittingly put the idea of a Dubai trip into her head, as he was away at the moment on one of his regular trips there to enjoy the horse racing.

She polished and scrubbed and ironed, all the time daydreaming of a world where she was telling Kevin about her trip face-to-face over cocktails; of him being enchanted by her wit and style, and eventually telling her he had fallen in love with her. As she wrung out the mop for a final time, she caught sight of herself in the kettle and smiled at the idea. Hair lank, face streaked with dirt and her tee shirt stained with perspiration, it was a laughable thought.

As she put the bucket away she heard a key in the front door. Leaning around the door jamb she saw Giles come in, a bag in his hand and a coat over his arm.

'Hullo Giles,' she sang out, 'Good trip?'

'Oh, yes thanks, er … Angela. Is my wife around?'

'Actually I've not seen her today, and she's not left a note. I don't know where she's got to.'

Not for Giles to know that when Angela came in this morning the bed hadn't been disturbed from the day before. Angela changed into her outdoor shoes and struggled into her coat.

'The Trafford Centre probably,' mused Giles half to himself, 'Retaliation for Dubai.'

Angela smiled back, 'I'm off then, Giles, see you tomorrow.'

'Not me, I have to be in the office. Thank you… Angela. Take care.'

By six o'clock Giles was beginning to get anxious. The Trafford Centre was open into the evenings, but it was unusual for Susannah to stay out until this time. He had expected her home by now and there was no sign of any preparations for a meal, which was unusual. He showered in case they were due to be going out somewhere when she arrived, and caught the local news and sport on the television. He saw that a football match in Manchester was causing congestion around the area, and decided to get himself something to eat.

'She's hardly a missing person yet, Sir,' said the constable patiently on the telephone. 'She's probably seen all the traffic and stopped off for something to eat.'

'She would have let me know.' Giles insisted. 'She never went anywhere without her phone. At the least she would have phoned to see if I'd got back.'

'I suggest you try to get some rest sir, chances are she'll come breezing in soon enough wondering what all the fuss is about.'

The description conjured up Susannah so vividly that Giles was irrationally reassured as he put down the handset.

Despite his worries, jetlag and a couple of large whiskies sledgehammered Giles into sleep in the early hours and he woke still in the armchair with a crick in his neck, and in complete darkness. He glanced at his watch. Just before seven, and still Susannah had not returned. Suddenly he realised that his assumption about Susannah going shopping may be entirely incorrect. She could have been missing for a lot longer than just yesterday.

He had no idea of Angela's phone number, or even her surname. If he was honest he had struggled to dredge up her Christian name. Presumably these details were in Susannah's mobile phone or committed to her memory. This thought prompted him to see if the phone was anywhere in the house, and to try to decide which bag Susannah may have with her, although searching through the wardrobe they jokingly called 'Bag City' he soon realised would be fruitless.

The other clothes cupboards were no help either. With so many clothes it was impossible to know if anything was missing. Giles tried but failed to conjure up a mental picture of what Susannah had been wearing when he last saw her. He rifled through a variety of handbags, in one finding a grocery receipt dated for Friday. This gave Giles some reassurance – the list included items she had presumably planned to serve to her friends on the Saturday evening.

The bedroom was immaculate as usual after Angela's ministrations, and a check of the rest of the house showed no evidence of anything untoward, until he came to the little storeroom beyond the drawing room. This was where the safe was situated under the floor, but although the access to the safe seemed unaffected there was a broken pane of glass in the small window. Immediately Giles contacted the police again.

*   *   *

By the time fingerprint experts had finished with the storeroom and moved on to other areas of the house, Angela could be heard letting herself in at the back door. Giles had been unable to say which clothes Susannah had been wearing and what else, if anything she had taken with her. He and Angela sat at the kitchen table with yet another cup of coffee. They had been able to establish that Susannah's laptop was not in the home office, but she often left it in the car. Televisions and other electronic equipment seemed untouched but her mobile telephone and possibly a handbag were missing, certainly there was no sign of her purse, keys or cosmetics bag.

Reiteration of the police questions seemed interminable, yet it seemed to Giles that they were no further forward. Angela had seen her on Thursday morning. She glanced at Giles and the police sergeant who was taking notes. Detective Sergeant Talbot noticed that she smelt less than sweet, and went to look out of the window, returning to a chair on the other side of Giles.

'To be honest, Susannah was a bit on high doh, getting ready for Saturday.' said Angela, 'She had me clean the drawing room especially, and the kitchen and downstairs loo. Funnily enough, she sat at the table there and put together a shopping list for Friday, then went upstairs and brought down her black skirt for me to press. Actually that was the last thing I did before I left on Thursday. I don't work on Fridays.'

The police checked with the neighbours. One

from next door had been included in the Saturday evening gathering, but had not seen Susannah since. She had seemed perfectly normal on Saturday. The neighbour was able to name some of the other guests. Some she met for the first time that evening and for these she knew only first names, but half a dozen she named were known to Giles. Susannah had been fine on Saturday night.

The only thing which came to light was that Susannah had offered to drive one of her friends home after the party. Although she lived close by, her journey on foot would have been dark and unpleasant. Susannah had drunk little and other guests heard her saying that she would take this Julia home herself. Julia's address was known to the neighbour, but there was no reply when DS Talbot called.

Was it usual, the Detective Inspector wanted to know, for Susannah to entertain whilst her husband was away? Giles explained that it was.

'She came to Dubai with me for possibly the first two years we were married, but she didn't enjoy it very much. She's not a good traveller, is very nervous of flying. Now she spends the time catching up with old friends and shopping, whilst I travel alone.' He missed the slight nod the inspector gave to the sergeant, who left the room to make a call.

'Funnily enough the bed hadn't been slept in last night.' said Angela. 'Actually I've just thought and,' she paused, considering, 'when I think about it, it hadn't been slept on Sunday night either. It was made already after a fashion when I arrived yesterday, and Susannah never made the bed when I was due in, she always left it for me to do. She said I could do hospital corners much neater.'

The detective inspector focused his full attention on Angela. 'Was there anything else different about yesterday? You clean here, what' he checked his notebook, 'four mornings a week? You must know the house and the routines very well.'

Angela thought. If she was strictly honest she was not in the least interested in Susannah and her routines. She came in, did her job and went. Glancing at Giles she decided it would not be prudent to say this.

'Well yes, funnily enough,' she said, qualifying, 'As much as there are routines. Susannah comes and goes at different times. She has some routines, the gym, the hairdresser each Wednesday, and so on, but otherwise it was very flexible. Actually there was one thing. When I came yesterday the burglar alarm wasn't set, although,' she paused, 'that wasn't so unusual. It was a complicated system and sometimes Susannah couldn't be bothered – especially if she wasn't planning to be out for long.'

Inspector Timothy tried another avenue. 'I'd like you to look at Mrs Scott-Ryder's clothes, to see if anything's missing,' but here too he was out of luck.

'Oh, really?' said Angela, 'Actually Susannah has so many clothes I wouldn't be able to say unless it's something very obvious, but I'll try.'

The constable accompanied Angela to what she called the utility room where she explored the washing machine drum, the tumble dryer and a large basket of clothes ready for ironing. She accompanied her search with a commentary for the officer.

'The stuff in this basket I usually tackle on a Tuesday morning, and I generally spend the whole morning ironing. Actually sometimes I iron on a Thursday as well, but that's usually if there's something special she wants to wear at the weekend.' She moved on to the principal bedroom where she opened the double wardrobe doors.

'That's odd,' she said, moving to another large basket, this time of clothes waiting to be washed. Angela frowned, rummaging in the basket.

'Actually that's very odd. I can't see the skirt she was planning to wear on Saturday. She asked me to iron it last Thursday, and I would have expected it to go either back in the wardrobe or in this basket.'

She returned to the wardrobe. 'It's hard to know which top she would have worn on Saturday, she didn't say anything to me and she has so many.'

She lowered her voice conspiratorially, so the constable had to lean forward to hear her, getting a whiff of her body odour in the process.

'Actually, between you and me, most weeks she visits the Trafford Centre, or Manchester a couple of times. She has some favourite out-of-town boutiques as well, and she seldom comes back without two or three designer name carrier bags. You can see all this stuff,' she gesticulated at the wardrobe, the overflowing laundry basket and a pile of boxes.

'There's another rail in one of the spare rooms upstairs. I'll check for that skirt up there, although I can't think why it would be there.' A quick check confirmed her suspicions and they returned to the kitchen.

'Funnily enough the only other place that black skirt could be is in the bin.' The constable looked surprised.

'Oh I know,' Angela interpreted his look. 'But I've seen things before where the zip breaks and she throws them away, even if they are designer labels, a wicked waste.'

She again cast a sidelong glance at Giles, hoping he wasn't offended, but Giles seemed to be unaware of what she was saying as he continued to gaze out of the window. The constable set off down the drive to the bin by the gate, returning a few minutes later to shake his head at the inspector.

'Then,' said DI Timothy, 'It seems that she was wearing the black evening skirt when she went out, which suggests that she went missing on Saturday night.'

They asked Giles about what blouse or top she may have been wearing. 'Really I'm not sure. Susannah buys so many clothes.' You've seen the boxes in the corner of the bedroom? She got those last week.'

The inspector had glanced through the boxes, Louis Vuitton, Chanel, and two Harvey Nichols' carrier bags containing scarves, perfume and a cashmere sweater. They did not look like the purchases of someone planning to leave home.

'Is there anyone else who may be able to help us with what's missing Mr Scott-Ryder?'

'Possibly Harriet, my daughter. She and Susannah have been friends for years and used to be flatmates, although Susannah is five years the younger. They spend a lot of time together.' Noticing the inspector's slight frown Giles gave a weak smile.

'Oh, don't worry inspector, I wasn't a cradle snatcher. Harriet had just gone through a messy relationship breakdown and gone on holiday with this old friend of hers. After that Susannah was round here a lot because Harriet moved back in for a while, and the rest as they say is history.'

'I believe your wife is an only child, and your cleaner thinks that her mother is out of the country just now. Do you have any other family from your first marriage, sir? Anyone your wife may have gone to visit?'

'That's right. Susannah's mother has gone to visit her sister in Cape Town. She goes every year from early December until well into the New Year. I do have a son, inspector, but Susannah would never have gone to Matthew's. She's only met him two or three times and he lives in the States. Susannah would never take off just like that. She hates flying, she would never fly alone. She always relied on me to deal with passports and visas and so on. I doubt she even knows where our passports are.' His voice broke. 'I've rung Harriet, she's on her way.'

Just then DI Timothy's phone rang and a brief conversation ensued. Snapping the phone closed, he said to the sergeant:

'That's the lady who was given a lift home on Saturday. She's been away overnight, but will be back in half an hour. We'll go and see her now.' He turned to the constable,

'You go back to the neighbour again and ask her to describe Mrs Scott-Ryder's blouse from Saturday night. Give a description to Miss...er,' he looked vainly in his notebook for Angela's surname.

'What is your other name? Mr Scott-Ryder was unable to say.'

'Actually it's Davies, Angela Davies.' She

said quietly, hurt that Giles did not even know her name, but she cheered up at the idea that he knew her so well he always used her first name, just like she was one of the family.

The Detective Inspector was still speaking and writing, 'Yes, Miss Davies, thank you. Once the constable has established what the top looks like, if you, Miss Davies will look for it and let us know whether it's here, that would be most helpful,' he flattered when Giles had left the room. 'You're knowledge of Mrs Scott-Ryder's lifestyle is very useful.'

The truth was that Angela despised the lifestyle her employers enjoyed and would have left them in a moment if she could have brought in that amount of income elsewhere. Frequently she had put up cards in the post office, the newsagent's and the village store, but people, as she said to herself were *feeling the pinch* and she had no responses that would anywhere near match the money she earned at the old farmhouse.

It was galling to her that Susannah showed not the least interest in her as a person, wanted to know nothing of her life, her hopes and aspirations, expecting her to sublimate her preferences to their petty caprices. Her contempt increased as she learned something of Susannah's background. In a moment of indiscretion fuelled by sweet sherry Susannah's mother had, during a visit, commented on how Angela was ironing Giles's shirts.

'It's a wonder Susannah hasn't put you straight,' she said over the rim of her Oloroso. 'She used to be a packer in a shirt factory in Manchester when she first left school. Nothing she doesn't know about looking after shirts.'

Angela smiled to herself. So it was only her liaison with Giles that had brought Susannah the trappings and attitude of wealth. And all the airs that she gave herself.

'Oh, how can you bear that instant coffee,' she had said once in the early days. 'Do help yourself to fresh from the machine.' Having eyed the machine askance Angela had decided to stick to instant.

Once when she had asked Angela to prepare potatoes for some fancy recipe, she had said out of the blue.

'I can't understand how people can bear to eat those oven chips, can you Angela?' and wrinkled her nose in distaste. Angela, in whose diet oven chips played a considerable part, had made no response.

*   *   *

Always with an eye to getting something for nothing, Angela had, in the earliest weeks of her employment, eyed up Susannah's wardrobe in some detail. It comprised mostly designer label items and they were much of a size. Angela decided on a ruse. She told Susannah that she worked for a local hospice charity shop part time, and if ever there was anything that Susannah was considering throwing away, then perhaps she might let Angela have it for the shop.

Reluctant to labour the point, she nevertheless occasionally dropped into conversation that she would be working for the shop that afternoon, or that she was going to collect some items to increase the stock. The result had been disappointing. Over all the months Susannah had offered her only a few old pairs of shoes of Giles's, which Angela had accepted with gushing thanks and put straight in the bin.

The only useful item she had acquired from Susannah had been a pair of bottle green Armani trousers with a broken zip, which she had retrieved from Susannah's bedroom bin. These she had mended and wore frequently.

Chapter 10

Julia Corner found the whole thing very distasteful. At least the detectives had arrived in an unmarked car, but even so she found herself hoping that her neighbours were out.

'I really don't know Susannah very well at all.' She stood in the hall, determined to offer the police inspector and his minion no more access to her home than necessary.

'Well enough to be invited to her party.'

'Really these parties were Susannah's way of passing the time. Giles was off somewhere – Abu Dhabi or Dubai or some such place.' Her expression of distaste damned the whole of the Middle East.

'I think anyone was welcome at these do's of hers. I really don't know her very well.' She made to move them to the door, but the inspector remained where he was, and changed tack.

'Tell me how it came out that she brought you home. How had you got there in the first place?'

With a petulant sigh Mrs Corner resigned herself to their questioning.

'I lost my licence, driving over the limit about a year ago. I got a taxi to Susannah's and intended to get one home, but she very kindly offered to bring me, pointing out that taxis are not easy to get at that time of a Saturday night and I may have a long wait.'

'Perhaps she wanted to be rid of you,' suggested the sergeant, earning him a glare from Mrs Corner and a slight twitch of the lips from his superior.

'I really don't think...' she expostulated.

'Mrs Corner,' the Detective Inspector interjected swiftly, 'please describe the route that you travelled in Susannah's car on that night.'

'Really,' she said, continuing to watch the sergeant, 'Really, we came the only possible route, from Scot Hay, down Crackley Lane, right through Madeley Heath, right onto the Betley Road, then left at the war memorial. I could have walked, but it's not well lit and I was glad of the lift at the time. I wish now that I had refused.'

Inspector Timothy inclined his head and continued his train of thought.

'What did you talk about?'

'Really, inspector,' it seemed to be her favourite word. 'I don't know that we talked about anything.'

'You sat in silence throughout a ten minute journey? Are you sure?'

'Yes, No, Really, I mean we didn't talk about anything particular. Just that so-and-so has lost weight; so-and-so hasn't worn the years so well etcetera. Really nothing of consequence.'

Resisting the temptation to refer to a load of old so-and-so's, the sergeant asked a question.

'How would you describe Susannah's mood on that , Mrs Corner?'

Pointedly ignoring him and turning towards the inspector she said,

'Well, she was quite as usual really. A bit tired perhaps but that's only to be expected after a party. She dropped me at the gate, and the last thing she said was that she would see me on Wednesday. We have regular hair appointments at Chez Michel at ten thirty. That's how I met Susannah.'

'What was she wearing on Saturday, Mrs Corner?'

'Really, I can't remember. Oh yes, a lovely pink and black top, no sleeves and a black skirt. Now if you'll excuse me.'

The detectives showed no sign of leaving.

'What about jewellery? Did you notice what she had on?'

This was clearly much more interesting territory for the woman, who visibly relaxed.

'Oh yes, she has some lovely pieces, lovely. On Saturday let me see, yes she was wearing her gold watch, she usually wore that. On her right wrist she had a heavy gold bangle, oh that matched the choker she wore. Giles had brought them back from Dubai one time, I believe. It must have been worth a fortune,' she finished wistfully. Once again she ushered them towards the door. There was nothing more to be gleaned from Mrs Corner.

Sergeant Talbot had barely got in the car before he exclaimed,

'What a bitch. With friends like that sir ...'

'Indeed,' mused the Inspector, 'I wonder what Mrs Scott-Ryder saw in her. She obviously didn't like her hostess much, but was happy enough to spend a spare evening sponging party food and drink off her.'

'And accepting a lift home from her. What a bitch.' The sergeant repeated. 'One thing though, sir, did you notice?'

'Mmmmm,' the Inspector concurred, 'she coveted that jewellery, didn't she?'

Returning to the Scott-Ryder's farmhouse the

detective inspector found that the daughter, Harriet had arrived, and was with her father in the drawing room.

Twice during the morning the front door bell rang. The first time galvanised Giles from his seat, but Angela who had been in the kitchen rinsing coffee cups, reached the door first. She opened it to reveal a pile of three white cardboard boxes, behind which was revealed the local florist.

'Mrs Scott-Ryder's Christmas order, he carolled, placing the boxes on the counter in the utility room at the back of the kitchen. He read from his order book,

'The usual lilies; white roses; rust and gold chrysanthemums – hope they're the right colours – for the bathroom, she said. The two wreaths, one for the front door, one for the porch, and mistletoe for good luck.'

'That's fine,' said Angela mechanically, signing his book as she did each week.

'Merry Christmas,' he finished. 'Best wishes to the family.'

'Indeed.' said Angela returning to the drawing room to a sea of expectant faces.

'Florist,' she said flatly. 'With the Christmas order. I'll put this lot in water.'

She saw Giles flinch. No sooner had she finished dealing with the flowers, than the back doorbell rang again. The police constable answered the door this time, closely followed by Giles, whose shoulders slumped at the sight of the baker's van parked on the gravel.

'Christmas,' spat Giles, 'It's going on all over the world – a frenzy of activity, and it means nothing.' He sat in the window seat and dropped his head into his hands.

'What on earth does Christmas matter under these circumstances?'

'You do have to eat Giles,' Angela said brightly, taking the bread order through from the kitchen, 'I'll just pop this lot into the big freezer shall I? Then I'll be off home.'

*　　*　　*

When the inspector arrived back at the house, the constable confirmed the information he had from the next door neighbour.

On Saturday evening Susannah had been wearing, he read from his notes, a smudge pink top, a bit Chinese in style with detail in black across one shoulder, very unusual. The neighbour had helpfully logged onto the Karen Millen website on her laptop and printed off an image of the top that Susannah had been wearing. The constable produced this image with a flourish.

'Nearly a hundred quid for a tee shirt,' he said, amazed. He confirmed that he had asked Angela to look for it, and as they spoke she returned to the kitchen shaking her head.

'It isn't here,' she said crossly, 'I was already sure it wasn't, and it's not. Can I go now? I actually only get paid for four hours each day you know.' She glanced again at her watch, a gesture noted by Inspector Timothy, and by Harriet who had silently entered the room behind her.

'I'll run you home, if that helps Angela,' she offered, fiddling anxiously with her earrings. 'You've been so helpful it's the least I can do.'

'Actually, I'm fine thanks.' Angela was brusque, shrugging into outdoor clothes as the Inspector gave permission for her to leave, 'I have my bike, and I have shopping to do. I'll come tomorrow shall I? Perhaps a bit later than normal, but I'll do my time.' She made it sound like a prison sentence.

Harriet was quietly spoken and beautifully groomed. She was considerably taller than the inspector, which to his surprise he found slightly disconcerting. Her clothes were classically elegant and she answered the police inspector's questions thoughtfully.

'Susannah is basically very insecure. I like her in spite of the nonsense she speaks. She had a difficult childhood. Her mother was very cowed and never spoke up for her, her father was often drunk, but middle class drunk if you know what I mean. He abused Susannah.'

The inspector's eyebrows rose questioningly,

'Oh not physically. More... intellectually, I suppose. Always putting her down, mocking her ideas. I can't tell you.' She paused. 'I think her initial attraction to Daddy was because he listened to her, respected the validity of what she had to say.' She sighed. 'Oh you don't want to know all this, it can't have any bearing on where she's gone.'

'At the moment anything may be useful to us. It was quite cold on Saturday night. Would you know if a coat was missing? Gloves? Boots?'

Harriet went to the hall cupboard, then up to Susannah's wardrobe, where she flung open the doors. 'Her pink coat,' she said to the police officer back in the kitchen. 'She has a favourite Dolce and

Gabbana pink coat, it's not there. She must have been wearing it. A faded sort of check, with a D & G logo inscribed all across the lining. It's wool I think and has epaulettes, and a sort of...' she demonstrated with her hands, 'a sort of military style detail from across the front of the neckline. Silver buttons. Big buttons. I'm afraid I can't help about gloves or boots.'

A nod from DI Timothy took the constable to the phone again. Mrs Corner confirmed that Susannah had been wearing 'some sort of pinkish coat, very creased.' More than that she was not able or not prepared to say.

'What about jewellery?' the Inspector asked Harriet. 'We have a description of a...' He referred to his notes, 'a gold choker and matching bangle, and a gold watch.'

Harriet put her head in her hands for a moment, gathering her thoughts.

'Daddy, where are all your photos of Susannah's jewellery?'

Retrieving a plain brown envelope from the study, where it had clearly been sellotaped to something, Giles handed it silently to the Inspector. Inside was a wad of A4 sheets, each covered with a number of photographs. 'Where was this Sir?'

'I keep it stuck under the desk drawer in the office. The insurance company suggested I keep a record of all the items of value in the house. There are photographs of all the jewellery in the safe, and of the more valuable ornaments and pictures in the house.'

'Just in case the envelope should be stolen in a break-in, we decided to keep an additional set at my house,' said Harriet. 'I don't have a safe, they are just shoved in the back of a drawer.'

'I'd like you to open the safe if you would please, Sir.' The Inspector had pulled out the sheet containing pictures of the choker and bangle. There seemed to be no picture of the watch.

Giles opened the safe as requested. The Inspector tasked sergeant Talbot with matching up photographs to the items stored there. There was an empty shagreen case, indentations in whose silk suggested these were of the missing pieces. Tasking this to be checked for fingerprints, the officers returned to the kitchen.

'It seems that only the jewellery described by Mrs Corner, and the watch are missing. Where was the watch usually kept?'

'It wasn't an expensive watch. Susannah wore it every day and kept it by the bed.'

DI Timothy sighed, closed his notebook and spoke to Harriet.

'We're going to leave you and your father in peace for now to try and get some rest, but we'll need to speak to you again. Where can we contact you?'

'Oh, I'll be staying here with Daddy for now. If I go home I'll let you know.'

Chapter 11

Angela had not enjoyed herself so much in years, and a rare bloom flushed her cheeks as she cycled over Alsagers Bank. Involvement in a crisis at second hand gave her a vicarious thrill such as she had never experienced. On her way home she called at the hairdresser and made an appointment for first thing the following morning, an almost unheard of event, to have her hair cut. She called in at the Co-op and picked up some mascara and blusher. Who knew, she thought, whether she may be caught on camera, perhaps have her picture in the Sentinel, or even on the television.

Unknown to her, the police had briefly explored her possible involvement in Susannah's disappearance, but had quickly eliminated her. That Saturday Angela had been at home all evening. She never closed her living room curtains until bedtime, the better to see passers-by; and several dog walkers and neighbours were able to confirm having seen her watching television at various points during the evening.

She had a bath at close to midnight and went to bed, confirmed by neighbours who were aware of the leaking downspout from her bathroom, and who discussed between themselves that it would have to be mentioned to her again. She then watched a film until the early hours, again confirmed by the unfortunate neighbours, who thought she must be hard of hearing, such was the volume.

The following morning there was a note on Susannah's kitchen table in Harriet's hand, would Angela please leave the principal bedroom as it was, the police wanted to go through it again.

Perhaps she would be good enough to start in the bathrooms, the bedroom Harriet was using, and the green bedroom. Angela tiptoed along the corridor to the main bedroom. She had always suspected that this room was Susannah's alone, with Giles usually sleeping in the green bedroom adjacent. Poor man, not even allowed to sleep in his own bedroom in his own house. She peeped around the door, and found that there were mounds of Susannah's clothes piled on the bed. It looked as though Harriet was wasting no time in assessing, perhaps for her own use, what Susannah had left behind.

There was one lovely jacket, tucked in the back of the wardrobe, which Angela had coveted as soon as Susannah had brought it into the house. She wondered whether it would be missed, and decided to move it and see if anyone noticed. By anyone's standards this was a very large house, and more of Susannah and Giles's clothes were housed on clothes racks on the attic floor. Angela took the jacket and put it on a hanger underneath a coat of Giles's that was hanging in one of the top rooms. If anyone noticed she would deny all knowledge and say Susannah must have moved it. If Susannah returned, she could replace it in the wardrobe and no-one would be any the wiser. When Susannah did turn up again, Angela decided that she would not carry on working for them. She had never liked the woman anyway, and Giles was far too good for her – a real gentleman.

When she had gently explained that she had not been paid for December, he immediately asked her how much, and apologized for not having thought. Harriet had given her a strange look, as if she should be above such things just now, but it was all right for her. She had no need to make ends meet, living as she was off her father at the moment, having taken Susannah's absence as an opportunity to move back in and start sponging. She had just moved to the green bedroom and was plugging in the vacuum cleaner, when Harriet appeared at the door, bringing her reverie to an abrupt end.

'Oh, Angela, I'm going to be using the gold bedroom and en suite for the moment, would you mind including them in your cleaning routine? Don't worry about the drawing room or the dining room for now if there's no time. Thank you.' With that Harriet turned and went back downstairs.

Her new hairstyle and colour had not been commented on, nor had her make-up on which she had spent some time. Typical, she thought, of someone like Harriet, who rated her no higher than the Victorians did their servants. She chewed on the skin of her little finger. Her own philosophy was that as she'd been invited to a party at Harriet's in the summer, she considered herself their social equal.

Harriet would not stay forever though. Angela knew she had a business of some sort to run, and she had taken what she called *a few weeks' break to help Daddy out.* Some sort of fashion and design thing she had called it, when Angela knew it was really just a knitting shop. For goodness' sake, even Angela's mother had been able to knit. It was nothing to give herself airs and graces about. Well, as far as Angela was concerned, Harriet was not welcome, especially not when she put on that prissy face as she had when Angela had asked about her money.

Harriet, upset on her own behalf and at her father's distress, disliked Angela's proprietorial attitude in the house and the way she levered her way into every conversation, like a child at the back of the classroom, jumping up and down shouting 'me, me'. She seemed to relish the attention from the police, and whilst Harriet had spared time only for the minimum of makeup and to pull a comb through her hair since being summoned by Giles, Angela had clearly spent some time with a hairdresser, and been beguiled into the current vogue for dying hair an impossible shade of red.

Angela ate heartily of the salad Harriet provided at lunchtime, although no-one had asked her to stay. Giles felt that as she had stayed on to help the police, it would be churlish not to expect her to join them in their meal, but Harriet simply picked at her plate whilst Giles ate nothing.

Harriet felt, perhaps unreasonably as she acknowledged, that Angela was enjoying the whole thing rather more than was appropriate. Then she reflected that in the woman's dull existence this was all probably very exciting, and not being close to Susannah, she could not be expected to share the family's feelings.

*   *   *

DI Timothy returned with more questions. He asked Angela about her car.

'Actually I don't drive,' she said, 'I had a

couple of lessons when I was younger but couldn't seem to get the co-ordination right. Funnily enough, I had a little bump.' Her embarrassed expression suggested something more significant. 'I had a little bump,' she repeated more confidently, 'and I never tried again. I use my bike to get here. That's it in the wood-store.'

Indicating out of the window, she saw the large Christmas tree that had been delivered on Saturday. For want of attention, it was already beginning to shed its leaves on the patio. The boxes of decorations were still in a pile in the corner of the living room awaiting Susannah's artistic administrations.

'Shall I bring the tree in Giles, and put some decorations on it?' She chewed on a fingernail, waiting for his answer. Angela loved Christmas and had always had a passion for what is known as *bling*. Her own home was laden down with tinsel and glitter and flashing lights, even though probably only she would see it. She had two Christmas trees and little village scenes all over the living room; holly and tinsel behind each picture, and twinkling lights draped over sprays of holly leaves in the hallway.

She watched Giles aim a desultory kick at the pile of decorations as he walked past. He made no answer. Angela turned to go back into the kitchen and found Harriet framed in the doorway.

'I think,' she said gently, backing away slightly from Angela and averting her nose, 'That we'll leave the decorations for now, Angela. It doesn't seem quite right to be celebrating in the circumstances.' Trying to lighten the mood, Harriet followed Angela into the kitchen and asked about her own Christmas plans.

'Nothing really,' she said sullenly, pulling at a snag of skin on her thumb, 'Susannah probably told you, actually I'm just back from a trip to York for a family wedding.' She was ready to expand on the story she had spent hours thinking about, but Harriet, gazing from the window with teary eyes was clearly not interested; she was distracted by her concern for Giles, and worry over her friend. Angela's resentment flourished, feeding the seeds sown in the hothouse of her self-righteous indignation.

*   *   *

The next morning Angela arrived bright and early for work, carrying in with her a supermarket bag of groceries. With a brief insincere smile at Harriet, she approached Giles flourishing the bag.

'I've brought some stuff for your lunch, Giles, and for a meal tonight. You won't have been thinking about food with all that's going on.' She began to busy herself unpacking vegetables.

Harriet relieved her of the bag. 'That's very thoughtful of you, isn't it Daddy? I can't tell you.' she said looking at Giles, 'but I plan to shop later today so we shall be okay for food.' She loaded the goods into the refrigerator. 'Now, how much do we owe you for all this Angela, oh, is this the receipt?'

Angela started to protest, 'Actually that's quite all right Harriet...' but the other woman counted the money out of her purse and laid it on the table, with as warm a smile as she could muster for Angela.

'Now, I wonder if you'd mind starting in Daddy's room and do his laundry from Dubai?' She was wearing stud earrings today, and she twisted one around nervously as she spoke. 'The police want the main bedroom left exactly as it is for now, so Daddy will continue to use the green bedroom. The top floor bathroom could probably use a clean as well.'

As Angela left the room, Harriet turned to her father, 'She never even asked whether we'd heard anything. And what's the point of putting on makeup when she evidently hasn't bothered with deodorant. Honestly Daddy, she gives me the creeps.'

Giles patted her hand absently. 'She's okay darling,' he said, 'I'm sure she means well.'

'Well, I wish I had your confidence. You are too soft, Daddy,' Harriet laid her cheek against his. She was perched on the arm of his chair, 'That can be a mistake.'

'That's what Susannah says. Oh, I wish it were over, this purgatory, but I'm so frightened of what the outcome might be.' Giles combed his fingers over and over through his hair.

Angela clomped furiously up the two flights of stairs. The bloody bitch, she muttered to herself. Why didn't she just go home and leave Angela to look after Giles. How could she move things forward with Harriet always around?

Angrily she turned on both the bath taps in the top bathroom, and re-hung damp towels on the heated rail. The towels were thick and luxurious; Angela stroked them, coveting them, comparing them with her own thin and scruffy ones.

'Just you wait, Lady Harriet,' she murmured, 'Just you wait till I'm living here.'

Day-dreaming that Susannah would stay away indefinitely, and imaging herself as chatelaine made the time pass more quickly as she worked. Angela watched Giles as she put away her cleaning materials. He was once again, or still, sitting at the kitchen table. Of Harriet there was no sign.

'Harriet gone then has she?' she asked through the open door of the utility room, as she fed dirty cloths into the washing machine.

'Sorry?' Giles looked up, his eyes haunted, 'Oh yes, she's gone to the supermarket, she'll be back shortly.'

'Actually, if she needs to get home you can always phone through a shopping list to me, and I can fetch some stuff in. There's no need for Harriet to stay.'

Giles surprised Angela by grasping for her hand.

'That's so kind of you, Angela, you are a great help, but Harriet wants to be here. She loves Susannah as much as I do.' He squeezed her hand briefly, and then released it.

At one o'clock, Angela cycled down the drive with a light heart.

Take it steadily Angela, she thought. She could still feel where Giles had squeezed her hand. As she reached the gate, Harriet's car turned in and Angela gave her a cheerful wave.

'What an extraordinary woman that cleaner is,' Harriet told Giles, after she had checked that there was still no news. When there was no response, she left the shopping and, placing her hands of Giles's shoulders, put her cheek against his.

'Oh Daddy.' She could think of nothing to say that they had not already said a dozen times. After a moment he patted her hand and pulled away.

'I think she's just trying to help in her own gauche sort of way.' He smiled faintly at her.

'I don't know, Daddy,' she said, 'I can't take to her and I don't trust her.'

'We don't have to like the woman,' he said, 'but she's useful, especially at the moment.'

'Okay, Daddy, you're right, but I think once Susannah is home again, we should persuade her to look for a new cleaner.'

*   *   *

DI Timothy felt that it was too much of a coincidence, the burglary taking place on the same night as Susannah disappeared and for there to be no connection. He considered whether kidnapping could be a possibility. There was plenty of money in this family. He cast his eyes across the room – why, that pair of vases alone must be worth thousands. Returning from taking a telephone call outside, he gently raised the issue of another man in Susannah's life, someone whom she may have arranged to meet on that evening whilst Giles was away. The idea was risible, Giles almost laughed aloud. Harriet shook her head slightly and patted her father's arm.

'Detective Inspector, it's difficult I'm sure when you don't know someone. I suppose everyone says the same sort of thing in this situation but Susannah adores Daddy, she isn't interested in anyone else. I can't tell you how awful all this is for him. She's been my friend going back to for years. I know her inside out.'

Abstracted, she fingered the tiny studs in her ears. Suddenly standing and looking out of the window onto Susannah's garden, she rubbed her aching shoulders. What the detective said next made her turn and stare at him.

'Mr Scott-Ryder, I want to put a tap on your phone. We may get a ransom call here if this is a kidnapping. I also want to leave her mobile phone, and her laptop unblocked for the moment. Contact might be made using either of those.'

'Kidnapping?' Giles looked incredulous, 'I had never even considered kidnapping.' He put his hand up to rub through his hair in a characteristic gesture, closing his eyes against the possibility of this new idea. It made it all seem more real somehow.

'Oh God, I would pay anything, give anything, go anywhere to get her back. Please Inspector don't let anything happen to put her more at risk, my poor Susannah,' and he broke down in tears.

Chapter 12

Angela was too cautious to enter Susannah's room. She had been told not to, the family were sitting below in the drawing room, and she knew only too well how clear footfalls were from above. Still, she was itching to go through Susannah's things. At eleven o'clock she went into the drawing room with three mugs of coffee and some biscuits on a tray. Intent on manoeuvring the tray, she failed for a moment to notice the third person present.

'I've made some biscuits, thought we'd have our coffee in here – oh, I didn't know you were here Inspector.'

'Never mind Angela, perhaps the Inspector could have the third cup – he needs to speak to Daddy and me.'

Thwarted again in her attempts to get close to Giles, Angela stomped back the door.

'Of course, Harriet, I'll have my coffee in the kitchen.' As she left the room she heard Harriet offering the detective a biscuit.

'Have one of these, Inspector – they are excellent. Angela buys them at Snape's and pretends to have made them.'

She heard their laughter as she headed back to the kitchen.

DI Timothy again took up the theme he had been pursuing.

'So we know that the tape used to deaden the sound of breaking glass was of the same type, fairly unusual although easy enough to get hold of,' he glanced at his notes, 'it's primary purpose is to fix together two pieces of tarpaulin. Now, you tell me that you know Mrs Chapman, and are in fact Godmother to her daughter, whose name is...?' He looked up.

'Pippa, Philippa, but she never gets her full title.'

'And her surname? Is she a married lady?'

'No, no, she's single. Her surname is also Chapman.' He noted down the details, then moved on.

'Is there anything else that either of you have thought of, however seemingly insignificant. We don't know at this stage what may be relevant.'

Harriet paused, then 'Well, I'm sure it's nothing, but I was really surprised that there were no quails' eggs in the fridge.

'I thought maybe Susannah had planned another trip to the supermarket before Christmas. She loved boiled quail eggs, and certainly would have had some in for Christmas.' She smiled remembering, 'She is really a very nice person. Do you know she won't shop at the supermarket on Saturdays?'

'Well, it is a horrendously busy day in the supermarkets,' he said, misunderstanding.

'No, it isn't that. She thinks it isn't fair when so many people have no choice but to go on Saturdays and she can go anytime.' Harriet massaged her hands together as she thought, then she took the plunge. 'I did wonder if Angela.... but no. I always felt that she didn't like Susannah, but she can't have anything to do with this surely? I was there once when Susannah asked her, perfectly nicely, to please polish the clean drinking glasses on kitchen roll before putting them away. I can't tell you, if looks could kill...' Hand to her mouth she realised what she had said, 'Oh God!'

'I wouldn't have thought it would matter to Angela what work she was expected to do,' said the inspector, redeeming the moment.

Harriet continued,

'No, of course not. Why should it? I'm just desperately searching for something out of the ordinary, anything that might make sense of this. I keep thinking I'm going to wake up soon, but I'm not am I?'

When he made no reply, she took a deep breath, and carried on more strongly. 'Angela does four hours' work each day, she gets four hours' pay. As you say, I would have thought polishing glasses much more pleasant than some jobs.

'And she is very well paid too. My neighbour has a cleaning lady, and I know Susannah pays Angela a couple of pounds an hour more, *and* she is planning to increase it after Christmas.'

*   *   *

Back at the station the Inspector spoke again to DS Talbot.

'Angela Davies is a weird woman though, isn't she? Do you think she may be involved, but with an accomplice?'

'Possibly.' The Detective Sergeant sounded doubtful, 'She hasn't much to gain though, has she? And she hasn't exactly a huge phalanx of friends and family to support her either. Who on earth could she have persuaded to get involved?

'Still, have another talk to the neighbours, check that they are positive about seeing her at home on that date.' The DS made a phone call.

The neighbours were sure it was the Saturday before Christmas. They had visitors staying, and had discussed between themselves the hope that these people had not been disturbed because of Angela's noisy bathing habits.

DI Timothy deliberated aloud to his sergeant, 'Who benefits? Apparently no-one. Susannah Scott-Ryder came from fairly humble beginnings. When she married Giles, he made a new will, he left everything fifty-fifty to his daughter and son, but leaving Susannah enough to buy a fairly standard house, take her pick of the pieces of antique furniture which, incidentally, she had assured both Matthew and Harriet that she did not want. Worried about legal protocol, she had written this down. We found a piece of paper in the safe, witnessed by two of her friends. Bizarrely, in law it probably fulfils the criteria of a legal will, but I'm not sure, I'd have to get that checked.

Her death really would benefit nobody. She has very little other than personal clothes, jewellery, accoutrements etcetera.'

He rubbed both hands across his face. Suffering now from tiredness, he tried to think. He really needed more to go on.

'Go back to Julia Corner, perhaps Susannah wasn't the intended victim. Put that to her, to all of them, see if it sparks any ideas.'

It seemed to both of them that they were clutching at straws.

*   *   *

On Christmas Eve, without knowing it, Angela Davies and Simon Napier bought a Sentinel newspaper from the same newsagent within two minutes of each other. To Angela's disappointment there was no photograph of her, just a copy of a studio shot of Susannah. Scanning the editorial, she found that she had not been quoted, nor even mentioned. She had been careful to wheel her bicycle very slowly past the two waiting reporters at the gate of the farmhouse, and had spoken to them both about what was happening. She reassured herself that it was early days, and there were plenty of chances to be in the paper yet.

Arriving at home after work, Angela wheeled her cycle round to the back garden. To her delight her next door neighbour was outside, placing something in her bin.

'Have you seen the paper?' Angela called over to her. The neighbour was not keen to talk, considering Angela to be a nasty woman who lowered the neighbourhood. She and her husband were still debating the best way to again raise the subject of the problematic downspout, but Angela's next words stopped the woman in her tracks.

'Did you see the Sentinel? It's the woman from the house where I clean that's gone missing.'

Propping her cycle against the wall she took the newspaper from its basket and began to read:

'Woman Missing in Newcastle. Mrs Scott-Ryder, aged 39 from Scot Hay has been missing since the early hours of last Sunday morning. She was last

*seen when she gave a friend a lift home to Madeley
after a social evening.*

*Her husband arrived home from Dubai the
following day, to find his wife was missing and he
raised the alarm at the end of the day when she still
had not returned. Her car, a red Lexus, is also
missing. A small window on the ground floor of the
house had been broken. The police are appealing for
information,* blah, blah, blah.'

Putting her bicycle away in the shed, she
wondered whether it was possible to get access to the
Sentinel on-line. If she did get a mention she would
forward the details to Kevin.

Thinking of Kevin, Angela deliberated long
and hard over what to say to him when she wrote. He
would expect her to be back from Dubai now, and
waiting for her news. Angela had planned initially to
tell Kevin all about the excitement, but she soon
realised that if she said that her employer was
missing, Kevin would know that she worked and may
quiz her about her job.

Looking back through their previous
correspondence, she had definitely told him that she
was a lady of leisure and she had described
Susannah's lifestyle, so that would not do. Nor could
she explain her involvement, being at the Scot Hay
farmhouse for hours every day without him becoming
suspicious, and if she described Susannah as just a
casual acquaintance, there would be no interest in the
story in Canada. She decided for the moment to make
no mention of what had happened. No, she was better
keeping it to herself and making herself useful to
Giles. For Angela had her plans.

Chapter 13

Simon was puzzled, but not yet unduly worried, by events and what had happened to Angela. She should have been in Dubai; the house should have been empty and yet, if Gary was to be believed, there were police cars gathered on the drive. How could that be? Surely it was too much of a coincidence that there had been another burglary of the house on the same night?

But maybe not, a house evidently empty, someone living there who had not the sense to keep her holiday plans to herself.

If she had told him, who else had she told? In fact, referring back to Angela's page on *findyourmates.com*, Simon recalled that she claimed two dozen or more friends. It would be ironic if amongst them there was someone with the same idea as Simon's, but who had beaten him to it by mere hours. Blast, after all his groundwork. Why had that cretin Gary not gone sooner? Then he thought again. Had Gary in fact gone to the right house?

Perhaps the police had actually been at a neighbouring property? In which case, Angela could be put on the back burner for a visit some time in the future. Simon went back to the photographs he had taken. He was sure that these fitted the description and location that Angela had given him. He had talked through it in detail with Gary, and had given him the address and copies of the photographs. Although Gary's literacy skills were sadly lacking, he was exceptionally astute when it came to diagrams and pictorial information, perhaps nature's compensatory measure. He must have gone to the right place. The house was very distinctive and very remote.

Concerned now, Simon logged on that evening and sent a tentative post to Angela, not knowing what response to expect. He was to be further confused by her reply, raving about Dubai, how interesting the racing had been; which horses won, and all about the wedding she had been to.

She posted photos too. Not very good ones admittedly, and she apologized for her lack of skill with the technology, but there were pictures of the Dubai racecourse, and a few fuzzy wedding photos that could have been taken anywhere. She expanded on details of her outfit and the bride's outfit and the food, and then said, of course he wouldn't want to know all this and sorry it was all very girly stuff she had to relate.

Dead right, he thought to himself, what I want to know is what went on in Scot Hay on Saturday night.

After a good deal of thought, Simon sent a post to the effect that he had a short holiday planned upstate, but was a bit concerned about the security of his house as his neighbors – he deliberately spelt it *neighbors* - would be away *on vacation* at the same time.

He went on to enquire whether this had been a worry to Angela whilst she was in Dubai, as she clearly lived in a very lovely, and apparently from her earlier photographs, quite isolated place.

He then wrote that if she could write girly stuff then he could write about boys' toys *ha-ha*, and went on to relate in great detail about a fictitious new car he had bought since last he wrote. After telling her about its make and model and all sorts of technical information in which Angela had no interest whatsoever, he finished with a seemingly insouciant enquiry as to what car Angela herself owned.

After a pause Angela logged off. She knew nothing at all about cars, but resolved the following day to check out Susannah's car documents, and relay this information to Kevin later. She decided that with that and a bit of help from the internet if he asked any difficult questions, she would be able to get by. She could hardly say that she was totally ignorant about everything to do with cars.

Someone in the position she had created for herself, Susannah's position, would be certain to have a car. About security she planned to be non-committal. Telling Kevin about the concept of Home Watch areas in the UK and something general about Scot Hay being a very quiet village, would no doubt satisfy his interest.

Again she considered and rejected telling him about Susannah's disappearance. She decided instead to let that saga unfold a little more before committing it to the internet.

This was Angela's second mistake.

*   *   *

Gary found that in the following days he doubled his nicotine intake. Every so often his hands would shake involuntarily and he would feel sick. He waited, poised for flight, but time went on and there was no news. He bought no newspapers of course, but nothing came on Radio Stoke or the regional television news. Nothing about a body, nothing about a burglary, nothing about anyone called Angela.

Coincidentally, some woman had gone missing from the same sort of area, but not recognising the double-barrelled name, Gary paid it no heed. Gradually he began to breathe more freely. His hands stopped shaking so often and he would go for whole hours at a time without reliving his nightmare. Now he needed to sort out Simon, who had landed him in such trouble. Simon, who had phoned several times on the Sunday morning and whose calls had gone unanswered.

Gary was furious at Simon for the mess he found himself in, but he also admitted to himself what he would not share with anyone else – that he was terrified of crossing Simon. Without Simon he had no income, and he was beginning to enjoy having money to spend. He sat for hours on his bed that day surrounded by the goods he had taken, and concocted a story which he hoped would satisfy. He knew that at some stage he would have to speak to Simon, so when he saw Simon's name on the display of his phone when it rang at something short of midday on the Monday, he took a deep breath.

Forgetting Gary's difficulties with reading, Simon opened with,

'Have you seen the Sentinel? What happened?'

'Hey mate,' said Gary sleepily, 'Not seen it yet. What's it say?'

'It says Mrs Scott-Ryder is bloody missing – last seen Saturday night, that's what it says. Now what happened?'

Hearing the threat in Simon's voice, Gary

plunged into his explanation. That Simon had seen this item in the paper could work to his advantage.

'So that's what was up! I got to the end of the lane early hours of Sunday morning, and could see police cars everywhere, well, more than one anyway. I just drove on straight past and back home. Who's Mrs Scott-Ryder anyway?'

'Why didn't you tell me yesterday?' Simon was suspicious.

'Never thought, mate, nothing to tell was there? I just went home.' He paused. 'Has she turned up yet, this Something-Ryder woman?'

'Nah, probably run off with some boyfriend while hubby was away. Her car's gone.'

'Hmm,' said Gary, 'You're probably right, mate. We'll just have to set something else up. Maybe next weekend?'

'No, old thing,' Simon was firm, 'I'll set something else up when I'm ready. Let's just see what happened up there Saturday night first. I'll call you.'

'Money, mate. I haven't any money,' began Gary, but Simon cut in:

'Don't contact me. Do you get it? I'll ring you. If you've run out of money you'll have to go and sign on, get the jobseekers' benefit or whatever it's called.' He laughed unkindly, 'or get that girl of yours to sub you.'

*   *   *

The suggestion of getting a loan from Janice seemed ridiculous to Gary, but it did give him an idea. She had helped him sell that camera on e-bay. It seemed quite straightforward, and though she had not raised a great deal of money, it would be better than nothing. He looked for items he could sell, and came upon the jewellery he had taken from Miner's Cottage and kept back for himself.

*   *   *

Over the following few days Gary was running low on patience as well as on funds. Simon said he had passed Maxine's jewellery on to his contact, to be told that he would *do what he could but it was only worth a few quid.* Gary was sure this was not the truth, but struggled to think of better ways to deal with disposing of the goods. He had his own stash of course, perhaps he could get Janice to help him get rid of it.

After drinking a good deal in the pub with Janice, he suggested they get a takeaway curry and go back to his house. Knowing full well what was implied, Janice agreed as the better of several evils. She had not previously realised the extent to which the drink had affected Gary, and as she procrastinated he became more and more bellicose. People were looking at them, and the last thing she wanted was to be recognised with him. She knew nobody who lived in the area near his home in Knutton, and to her knowledge, neither did Ken. News of her exploits was unlikely to get back to him, but she did not want to draw attention to herself.

Paradoxically, back in the autumn she had found the idea of sex with someone different, exciting. Ken was a steady if unsurprising lover, and Gary's volatility made for an interesting contrast. A fling with Gary had seemed like a good idea. They would meet for a drink or a meal, then adjourn to his room for sex. But as time had gone on he had become more and more aggressive, and Janice had become concerned that it was taking increasing violence in order for him to be satisfied. Also, she now had another reason to be a very worried girl.

Chapter 14

Pippa visited Maxine on Christmas Eve, arriving unexpectedly in the middle of the afternoon. The weather was closing in, the sky leaden with unshed snow. The festive lights that could be seen across the village, glistened on grass white with frost. Maxine had lit the fire, and she hurried her daughter into the warmth.

'I thought,' said Pippa, turning away from her mother to hang up her coat, 'that as Mohammed wouldn't come to the mountain for Christmas etcetera.' Realising the mixed metaphor, she turned to Maxine and laughed.

'And Clyde?' Maxine said lightly, 'Is he joining us for tomorrow?'

Pippa paused, then sighed deeply, 'Oh Mum, you know he's not. You're so diplomatic. He says that spending Christmas with two old biddies, miles from his mates isn't his idea of Christmas. I suppose he has a point.'

Maxine wondered what made Pippa an old biddy, and Clyde had originated from the Potteries, surely he had friends around here still. However, she kept her counsel and changed the subject.

'What's in the box?' Maxine had taken Pippa's overnight bag from her and put it on the stairs.

'Aha,' said Pippa, taking the box into the living room. 'It's the magic decorations. I thought they could cope with one more year here on your tree. You haven't dressed it yet?'

'Of course not. You know I always do that on

Christmas Eve evening.'

'Good. Then we'll do it together, and then I'll take them back with me afterwards, and see where we go from there.'

It seemed a strange way to put it, but Maxine decided not to pursue that thought for the moment.

The two shared a companionable meal of beef casserole with red wine, followed by Wenslydale cheese and Christmas cake, their favourite. They had settled down before the fire with the dogs when Pippa's mobile phone rang.

'Oh Hi Clyde. Is everything all right? Oh sweetheart I told you. Probably till Boxing Day, I said. Yes. Yes. Clyde how much have you had to drink? Clyde! Clyde!'

The connection had been cut. Maxine picked up her knitting.

'They say, don't they, that Christmas is one of the most stressful times for relationships?' Pippa seemed not to require an answer. The ache of longing and the humiliation vied for dominance in her voice.

'Is everything all right?' Maxine ventured at last.

'Oh Mum, you know it isn't, but we'll work through it. It's difficult for Clyde.'

Maxine kept her thoughts to herself. She found she was becoming an expert in diplomacy.

'What are you knitting?' Pippa had turned on the television to a programme of carols, and they watched companionably.

'It's one of Harriet's designs. She has a whole fleet of home knitters now producing her clothes, but occasionally she asks me to try a pattern before she distributes it to them. I'm a pretty basic knitter so I tend to spot any mistakes or difficult bits, so she can make sure that the patterns are clear. The jacket I had on when I came up to yours was one of hers.'

'That was gorgeous,' said Pippa.

'I find it relaxing. I've always enjoyed knitting, although …' one of the dogs snuggled closer to her on the sofa, 'it is quite difficult with a retriever under each arm.'

As the carols finished she reluctantly put the knitting away. 'Come on,' she said, kneeling on the floor in front of the Christmas tree, 'let's get these decorations on the tree.'

'I wonder how Harriet and her father are coping?' Pippa mused, hanging silver baubles carefully.

'That bauble looks a bit tatty Pippa, nearly all the paint is rubbed off. Are you sure you want to use it?'

'Most definitely,' said Pippa, her hand on her stomach. 'It is very worn but in its heyday it said *Baby's First Christmas*, it's nearly as old as me.'

'Let's get this finished and then I want to sort out wine for tomorrow's dinner. Anne and Tom from next door are coming in, and old Mildred from opposite. She's as deaf as a post and will sleep all through the afternoon, but I don't like to think of anyone being on their own at Christmas.' Both of them thought of Susannah, and wondered whether she would be alone this Christmas Day.

Reverting to the previous train of thought Maxine said,

'It must be awful for them, Harriet and Giles, with Susannah still not home. I feel I want to keep phoning to see how they are, but Harriet says every phone call gives Giles such hope and then he's so downcast when it's not her. And all the surveillance and everything – policemen listening in to every call. I don't know how they can bear it.'

*   *   *

'I can't bear it sweetheart, I really can't. How am I going to cope?' Giles begged of his daughter the next morning. She had stayed over again at the Scot Hay, and had asked if he wanted to go to church as usual on Christmas morning. He had decided that he would prefer to stay close to the phone. If Susannah had left voluntarily, which he could not believe for a moment, but if she had, then Christmas morning was the time when she might phone. The vicar, in the vain hope of offering solace, had phoned and said he would call round later.

Relentlessly, perversely almost, the telephone remained quiet. Normally there would be calls of good wishes throughout the day from friends and from family. Matthew called from New Hampshire, more to find out if any news had come in than to wish them Merry Christmas. It could hardly be that, for any of them. Maxine and Pippa had phoned too, and invited them over if they found that they could not bear to stay at home any longer. The police after all, were monitoring calls, and would get hold of Giles straight away if there was any contact, but he was adamant that Scot Hay was where he wanted to be, just in case.

The tree, carefully chosen and ordered by Susannah, remained undressed and dying outside the back door, eventually to be removed by the recycling collectors in February. Angela had offered to come and cook them Christmas dinner, but Harriet had shuddered so violently at the prospect, that Giles had thanked her and said that they would rather be on their own, just the family, thank you just the same.

*   *   *

Angela looked again at the quails' egg box then slammed the fridge door on it and took the wine glass back through to the computer.

She took a big gulp, and gasped as the smooth Merlot warmed her throat. She raised her glass in mock salute, commending herself for choosing this bottle from one of Giles's wine racks.

After all, she would need to be familiar with the quality of wines ordered from a wine merchant, rather than picked up from a supermarket, once she was installed at the Scot Hay farmhouse. She could see the hand of that prissy Miss Harriet behind Giles's refusal of her company at Christmas. Just you wait till next Christmas, Missy – it'll be me refusing your offer of a visit to Scot Hay then.

She switched on the second bar of the electric fire – it was Christmas after all. The smell of dust caught the back of her throat and made her cough. She had a single portion of turkey breast – courtesy of Marks and Spencer, via Susannah's freezer, and had treated herself to a bottled prawn cocktail mix and a Christmas cake slice. Susannah's fridge had yielded a tub of long-life cream to top off the feast.

She took another swig of the wine, admiring the way the ruby liquid caught the light. In an approximation of Susannah's voice she said aloud,

'Angela may I ask that you always polish the glasses on kitchen towel once they are dry? It is too unpleasant drinking out of a smeared glass.'

'Yes, you may ask,' she replied to herself, picking at the skin on her forefinger, 'once those cut glasses are all mine, I shall see to it that they are polished each time, only it won't be me doing the polishing.' Plonking the glass down on the computer desk, she turned her attention to Kevin's message.

Hope Christmas is good to you this year, she typed, we have friends coming over for Christmas luncheon, but everything is under control in the kitchen. My cook is really very good. Going back to your last message - men are always interested in cars, aren't they? Then she went on to give details pertaining to Susannah's stylish red model, as she had gleaned them from the folder in Giles's office.

Fuelled by the wine, Angela gave her imagination its head, inventing proposed trips to Scotland for the shooting, and a considered visit to Glyndebourne to see La Bohème. After a few moments, her thoughts turning again to the contents of her fridge, she wrote: Have you ever tried quails' eggs? Actually they are fast becoming a favourite of mine. At first, I was unsure about them, but pride myself that now I've become something of an expert, and cook has it off to a fine art.

I notice that you haven't mentioned your son in messages lately. Are he and the rest of your family well? I know that your daughter lives near to you. Are the boys in the photograph you sent, hers or your sons? Where does he live – I don't think you said? Oh goodness, I have just noticed the time. I shall have to go and change, we always wear formal dress for

Christmas dinner – it makes the day so much more of an occasion, don't you think?

With a wine-induced flourish, she logged off and poured the remaining wine into her glass. After all, it was Christmas. Unsteadily, she got up and switched on the Christmas lights. There was plenty to celebrate.

*   *   *

Simon too was celebrating Christmas. He was in bed in his room with Emma. Having made love, he had gone to the bathroom, leaving Emma, as he thought, asleep. Stirring as he closed the door, she sat up feeling cold, and got up to turn on the gas fire. Simon always insisted on the windows being open, whatever the weather. She wrapped the duvet around her, and crouched down to look how the fire ignited. As it flared and she sat in front of it for warmth, she looked at a pile of books and papers pushed down the side of the bed.

Amongst them was what looked like a painting. She pulled it out for a closer look, and found that it was a framed print of three girls; all three with breasts revealed, and lying and sitting in various quasi-erotic poses. She could see that it was good, it was well-painted, and the girl seated to the right of the three looked rather like herself. She assumed the pose, and was sitting, legs akimbo and arms up, when Simon returned.

'That's a vision, that is,' he said, putting on his glasses, his eyes feasting on her.

'It's gorgeous, don't you think she looks like me? What was it doing just stuck down by the side of the bed? It should be on the wall.'

'Tell you what,' he said. 'You can have it, Merry Christmas. Now come here.' And he led her back to the bed.

Chapter 15

Emma's brother had been in property development for three years. He had started his working life jobbing for his uncle, who was a general builder. Three years previously, the uncle had succumbed to lung cancer and left the business, such as it was by then, to his only nephew. This misogynist also had a small life policy, the proceeds of which went the same way.

Seduced by a rash of television programmes, the young man had turned his attention to buying small terraced houses at auction, and letting them out. With two university sites in the immediate vicinity, he focused on Fenton and made a good income, salving his conscience over his good fortune by accommodating his only sister rent-free in one of the houses.

Emma had thought for a while before Clyde was due to phone her back about the possibility of a room. Her brother currently had a vacancy in the house where she herself lived. She wanted to consider whether Clyde living in the same house would compromise her in any way. She decided not. Clyde was very attractive, much more so than Simon, but he never had much money, and Emma was nothing if not a good time girl, who loved a boyfriend to spend his money on her.

By the time he rang she had made her decision.

'Oh, hi Clyde. I've spoken to my brother. You can have the room from Friday if you want.' She named her brother's price for the rent and Clyde arranged to move in at the weekend.

'Tell you what,' she said, 'once you're sorted, knock on my door and we'll do a takeaway. Simon'll be coming over.

It took Clyde no time at all to stash his few belongings, and by seven o'clock he was knocking on the door of Emma's room. Simon was already there and the couple had obviously just got up.

'Okay, let's eat,' said Simon, 'sex always makes me hungry.' He leered at Emma, who smiled back at him as she picked up the phone.

'Who wants what?'

Having given his order Clyde looked around. She had arranged the room prettily and had a good eye. It was not as big and nice a place as Pippa's, but it looked good, and she'd got some good quality stuff – ornaments and pictures. It was very homely. Clyde nodded his approval.

*   *   *

On the Friday between Christmas and New Year, Harriet phoned Maxine and they arranged to meet at Bridgemere Garden Centre for lunch. Giles had gone into the office for an hour or two, and it was not Angela's day to clean.

Maxine had spent the first part of the meal bringing Harriet up to date with her concerns about Pippa.

'But here I am rambling away about myself, when I really wanted to see if I can be of any help to you. Is there no news at all about Susannah?   It must be nearly two weeks now?'

Harriet paused and shook her head, flicking a lock of hair behind her ear, then fingered her earrings in turn.

'It's eight, no nine days now, and there's been nothing. I can't tell you the state Daddy's in. The police told me, out of Daddy's hearing, that the more time goes on, the less likely it is that she's been kidnapped. Kidnappers don't want to take the risk of having someone to hide for long, they make contact very soon, so that's looking less and less likely as time goes on. Apparently it's very hard to hide a live person, whereas ...' her voice broke. She took a deep breath, 'It makes it much more likely that she's gone off of her own accord, or that she's dead. I can't tell you ...' Harriet's eyes filled with tears, as she fought to compose herself, 'just how awful it all is. Thank goodness it's a quiet time at work now Christmas is out of the way, I can take time to spend with Daddy.'

'Would Susannah have gone off with someone do you think?'

Harriet considered this, hands up at her throat.

'I really doubt it. She seemed to have everything she wanted with Daddy. Well not strictly true. She desperately wanted children, when she was younger. A rich man and big family was all that she wanted when we were at school. They seemed such modest aspirations in a way. They went through IVF for years, but it never worked out, and now she's too old. But she seemed happy – full of nonsense of course, but I think Daddy was what she needed in a husband.'

'Which was?'

'Love. Security. Money.' Harriet paused, 'What we all want really, only,' she smiled wanly and smoothed a crease in the tablecloth with a long, red fingernail. 'Money may have been higher on Susannah's list than some people's.

'Someone to keep her grounded. She was a bit wild at school so I understand from what she said, but now she seems happy and settled with her social life and entertaining, and of course with Daddy. It's such a cliché but I'd say they were ideally suited. He's gone into the office today, but really he's like a zombie. He has aged dramatically. The realisation that Susannah is really missing has dawned on him gradually, and now he's actually having to face up to it.

'I think initially he thought that there was some mistake, well, we all did. He has become an old man. Yesterday he was shuffling about wearing what should have been a smart cardigan, but he had it on inside out. I encouraged him to go into work today for a few hours, to give him something else to think about.' The two looked at each other. Maxine ventured gently,

'What do you really think has happened Harriet?'

'I just don't know.' Harriet's fingers crept unconsciously to her earrings. 'I've been over and over it, by myself and with Daddy, even with that creepy smelly Angela, and with the police, of course. It seems ridiculous that in the early hours on that Sunday morning after a perfectly normal party, of which she's hosted dozens, she got into her car and drove off for no reason. And where on earth is the car? It's really distinctive, it can't have vanished.

'Of course they've checked us all out. Daddy really was in Dubai that Saturday – no surprise there.

Matt, of course, was at home in the States. They even checked Angela! Apparently her neighbours could vouch for her, she snores or something.'

'You really do dislike her don't you?' Maxine was interested.

'Don't get me started. Anyway, I was at a knitwear convention in London on the Friday, all sorts of contacts have been able to confirm that, and several of them stayed over to make a weekend of it.'

Her fiddling loosened one of the earrings, and she paused to secure it properly, 'Imagine, we actually went to see *Phantom of the Opera* that Saturday night, six of us, then on to a late supper in Covent Garden, while Susannah was... If I hadn't been away I'd have no doubt been at Daddy's. Maybe whatever has happened wouldn't have happened. I go round and round in my head trying to figure it out. It's too awful, I can't tell you.

'I can't stop saying *What if*? and *if only*, but who knows what would have made any difference? Wherever Susannah is now, maybe I'd be there too.' She shook her head,

'I look at Daddy's face, and almost wish that I was. Oh I don't really mean that,' as she saw her friend's horrified face, 'But it's so hard to see what Daddy's suffering and not be able to do anything to help. I feel so guilty for saying this, I couldn't say it to anyone else, but in a way I almost wish Susannah would phone and say she's left Daddy, or that a ransom letter would come. At least then we'd know what we're dealing with. It's this limbo that is too awful. I can't tell you.'

She glanced at her watch.

'I'd better go, I want to be back before Daddy.

I don't want him to go home to an empty house.' She stood up, 'I'm going home tomorrow. I have to go into work. I also think, although it may sound harsh, that whatever the future holds for Daddy, it doesn't include me living there long term, and sooner or later he'll have to get used to that. But for now, I'm going back to Scot Hay. This first time he's been into the office, I want to be home first.'

Chapter 16

Gary was struggling. He was short of temper and short of funds. Having watched Janice help him sell the camera on e-bay, he decided that his memory was sufficiently good to have a go at selling the jewellery and laptop he still had hidden away. He had never acquired a computer, his literacy skills were too poor to make it useful, and he had never had enough money.

With some trepidation, he retrieved the laptop from his wardrobe, along with the various leads he had grabbed up in his panic, and opened it up.

Plugging in the lead, his first reaction was relief when the screen sprang into life with its various icons displayed. Having watched Simon use his computer on many occasions, he was aware that Simon's laptop needed a password to get any further, but that did not seem to be the case here. This one was clearly set up differently.

For half an hour he persevered unsuccessfully in trying to access the internet, and eventually had to accept, to his frustration, that this was not going to work. Unplugging and slamming the lid he wondered about the Sentinel. He knew it carried small ads but doubted he could compose anything suitable.

He was currently buying the newspaper each day, to check the headlines for recognisable information about the Scot Hay woman. Today, the leader was all about predictions of bad storms for the spring, the worst for years. He paid little attention to that, these things were always wrong anyway. He found it difficult to follow smaller print, but reassured himself that if a body had been found it would be the front page headline.

Gary evinced that common trait of illiterates – he had excellent recall. Generally he had to be shown something only once to be able to repeat it, and he was frustrated that this computer had defeated him. He racked his brain for an alternative source of funds.

For Christmas, his mother had sent him a mobile phone, possibly in the vain hope that he may use it to keep in more frequent contact with her. Gary, unimpressed, wondered how much it was worth. If that other source of information, the internet, was not a closed book to him, he would be able to look it up. As it was, a journey to Hanley was needed.

The shop assistant was very eager and helpful, although less so when he realised that Gary was interested in selling, not buying. He fetched the manager, who quoted a price just over a third of what had been paid for the phone.

'But it's bloody brand new. You can see it's not been out of the box.' With an effort Gary kept his voice calm.

The manager launched into a polite spiel about *second hand the moment it left the shop; was he the purchaser? did he have the receipt?* but Gary heard only half of it as he stormed out of the shop, slamming the door behind him so that the glass shook, and a window display of, fortunately empty, boxes toppled.

Temper rising, he set off for home. As he pulled up for cigarettes at the shop opposite the Community centre, a man of about his own age was putting up a notice on the centre railings. He crossed the road to gauge the effect, as Gary stepped out of the shop and lit up.

'Now, young man,' he said cheerily, 'Wouldn't you like to make better use of your phone and computer? You must have apps and functions you don't fully understand. We're running courses of six sessions, heavily subsidised so they're really reasonable. Would you be interested at all?'

He tried to thrust a leaflet at Gary, who took a deep drag on the cigarette and was about to tell him to fuck off, when something stopped him.

'I'm no good with technology,' he said, 'It wouldn't be any use to me.'

'Now, that is exactly where you are wrong. You are just the sort of person who would find this course useful,' said the young man, 'These classes are aimed at people who say exactly that - *I'm no good with technology.*' He seemed pleased, as if he had discovered some fundamental truth. 'I'm going to help you to conquer your fear of technology. And you have a phone,' the man continued, indicating the carrier bag visible on the back seat, as Gary opened the car door. 'Do you understand fully everything it can do for you?'

Slowly Gary turned to him again, squinting through a stream of smoke.

'No, no, I don't.'

'Well, I can help you with that. The first session's free.' he added earnestly. He leaned into the car, as Gary got behind the wheel. 'Come along and try it, tonight. Six thirty. You've nothing to lose.'

'I might,' Gary was non-committal.

'I'm Dave.'

For some reason he could not have explained, Gary said,

'Simon, Simon Napier.' He watched Dave's face closely, ready to accelerate away at any sign of recognition, but there was nothing.

'I'll think about it,' he called out of the window as he drove off.

*   *   *

Dave opened the session with what he called ice-breakers, asking them in turn why they had come.

'Now Simon,' He said as he turned to Gary, who had almost forgotten that this was supposed to be his name. 'I think I know why you're here.'

Gary felt cold, and sweat broke out under his armpits. Dave addressed the group as Gary prepared for flight.

'Simon has a rather lovely new phone, and I think it's those advanced apps you want help with, isn't it, Si?'

Gary smiled with relief, 'That's it mate, yeah.'

Dave went round the rest of the group to see what had prompted each to come to the class. Gary surveyed each one. There were only two other people, obviously a couple, who were anywhere near his age group. The other six were much older, several of them looking for really basic information about their phones and computers.

Relieved that he recognised no-one, and that the false name he had given had brought no response, Gary settled down and possibly for the first time ever, looked forward to learning something.

Everyone was asked to put forward a question,

something that was a key issue for them, so that Dave could assess the best way forward. Again they went round the room in turn. A middle aged man, who said his name was Charlie, asked how to protect his phone in case it was ever stolen. The next man asked what to do if he had forgotten his password. Several questions were about sending and retrieving texts and voicemail messages.

Dave noted down the questions on a whiteboard, then set one small group of people instructions, and tasks on phoning and texting each other. The rest, he addressed as a small group, settling down to enjoy listening to his own voice, as he imparted wisdom to the uninitiated.

'The crux of your two questions' he started, indicating Charlie and his neighbour, 'lies in the difference between unlocking and unblocking your phone. If you forget or mislay your password, most phones will give you three attempts then freeze you out. There are some simple downloads which you can use to unlock the phone, or there are people who will do it for you for a fee. It's also useful if you are tied in to a particular network and want to change, perhaps to a different one offering better terms.' He mentioned sites at the entrance to local shopping centres, and on the markets.

'Unblocking' he went on pompously, 'is quite different – one key difference being that it is illegal. If a phone is reported as being lost or stolen,' Gary's heart sank, 'its individual number is notified to a central body, where there is a national register. The SIM card is *fried* and becomes unusable, and the police can track the handset itself, get a geographical fix on it, and then it can be confiscated.

'I hope you're not thinking of taking up a life of crime, Charlie? I can assure you, it's not worth it. These are safety measures that can be overcome, but it takes a level of expertise. Believe me, I know.'

Gary looked at him through narrowed eyes, but Dave remained inscrutable.

'Every police force in the country checks regularly for stolen phones on that national register.

'Now,' he glanced at his watch, 'I'll just talk a little about how this works with your laptop, although basically the same applies; and then we'll break for tea.'

Gary got up and wandered over to the group practising using their phones. They were now sending and receiving texts between themselves, and Dave had provided them with typed sheets of accepted abbreviations. Gary stood behind two of the ladies' chairs, watching and learning.

At the tea break, he headed for the door.

'It's this way, Simon,' Dave called after him.

Gary waved his cigarettes and lighter, and kept walking.

'Fag break.' He got to the door, his new phone tucked under his coat, and kept walking.

Gary lit up directly he was out of the door. Finishing the cigarette, he went over to the off licence for a four-pack of beer. Emptying his pocket of the requisite coins, he realised that walking out may have been too hasty. This first class, after all, was free. He may as well get as much information out of it as he could. Arriving back in the centre, he met the others finishing their break. Dave clapped him on the back,

'Thought we'd lost you, mate.'

'Nah, just went for fags and to check if my

laptop was in the car, but it must be at home. I wanted you to remind me how to sell stuff on the internet.'

'There are a few people saying they want similar. We'll spend the rest of the evening on that, Simon.'

Gary managed again to hide his surprise at the name, he must be careful not to give the game away now. For the next hour, Gary concentrated hard on the information Dave was sharing. The screen images on the white board looked just like those he had found so inaccessible on the stolen laptop – not at all like those he was familiar with on Janice's.

At home later, with a half-consumed lager at his side, he steeled himself to try. The screen came up exactly as Dave's had, and, following the carefully remembered instructions, within the half hour he was familiarizing himself with the machinations of e-bay. Gary used the stolen phone to photograph the cheaper pieces of jewellery – those he had taken from the green jewellery box in the bedroom, along with those picked up at Miner's Cottage.

But the instructions for selling items still proved insurmountable. He kept bringing up dialogue boxes that were meaningless.

Description of the item – He picked out the letters carefully. As if he could write a description of anything. Furious with himself, he slammed the laptop closed again. Even stupid people could manage computers, and he was unable to get the blasted thing to do what he wanted.

He was really regretting having given the pendant to that slag Janice. He should have kept it – he could have sold it himself. Even at one of those gold places he would have got something. He slammed his fist down on the desk. Money was running out, and he had heard nothing from that bloody Simon. He opened the drawer to examine the jewellery once again. He had to find a way of getting some money for this stuff.

He had not previously explored the medals. There were five of them in two boxes, one on its own and the others, all four crammed into a tiny cardboard box covered on one side with spidery writing. None of them were engraved with anyone's name. The only marks, which he could not decipher properly, were obviously a part of the design of the medals themselves.

He wondered where he could sell untraceable medals, without travelling too far or resorting to the internet.

Chapter 17

Giles was not really needed at the office. The place ran like a well-oiled machine, and was in any case, quiet in this somnolent period between the Bank Holidays. He spent some time tidying his desk and checking diary entries for the following couple of weeks, drank the three cups of tea brought to him by various concerned employees in the space of an hour, and then headed for home. Perhaps Susannah would have returned in his absence.

He scanned the roads and lanes as he drove, but there was no evidence of Susannah's red Lexus. As he approached the house, he passed Angela cycling in the opposite direction, but failed to notice her. She saw his car but made no acknowledgement, and her visit would have gone unnoticed, had Harriet not turned into the lane shortly afterwards. She pulled up alongside him on the drive.

'Daddy, was that Angela?'

'I didn't notice.'

'I did, Daddy she's been here whilst we've both been out.'

'She's often here when we're out, Harriet.'

'I suppose so, but why has she been here today? She doesn't normally work on a Friday.'

'Harriet,' Giles put his arm across her shoulder, 'Things here are hardly normal.'

'No,' she admitted, giving her father a hug. She made no mention of the bulky, and very distinctive Gucci carrier bag with its gold logo, bumping along on Angela's handlebars, but she drew her own conclusions.

Following Giles into the house, she heard him shout immediately,

'Susannah! Susannah!' Then, 'I don't know why I did that. I know she's not home, or the car would be here. Oh Harriet, I've a terrible feeling that she's not coming back. I'll check with the police officers in the van.' He went through to the back door.

Harriet could say nothing. Her hands fluttered unconsciously to her earrings. If the officers had heard anything in their absence, they would have contacted Giles immediately on his mobile. She was sure that their agreement for Giles to leave the house today, was an indication that they were not expecting any calls.

She shared her father's misgivings, and resorted to the coffee machine to provide them both with some modicum of comfort, as she saw his blank expression when he came back to join her.

She left Giles staring unseeing at the morning paper, and went up into the main bedroom. There was no way of telling what Angela was doing here, there certainly had been no cleaning done today, but Harriet was not able to identify what, if anything, had been taken.

Retrieving her mobile from her bag, she took pictures of the contents of each of Susannah's drawers; the hanging rails in the large wardrobes, and the piles of shoeboxes in their base.

She looked at what was obviously a Christmas present, and saw that it was labelled to Angela from Susannah and Giles. This she put to one side. She also photographed the top of the dressing table, with its range of expensive lotions and creams. She smiled to herself, Susannah was a sucker for a cosmetic bargain.

Harriet sighed at her own paranoia, but she was becoming less and less comfortable around Angela. *Bad vibes*, she called it to herself, replacing her phone and considering carefully the implications of what she thought had happened. She wondered whether to go to the police, or to tell Giles, but rejected both. The police could do nothing based on her suspicion alone, and her father was too fragile to be burdened with this at the moment.

So Harriet shared her fears when she called on Maxine.

'What on earth do I do? She's taking Susannah's stuff. I know she is.'

Maxine was quiet for a while.

'I know it seems like that, but do you know? Do you really know?' she said at last. 'Who else has been in the house?'

Harriet thought.

'The next door neighbours both came in, but only went through to the drawing room. Then that Julia called round with a casserole, and a lady from down the road brought a cake. All sorts of friends and neighbours, I don't know some of them. People have been really kind.'

'And the police have been in,' added Maxine.

'Oh but surely ...' Harriet looked aghast. She swept her hair back behind her left ear and fiddled with her earring.

'No, of course, but you do see don't you, that if you challenge Angela with any of this she will point out to you that all these people have been in?

You and I both know that the likelihood is that she has taken stuff, but we can't prove it. What have you done?'

Harriet told her about taking the photographs of Susannah's things. She sounded sheepish.

'Of course, even if things move or go missing I couldn't prove it was her could I? It's too awful for poor Daddy, as if he isn't suffering enough. I can't tell you.'

'No, but if anything else comes to light, it may be something the police can use in the future. I can't think of anything else to suggest. Now, tell me about Susannah. What is she like?'

Harriet smiled as she collected her thoughts, again smoothing her hair.

'She is great fun. We shared a flat you know, when I first moved out of Scot Hay. It was in a lovely Georgian house near the hospital. All elaborate cornices, and a beautiful ceiling rose in the living room, from it was hanging a wire with a bare bulb. Susannah decided that it should have nothing less than a chandelier, and in a way she was right – it was what the room called for. But she couldn't afford a real one, so she bought a plastic one, can you imagine. In fact it was quite realistic, but anyone who had lived, as I had done, with the two chandeliers in the drawing room at Scot Hay, would have no difficulty in spotting it.

'She was a quick learner though. When she and Daddy got engaged, I found her one day in the small sitting room with a pile of books about antiques from the library. She was obviously going through Mummy's ornaments and things, seeing if they were worth anything. It's the one and only time we nearly fell out, and it would have been my fault.' Harriet shook her head, remembering.

'My first thought was that she was an avaricious cow, checking what Daddy's worth, although that didn't seem to tie in with happy-go-lucky Susannah.' She smiled at the thought.

'She wasn't baptised Susannah, you know. She was just plain Susan, but that was too ordinary and there were several other Susan's in her class at secondary school apparently, so she changed it. When she married Daddy of course, her real name was read out. I don't think anyone else apart from her mother had remembered she was just Susan.

'Anyway, when I found her going through Daddy's things, I tackled her. I felt really bad about it afterwards, but she never held it against me.' She tapped a long fingernail against her throat as she recalled Susannah's reaction.

'She just said calmly, *Harriet, if I am to be custodian of these beautiful things until they come to you and Matthew, I need to know how best to look after them. These miniatures, for example, are really quite valuable. I think they should be in the safe or at least in a locked cabinet.*

'This was long before Angela of course, and Daddy had employed a succession of people – nurses for Mummy, cleaners and cooks. There were all sorts of people in and out of the house. What Susannah said made perfect sense.'

'God! And now this awful cleaner woman is making off with all these things Susannah cared so much about.' Maxine reached out her hand to her friend.

'You do believe me then?' Harriet looked

troubled. 'I thought I might be going mad. I really dislike that woman. I don't know why Susannah keeps her on.'

'Good cleaners are hard to find I expect. You said she does seem to keep the place neat.'

Harriet smiled for the first time in what seemed like weeks.

'Maxine, I can't tell you what I'd do without you. God forbid that Susannah should come back and find we've dismissed her cleaner! I'd better not interfere, but I'm going to keep a very close eye on her. Pity I have to go home tomorrow, but I'll come back often.'

* * *

Angela considered herself to have had a lucky escape. Giles had certainly not seen her as she cycled away from Scot Hay. She tried on the beautiful sandals. She had, commending herself on her prudence, taken one of the bottom shoe boxes from Susannah's wardrobe, reckoning that these were less likely to be missed. Taking them off reluctantly, she stashed the shoebox and its contents in her own wardrobe.

Trying them on now and then and daydreaming would be a real treat, but she would have to be careful. She noticed the price label on the box. Over four hundred pounds for a few straps! She might be able to sell them, but she would have to bide her time and see what occurred at the old farmhouse.

The following lunchtime, as Angela was about to leave and Harriet was checking the contents of Susannah's wardrobe, she again came across the

Christmas present for Angela. She went down to the kitchen and gave it to the cleaner, who was changing into outdoor shoes. Today she clearly had not taken anything that was not her own.

'We're all at sixes and sevens as you know Angela. I'd like you to take this now please.'

Angela thanked her briefly, then, 'Actually, I'll just thank Giles before I go,' but Harriet interrupted.

'I don't think so,' she said, placing herself between Angela and the door to the study. 'I don't want him upset any more than he is already. He probably doesn't know about it anyway.' She was dismissive, 'Susannah deals with that sort of thing.'

'Of course,' said Angela. She knew what it was – she could smell it through the wrapping. Fancy soap! It was the same gift as last year – that Susannah had no imagination - some really strong smelling soap from a so-called specialist shop.

In Angela's opinion, it smelled far too strong, and oozed disgusting puddles of vibrant colour all over the bathroom. Last year she had opened the stuff – even started to use one tub before she realised how awful it was. Now she was wiser. Even on her way home she called at the post office, had it weighed, and found out the cost of sending the box inland. Once home, she checked the cost of the soap on the outlet's website, and by evening it was for sale on the internet.

Angela was seething. She sat and chewed her nails thinking of the injustice she had suffered. After all she had done these last few days, and this was all the thanks she got. It confirmed her in her dislike of Susannah, and of Harriet. Giles not even to be thanked indeed, she'd see about that once that Harriet was out of the way.

Next morning, she retrieved the jacket from the attic when Harriet was not around. She carefully packed it in the supermarket carrier bag in which she had brought her slippers and rubber gloves, but she need not have bothered hiding it, Giles had not emerged from the drawing room throughout the whole morning. When she was ready to leave, the carrier bag safely stowed on the handlebars of her bicycle, she sought him out.

'Bye Giles. I'm going now.'

He looked up from the pile of photographs on the coffee table.

'Oh goodbye er, Angela. Thank you. Oh I meant to check, you do have a key, don't you?'

'Oh yes, and the alarm details. Susannah has always trusted me completely.'

'Of course, yes, only I may not be here tomorrow. I wanted to be sure you could get in.'

Angela smiled at him, picking at a fingernail. 'Is there anything particular you want me to do tomorrow? I could get you something in for lunch? Leave you something in the oven for your dinner?'

Giles remembered Harriet's doubts about Angela and said, somewhat repressively,

'That won't be necessary thanks. Hopefully my wife will be home soon, so I think it best if you just stick to your normal routine please, Angela.' His voice softened, 'And I'm quite handy in the kitchen. I shall cope for as long as is necessary.'

'Okay', Angela was downcast. 'Well, if there is anything just let me know. Do you want my telephone number?' Angela fumbled in her pocket for a pen.

'No, that's fine. I can always leave you a note.' And Giles had already turned back to his perusal of a photograph of Susannah.

Trying on the jacket at home was some consolation, but it was a sombre Angela setting off for work the next day. Harriet phoned during the morning and, in Giles's absence, Angela took the call.

'Any news?' Harriet asked, without preamble. Angela had not even bothered to check.

'No, the police in the van have said nothing, and …' She glanced down at the handset display, 'Actually, there haven't been any calls. Sorry.'

She said, in what she considered a suitably lugubrious voice, 'Your father's not here.' She picked at a cuticle. She badly wanted to know where Giles had gone, and how long he would be out, but Harriet was not including her.

'I know. What time do you finish today?'

Same as I do every day Angela thought, but she told Harriet, wondering why she wanted to know.

In the middle of the afternoon, once she was sure that Angela would have left, Harriet arrived at her father's. She had arranged to meet him for dinner, and wanted to go through Susannah's room again first. Nothing seemed to have changed. Before Giles came home, she took the opportunity to phone Maxine, she needed to talk about her fears.

'I hope you don't mind me ringing again. I can't tell you how upsetting this business with Angela is, I can't get it out of my head. I've checked Susannah's room again, but can't make out anything that's different from the photos. Of course, she's been told not to go in there at the moment, so maybe she hasn't. She's making me feel very uncomfortable. I can't tell you.'

Harriet went to the window and looked out,

'The way she looks at me with her head to one side? It looks weird, and her hands. She's forever picking at her nails and her cuticles and they bleed, and, oh, it turns my stomach.' She sighed deeply, 'Oh it may be an affliction and she should be pitied, but just now I'm afraid I feel sorry for Daddy and for myself, and I've no more sympathy to spare for Angela.

'She strikes me as being really malevolent, and I can't explain it. And another thing,' she paused, then ploughed on, airing her concerns outside the family for the first time. 'I've remembered something else.' She told Maxine about the Christmas flowers.

'I thought nothing of it at the time, but now I'm sure she took them. I overheard the florist saying what was ordered, and Angela signed for them and took them into the utility room to put in water. The next day I was in there, changing into my boots because it had been raining, and there were no chrysanthemums anywhere. I know the florist brought them because he particularly mentioned the colours.'

Harriet sat down and shook her hair back, then twisted the stud in her ear.

'I asked her about the copy receipt from the florist's record book, but she blustered a bit and picked at her fingers, then said in all the fuss with the police here, and the baker's van coming just afterwards she couldn't remember where she'd put it, and she couldn't remember exactly what the order comprised.

It all sounds so plausible, but she's lying. I know she is, and I feel so petty making an issue of a bunch of flowers at a time like this, when really nothing matters less.' Harriet heaved another sigh.

'What does Giles say?'

Harriet smiled down the phone.

'Daddy's so tolerant, he just dismisses it. He's the perfect partner for Susannah, you know, he lets her live her life just as she wants to, indulges her whims, and doesn't interfere with what she does – just accepts her for what she is. But with Angela he's being the same, and I'm positive I'm right. She's so manipulative and shifty, it just pulls the wool over Daddy's eyes every time.'

'God, that's awful. As if things aren't bad enough just now. Is there anything I can do?'

'I don't think there's anything anyone can do.' Harriet sounded resigned, 'But it helps to talk about it.'

*   *   *

The next afternoon, with promises to speak on the phone at least twice a day, Harriet kissed goodbye to her father and went home to Nantwich. She was not destined to stay away for long however.

She returned to her father's when news broke that Susannah's car had been found.

Chapter 18

Dan Fairley had started work at the airport at the beginning of the coldest December for a hundred years – not quite, but not far off *since records began* as they are wont to say on the News.

He was keen to make a success of this job, but wondered how he would cope with the cold and the damp. As the newest member of the team, he had been entitled to no time off and had worked for several different supervisors over the holiday period. On the second Monday in the New Year his regular boss was back, and at the end of January they met in the office for Dan's second monthly review.

Dan asked again exactly what it was that he was to look out for on the regular patrols he carried out. His supervisor was experienced in airport protocol, as well as being very fond of the sound of his own voice.

'We,' he began, puffing out his substantial chest like a superannuated sergeant major, 'are the security frontline of the airport – a very important job, Dan my boy. Our customers rely on us to keep their cars safe. So anyone hanging around, you let me know; any bumps or breakages or things that seem out of the ordinary, no matter what, you tell me, see?'

'The truth is...' Dan stopped.

'What? Have you seen anything like that?'

Dan hesitated for a moment then shook his head, but he made a point on his next patrol of checking on the red Lexus he had first noticed just after Christmas. The car was an expensive model with a personalised number plate, and the dust and grime was now thick, and still undisturbed. Peering through the passenger window he could see that the handbag was still there. He felt guilty at having to mention it to the supervisor – perhaps he would be sacked for peering *inside* the car, but this was definitely something odd. Ladies did not leave handbags poking out from under the passenger seat of their cars when they went on holiday.

*   *   *

It was reaching the close of the day when the call came through from the Manchester police to say that the missing car had been found at Manchester Airport, in the Terminal Two long-stay car park. Detective Inspector Timothy was delayed in the rush hour traffic on the M6, and reached the car park control centre just short of seven o'clock. The assistant was waiting in his supervisor's office, keen to tell his tale.

'It's a brill car. I want to have one of those when I get enough money – that colour too. I noticed its number plates. I'd love to have my own numbers like that – when I get a decent car to put it on 'course.'

DI Timothy waited patiently for him to continue.

'Those is my mam's initials, so I noticed it p'ticular.' He paused, looking backwards and forwards between his supervisor and the policeman, who smiled encouragement.

'How do you know how long it's been there?'

'I noticed it first on a Monday. 'Cos I'm the newest, I had to work Christmas and New Year, but I had the weekend before Christmas off. It wasn't there on the Friday when I finished at six, but I noticed it when I did my first patrol on the Monday morning. It was very clean then and shiny, like it was newly polished.'

As he spoke, the car, shrouded in plastic now and on the back of a police transporter, passed the office window en route to Staffordshire for forensic examination. The conversation stopped as the three watched it out of sight.

'You've done well, lad,' said the supervisor, earning himself a look from DI Timothy, who spoke again to Dan.

'If you'd mentioned it sooner it would have helped us more, but there we go. You've told us now, that's the main thing. We'll need a full statement from you tomorrow morning. Off you go home now, you've had enough excitement for one day.'

*   *   *

Clyde was reading aloud to Emma from the Sentinel, as Gary arrived at the pub.

'What's that you're reading, Clyde?' he was hopeful for elucidation about the conversation he had overheard whilst buying cigarettes.

'*A car found yesterday at Manchester Airport's T2 long stay car park has been identified as belonging to Mrs Susannah Scott-Ryder, who was last seen during the weekend before Christmas.*' Clyde read,

'*The car is believed to have been there since soon after Mrs Scott-Ryder's disappearance, which took place in the early hours of Sunday December*

22nd. She was last seen when she gave a friend a lift home after a social event at her home. Mrs Scott-Ryder was wearing a black skirt, pink and black silk top and a distinctive pale pink coat. Detective Inspector Timothy, who is in charge of the investigation, stated that they do not believe Mrs Scott-Ryder is travelling abroad. Any information please telephone ... etc. etc.'

Clyde lowered the newspaper.

'Bet she's dead, probably raped and then stabbed. There's loads of places by that airport, countryside and that. I used to live near there, loads of places.'

'Oh, don't,' Emma made a moue of disgust.

'What's up?' said Clyde, leaning over her, 'You squeamish or somethin'?'

'I don't like anything like that, people getting hurt. It's horrible, I won't sleep tonight.'

'Good,' said Simon, putting his arm tightly round her waist and grinning at her.

Gary remained quiet.

*   *   *

'We've got the initial report from forensics on the car, Sir. Susannah's hairs and secretions in the boot, almost certainly that's how he moved the body. Scuff marks that may have been from her shoes, they're doing a check. The handbag and contents under the seat contain nothing unusual.' The Sergeant looked up, 'No phone though, that's pretty unusual.'

He flicked back through one of the boxes of reports on the desk. 'She had an i-phone, it's not been found in the house.'

Turning again to the report he said, 'The bag itself has her prints and those of one other female, not the cleaner or Harriet Scott-Ryder. The prints are smudged, not surprising, we know the attacker probably wore gloves. The position of the driver's seat suggests someone of over six feet tall, probably nearer six two, so most likely a man.

'There is also a cigarette stub on the floor of the car. Ashtray empty. Mrs Scott-Ryder had never smoked; it doesn't look as if the ashtray had ever been used. All we need now is someone to match that stub to.'

*　　*　　*

Harriet phoned her brother in New Hampshire as soon as she heard, and told him about Susannah's car. They had spoken several times, and now they discussed whether he should fly over.

He spoke too to Giles, and they agreed that his presence would serve no practical purpose.

He did however catch the first available flight in the middle of February, when Harriet phoned him to say that Susannah's body had been found.

Chapter 19

The forecast storm hit Staffordshire late that night. Perched on the hillside outside Audley village, the spectacular view afforded Miner's Cottage, gave it a vulnerability to the winds blasting across the Cheshire plains. Usually the area seemed to avoid the worst of the British weather, but nature seemed intent on addressing that oversight. In normal conditions, the back of Miner's Cottage took the brunt of the prevailing north westerly winds. That night it was gusting so strongly that the cottage seemed buffeted from all sides. Blowing and swirling alarmingly, driving torrential rain intermittently against the windows, before calming briefly, only to build up pressure for the next onslaught.

Huddled on the sofa with both the retrievers curled up anxiously beside her, Maxine focused determinedly on a television comedy, ignoring the flickering lights and the worried expressions on the faces of the restless dogs. Heading for bed eventually, and determined not to rescind the ban on dogs in the bedroom, she softened enough to leave the pair in the living room, where they lay together on the sofa.

Maxine woke at three o'clock to the sounds of something metallic blowing down the road, and of Hettie howling. She went down to make a drink and put on the gas fire. Jasper was happy to lie in front of it, but Hettie sat upright, still shivering and flinching at every loud noise.

'Come on you two,'

Maxine resigned herself to the rest of the night

on the sofa, with Hettie cuddled up beside her, still galvanised with shudders, and it was there that she finally gave up the pursuit of sleep just before seven o'clock. Her neck was stiff and her head aching, but the storm had abated to some extent. There were still strong gusts of wind, but for the moment at least the rain had stopped.

During the restless night dustbins and water butts had left their moorings; the greenhouse had lost several panes of glass, and three roof tiles lay smashed and broken.

By the time sun rose fully an hour later, the storm had completely blown itself out and an apologetic sun rose on a clean washed hillside as Maxine opened the curtains. Putting a couple of towels in the porch to dry Jasper and Hettie on their return, she set out with them on their morning walk.

Maxine surveyed a sodden landscape. There were fallen branches everywhere she looked, and she could see that tiles had blown off the roof of the cottage on the corner of the road. Her neighbours' corrugated lean-to lay snapped on the lawn, and down the unmade path to the nature reserve, one of the farmer's sheds leaned at a precarious angle, its roof twenty yards away across the field. Reaching the entrance to the car park, she bent to unclip the leads and slung them around her shoulders. As usual *off you go* was enough to send Jasper and Hettie galloping ecstatically across the fields, tails high and ears flapping as they ran.

Time to think, she reflected, I need time to think. Whatever am I to do to help Pippa? She stood awhile, watching the mist hovering over the lake, listening to the torrents of water burbling and tumbling down the hillside ditches. With a slight shiver, she closed her mind and set off resolutely along the bridleway after the retrievers. For ten minutes she walked alone, occasionally catching site of one or other of the dogs, as they monitored her progress along the familiar morning route.

At a point where a path debouched from the bridleway to the right, Maxine hesitated and then turned, plunging between the silver birch trees. It was mild for February and a light mist hovered over the water – a portent of approaching spring. The trees, washed now, spread to left and right and brambles, naked in the February air, stitched themselves along the path edge.

Evidence of the devastation caused by last night's extreme weather was everywhere. Many trees were damaged, and two or three along the path were uprooted completed. One old oak tree had fallen across the path, damming one of the many artificial drainage ditches that hatched the area. Approaching the culvert, Maxine could see that the water had flooded across the path, washing away its surface and piling the gravel to one side. As she rounded the bend in the path, she saw the dogs ahead of her chasing off to the right down a narrower path, the path they had always called Narnia.

Approaching the junction, she could here low unearthly howls from Hettie. From Jasper there was no sound. Maxine ran down the path, then stopped as she saw the dogs in the trees way off to her left. Jasper was rolling again and again against something on the sodden ground, whilst Hettie bounded around him barking.

Oh no, Maxine thought with a grimace and a

quick glance at her watch. Chances are it's some dead animal, a rabbit maybe or a fox. Now she would have to bath him when they got home. She blew into the whistle to which both dogs were trained. The young bitch dashed towards her, then back to Jasper, hackles raised as if in some macabre dance. Jasper continued rolling, impervious to the command.

Anxious now to know what was disturbing the dogs, Maxine moved slowly forward into the dense undergrowth between the trees. As her eyes adjusted to the change in light, she could make out a shape far too large to be a dead animal, apparently draped in some type of pink fabric. Her heart thumped at the sudden image of human death, and holding the bough of the stoutest birch tree, she turned and retched into the bushes. As her stomach calmed, she wiped her cold, clammy forehead on a tissue with shaking fingers, and reached for her phone. She caught Hettie and clipped on her lead, but Jasper was reluctant to leave this prize, nuzzling and rolling against it sickeningly.

Holding her breath Maxine approached the body that was part-submerged in ditch water, and physically pulled the resisting dog away, noting as she did that this was a woman, perhaps middle-aged – not a child anyway, and that she was very definitely dead. As the water disturbed the corpse, a nauseating stench rose, and the grotesque figure turned towards her, eye sockets empty and face black.

Not wanting to be alone with the body, Maxine hurried back up the path and sat at the picnic table to phone the police. Suddenly very tired, she felt she could no longer stand up. She hoped that there would be no walkers along before the police arrived. She didn't feel she could cope with having to explain to someone what she had seen.

Sensing her mood and deprived of their fun, the two dogs threw themselves down at her feet and lay panting after their excitement, seeming to realise that there would be no further walking this morning. As Maxine listened for the arrival of the police the only sound was the mocking laughter of the ducks on the lake. Mocking is right, she thought to herself, embarrassed at her call to the police:

'In Bateswood,' she had said into her mobile phone, hands shaking, 'the Narnia path by the big silver birch.'

The voice at the other end was gentle. 'Narnia? I haven't got any Narnia on the map Madam. Are you sure?'

She could hear the laughter in his voice, imagine the ribaldry when she had rung off.

'Oh, sorry,' Maxine said, realising her mistake. 'A family name. Along the bridle path from Podmore Lane, to the picnic table where there's an information sign. Down the path to the right, about two hundred yards.'

As she rang off, she felt very foolish. Narnia was the name Pippa had given the path when she was small. It had reminded her of a line drawing in a C S Lewis book. She had said that there was even a silver birch, taller and more sturdy than the others, where the lamppost should be. She and Richard had laughed together in those happier times, encouraging Pippa to fetch the book out to check, and the family had used the name for this path ever since.

'They had a good walk today,' Richard would say, returning with the dogs. 'I took them through

Woodpecker Woods; down Narnia and round the lake, then out through into Red Hall Lane and as far as the motorway bridge. They should be shattered.'

After taking the briefest of details, the police had brought her and the dogs home. She sat in the living room with the two officers who had arrived first in the woods. Her hands held a cup of hot coffee that the younger officer had made for her. Somehow she had managed to hold herself together as they brought her home in the car, but as she tried to unlock the porch door, her hands started to shake and the young constable took the key from her.

Gently, the constable sat her down in the living room, then went through to the kitchen. She heard her filling the kettle and the dogs' water bowl, then opening the back door and shutting the dogs out in the garden. Seated on the sofa with a mug of coffee in her hands, Maxine wondered whether she would ever stop shaking. She cradled her coffee and looked up at the sergeant.

He looked vaguely familiar, she thought, but she fought to bring her attention back to him as he gently encouraged her,

'In your own words, Mrs Chapman.' The constable looked about twelve. She had taken up her position at the table and got out a notebook. Maxine took a deep breath and recounted the events as well as she remembered them; the time she left the house; the single car in the nature reserve car park; the lack of human presence as she walked the bridle path, and then the dogs' unusual behaviour, alerting her to something wrong.

'Is that the way you usually walk with the dogs, Mrs Chapman?' She hesitated, and both police officers looked up.

'Well, sometimes,' she said, 'I always walk them in that area, but sometimes I change the route for a bit of variety, you know.' Her hands shook as she tried to sip her coffee.

'If it's really wet like this morning, then the woods are too muddy and the dogs get filthy, so I tend to stick to the paths. It doesn't help much,' she added ruefully, looking where Jasper had briefly wiped his dirty paws on a cushion, before the constable shut him out, 'But I do what I can. Normally I dry them on a towel in the porch when we come in, I …' her voiced trailed away, and she dragged her reluctant thoughts back to the present morning.

'You're doing very well, Mrs Chapman,' prompted the sergeant. She couldn't remember his name. 'Now tell me exactly what you saw when you followed the dogs.'

'The body, her feet were pointed towards me, and she was more or less on her side. She was in the culvert and sort of billowing towards to edge of the ditch.'

'You knew it was a woman then?'

'Oh yes, the shoes and tights and the pink coat. When I got nearer, I had to go nearer to pull the dog away,' she defended herself, 'He was rolling and nudging, and I thought...' she glanced up at the inspector, and noticed a glance shared with the constable.

'Of course,' Maxine babbled on, 'I knew about disturbing a crime scene, I read a lot of murder mysteries.' Her voice fizzled away. Was that another glance between the two professionals? Pity perhaps?

She cleared her throat and continued.

'I knew I should stay away, but I was afraid the dog was making more of a mess if I left him there. Sorry.'

The sergeant picked up a thread as if she had not spoken this last.

'What made you think it was a crime scene?' he interrupted.

'Did I say that? I'm not sure, only that she was so very obviously dead. I thought I should be trying resuscitation or something, but I wasn't sure I could do it properly, and anyway when I looked more closely, I could see she was all swollen and black, the face and the eyes, the eyes were empty and …' Maxine shuddered. 'There was mould on her clothes, and a fly crawled in her eye socket and,' she hurried on with a sob, 'the skin was peeling off. I was sick.' For a moment Maxine looked down on herself from above, that disembodied feeling before a faint.

'Mrs Chapman. Maxine.' The constable spoke making her jump. 'Take some deep breaths and have some of your coffee. It will be cool enough now.' They must have thought she would be sick again.

'I think we've troubled you enough for now, Mrs Chapman,' said the sergeant, and the constable closed her notebook in response. 'We'd like you to call into Merrial Street at about ten tomorrow to sign a statement. Ask for PC Thomas here, she'll come down and meet you in reception. In the meantime, if you think of anything, anything at all give us a call.'

He wrote on the back of a card and handed it to her. *Detective Sergeant Talbot*, she read. On the back he had written *DI Christopher Timothy*.

'That's my boss,' he explained. In spite of

herself she suppressed a smile. Like the TV vet from long ago, she thought. Then she recalled why DS Talbot looked so familiar. She had seen him at Christmas, at the time of the burglary of her cottage; only then he had been in uniform. He must since have moved into CID.

'Is there anyone I can call for you, Mrs Chapman?' asked the younger officer, watching her carefully, 'A neighbour, family? You shouldn't be alone just now.'

'No, thanks.' said Maxine shortly, 'I'm going to bath the dogs, then I'll phone my daughter.'

Once the police had left, Maxine glanced out of the patio door. Both dogs were asleep on the flags. Bathing them could wait.

She made herself a hot cup of coffee, and took it to her bedroom where she sat at the computer. Instead of switching it on however, she swung the office chair round to look out of the window.

The view was what had attracted her to this cottage when she and Pippa had hurriedly moved out of their family home in Bignall End, and needed somewhere to live. Now that the sun had broken through the last remaining remnants of the morning mist, she could clearly see the power station on the horizon, and the Welsh hills. Looking to the right, she could see the strange orb glistening in the sun. She smiled as she remembered Pippa's delight in the little miners' cottage.

'It's great Mum,' she had said, unpacking binoculars and searching for Ordnance Survey maps. As Maxine continued to unpack boxes of books, Pippa had shouted her to come upstairs. In this bedroom she had the maps spread over the as-yet bare mattress.

'Look,' she said, pressing the binoculars on her mother. 'That's Crewe, and over there is Jodrell Bank, that white curve is the telescope. That's over fourteen miles away. That's cool, Mum. Can I have this bedroom? Please?'

Maxine had agreed. She would have agreed to almost anything to make this transition easier for Pippa. Even the inconvenience of the smaller bedroom with the noisy central heating boiler tucked in one corner, was a small price to pay for Pippa's smiles and hugs of thanks.

Now, of course, Pippa was elsewhere with her own home, and shortly to have her own family. Maxine had waited two years after she had left home, then without comment to anyone, had moved her own bed and belongings into this bedroom, the view from which always reminded her of her daughter.

As she continued to sit inactive, Maxine wondered whether she should call her and let her know about this morning. She glanced at the clock, and decided that it was not worth worrying Pippa, especially at this stage of her pregnancy. She would telephone her in the morning. She curled up on the sofa with the two dogs, taking comfort from their warmth, and watching the snuffling dreams of the soft velvet muzzles, and the distressed-leather tips to two noses.

*   *   *

The following morning Maxine found herself reluctant to revisit the nature reserve. At the front gate, she hesitated for a second then turned left up the hill. The dogs, after a longing look in their usual direction, fell into step on either side.

The sun was bright this morning and they were walking directly towards it. The damp autumnal feeling of yesterday had gone. It could have been June. Maxine strode quickly up the hill to the cenotaph outside St John's church, then on to the top after a pause for breath, crossing the road to take in the spectacular view from the Gresley Inn car park.

This looked out over Woodpecker Woods, beyond which she knew would be the blue and white crime scene tape beloved of television producers. She forced herself to walk across the fields towards the nature reserve, then cut back through Woodpecker Woods, although it was really too muddy. She felt that this walk had exorcised the ghost of the previous day, not sure that she would ever again want to walk down the Narnia path again.

After walking the dogs, she drove to the supermarket for groceries, leaving Jasper and Hettie dozing in front of the lounge window. As she parked outside the house and carried her shopping bags in, she didn't recognise the sporty silver car parked on the hill. Once she was inside however, the doorbell rang almost immediately. She answered it, shopping bags still over her arms.

'Hello, Maxey.' Only Richard had called her Maxey, then when she was pregnant and in those first few months with Pippa, 'Maxey-mum.'

Richard asked, 'Aren't you going to ask me in? I was worried about you.'

'All the way from Manchester?' she asked mocking him.

'Please,' he said, as she knew he would, 'Not

Manchester, Hale.'

'Snob,' she responded, moving into the galley kitchen and putting the bags on the counter. He raised his eyebrows and put on the well-practised face she had used to call *Poor little me*. He put up his hands in surrender.

'Guilty as charged,' he smiled, 'Blame my upbringing. Are you going to offer me coffee?'

Maxine hesitated just long enough for him to notice, then crossed the kitchen. Her hand hesitated over the jar of instant.

'It's ages since I had real coffee,' he said, 'Sonja prefers decaff.'

'It'd take too long,' Maxine said, hoping he'd take the hint. 'I tend towards decaff myself.'

'I have all the time you need,' he said easily, 'I came to see that you're okay.'

For the first time in hours, Maxine laughed aloud. Turning she looked at his face properly for the first time since he had arrived. He wore the *poor little me* face again, but it couldn't hide the receding hairline or the age lines.

'What?'

'You,' Maxine told him, pouring water into two mugs, 'The idea of you seeing that I'm okay is rather ironic.'

He sat down on the sofa, where he could watch her.

'Have you spoken to Pippa?'

'I didn't think it worth it,' she passed Richard his coffee then stood leaning against the bookcase, rather than sit near him, 'There's nothing much to tell. I don't want her worrying and she won't hear about it any other way.'

'Ah,' said Richard, dropping his eyes, 'I phoned her this morning before I left, saying I was coming to see you.'

The anger burst through her.

'You had no bloody right...' she started.

'She's my daughter too,' Richard butted in, 'Anyway, there wasn't any reply. I left a message. How is Pippa? You saw her at Christmas didn't you?' asked Richard.

'Okay, I think,' Maxine diluted her feelings, 'can't say I'm really taken with Clyde, but that's up to her.'

It was not Maxine's place to share Pippa's news with Richard.

'Do you mean you haven't been in touch with your daughter since before Christmas, and now you've just phoned her to gossip?'

'I tried last evening as well,' Richard looked at her steadily. 'There was no reply then, either.' He relaxed back into his chair. 'Why don't you tell me what happened?'

Maxine pushed to the back of her mind where her daughter may be at this time on a Sunday, and why she had not returned her father's call. She drained the last of her coffee and put the mug down.

'Because,' she said rubbing her eyes, 'I've been over and over it, in my head, and with the police, and with every neighbour and friend who saw the cars or the crime scene tape, or who spoke to any of the above.'

An impasse in the conversation, interrupted by a scratching at the back door prompted Richard uninvited, to let the dogs through. To Maxine's chagrin they greeted him excitedly.

'Traitors,' murmured Maxine, fondling their ears as they dashed from one to the other. 'He left you too.'

'I would have loved to have more dogs,' mused Richard, 'but Sonja wasn't keen on the children having pets.

Maxine bit back several pithy retorts.

'Anyway, how do you know about this, and why are you here?' She put down her mug.

'I spoke to Joseph Traynor. We're organizing a trip to Torevieja for the two golf clubs.' He looked hurt, 'I do have some friends still round here you know.'

'But how did he know about it?'

'His son's a PC in Newcastle. Most exciting thing that's happened there for years, according to Joseph.'

Maxine looked away in disgust. 'And you came to do what exactly?'

'To help of course, I came to help.' His smile was disarming. 'I thought you might want to talk it all through – the experience of finding that old woman, it must have been weird.'

'Not the word I'd have used. She wasn't particularly old. At least,' she drew in a faltering breath, 'I didn't get that impression, it was hard to tell. It was horrible, so horrible that, far from talking it through yet again.' She gave an involuntary shudder. 'I have talked it through endlessly. What I want is to try and forget it.'

Richard looked crestfallen. 'I've come all this way, Maxey. I thought I could help you to cope.'

'I've coped with worse things,' said Maxine, watching him steadily.

'Oh, of course,' he raised his eyebrows, 'That break-in. That was awful for you, too. Poor thing.'

Maxine's hold on her temper snapped. 'I was not alluding to the break-in.' She was aware that she was sounding more and more pompous. 'I was referring to finding out that my shit of a husband was sleeping around, and had fathered a child on one of his conquests.' All Maxine's vitriol poured into the sentence, surprising her as much as Richard.

Richard rocked back on the two legs of the chair, then seeing Maxine's glare, righted it again.

'It still hurts, doesn't it my love?' He sounded like a cat that had stolen the cream, 'I had to choose, Maxey.' The petulant whine was back. 'Sonja needed me more, and so did little Florence.'

Maxine swept up both coffee mugs, despite Richard's still being half full.

'You did not choose,' she pointed out, her back to him at the sink, 'I threw you out, and now I'm doing it again. Go, Richard. You are not wanted here. Don't interfere in my life anymore.'

She pointed, 'Dogs. Basket.'

Unquestioningly the two animals went to sit in the basket in the corner, and looked from one to the other. They knew better than to argue with that tone of voice. Maxine went and opened the front door, giving Richard little choice but to leave.

She hurriedly put away the shopping then, glancing at the clock, set off again to the police station.

*   *   *

'Tell me about the car Mrs Chapman, the one

you saw parked,' said the Inspector.

'Oh, I'm not very good at makes and models, it's metallic, pale gold in colour with a dog guard behind the back seats. Always very clean.'

'Always? You've seen it before then?'

'Oh yes, it's a regular dog walker, I don't know their names but the dog's a chocolate Labrador, called Murphy. I know the first bit of the registration because it's like the cricketer, Grace?'

The sergeant looked blank.

'WG,' Maxine went on, 'and the figures are the same year as mine,' Both the officers glanced through the window at her car outside. The police inspector nodded slightly to DS Talbot, making sure he had noted this,

'Not local then.'

'Oh, they are,' said Maxine, misunderstanding. 'At least, not as local as me, as they usually drive to the nature reserve rather than walk, but I see them around fairly regularly.'

'How often do you see them?' Detective Inspector Timothy asked,

'Oh, a couple of times a week I'd say, usually one or other of them, but occasionally they walk Murphy together. I don't always see them to speak to, it's a big place.'

DI Timothy made a note. Something more to check, almost certainly irrelevant, but at this stage in any enquiry it was difficult to tell. He looked across at the dark-haired woman sitting opposite. The shock was taking its toll.

'Is there anyone I can contact for you, Mrs Chapman, you look all in?'

Maxine smiled at him, 'A visit from my ex-husband is always a trial Inspector. Once I get home, I'll phone my daughter.

*   *   *

'Mum, how are you? Dad phoned.'

'I'm fine, Pippa,' Maxine wondered when she had started to need to lie to her daughter. 'Really, I'm fine. How are you? I was a bit worried when your Dad said he'd phoned a couple of times.' She tried to keep her tone light.

'I'm coming down to see you Mum, I'll be with you later this afternoon, and I'll tell you all about it then.'

'Darling, are you sure? Not that it wouldn't be lovely to have a little moral support just now. I have made a statement to the police this morning, but they may want to talk to me again, so I'd better not come up to you.'

'Oh Mum, I'm longing to see you.' She sounded a bit tearful. 'But a statement to the police? That's really why I phoned. Dad's message said you'd found a body. What on earth is going on?'

Maxine told her briefly what had happened, trying to keep her voice from shaking as she revisited the horror of it all.

'Now, don't worry about me,' she finished. 'I really am okay. Just take care coming down here.'

Chapter 20

The first ring at Maxine's doorbell yielded nothing, drowned as it was by a raucous grating noise emitting from the kitchen. As the noise subsided, DI Timothy tried again.

This time the door was opened by a pale young woman of medium height, slim but with strikingly similar hair to her mother's. He flashed his warrant card, and asked for Maxine.

'She's not here,' Pippa opened the door wide, welcoming him in, and leading the way to the kitchen.

'I'm not sure where she is, I expected her to be out with the dogs but the car isn't there. I thought I'd just make coffee – I left home in a hurry, and I'm desperate for a cup, then I'll phone her.'

She looked gloomily at the results of her labours.

'I never seem to be able to do this – I end up either with lumps or powder so fine it blows away.'

'Let me.' He rinsed away her efforts, and measured beans like a scientific experiment.

'When I was at school, I had a Saturday job in a coffee shop.' He paused and looked at her over his shoulder.

'A proper coffee shop, not these American chains that are everywhere now, and only require some youth to press a button. Mr Galleti was a second generation Brazilian immigrant, and was passionate about good coffee. Some of it rubbed off on me.'

As he talked, he deftly adjusted quantities,

warmed the coffee pot, and then when he was satisfied, poured out two steaming mugs. They chatted on companionably.

'Is that coffee I smell?' Maxine had entered the house unnoticed, and appeared at the kitchen doorway. Immediately the officer disentangled his long frame from the bar stool where he had perched, and went to pour her a mug.

'I didn't expect you yet, Darling.' Maxine raised her eyebrows to her daughter.

'No,' Pippa glanced quickly at the visitor, 'but where are the dogs, Mum?'

Maxine took an appreciative gulp of the coffee, and nodded approval at the detective over its rim.

'I wasn't entirely truthful with you yesterday Inspector. I said I would bath the dogs when you had gone, but I couldn't face it. It just seemed too much effort.' She turned to Pippa, 'You know how news spreads in the village – especially sensational stuff like this? I had a call from Woofs and Whinnies – would I like the dogs shampooed this morning, so I've grabbed the chance, and just dropped them off. People are so kind.'

The Inspector glanced at his watch and drained his coffee. He stood and faced Maxine.

'This has been most enjoyable, Ms Chapman, but I do have a serious reason for this visit, and I wanted to tell you myself. I'm afraid Mr Scott-Ryder has just positively identified the body you found yesterday, as his wife Susannah.'

'Oh, my God.' Maxine was stunned. 'I was afraid that...But I hoped... He didn't have to look at her did he? To see her like...' she couldn't continue, put her hand over her mouth in horror.

'Good grief, no,' the Inspector was shocked at the idea.

'We do have to be one hundred percent sure of course, but Mr Scott-Ryder identified her by the clothes she had been wearing, and by her jewellery, which seemed to be intact. Dental records will confirm the identification.'

Pippa went paler even than before, and started to slide off the barstool. The officer caught her and took her to the living room sofa, where he gently pressed her head down between her knees.

'I'm sorry, that was crass of me,' he apologized to Maxine, 'I should have brought a female officer with me, I had no idea she would be so affected.'

Pippa struggled to sit upright, and put out her hand to his.

'No, no,' she patted his hand gently over and over. 'It wasn't you, it's me. I haven't been well, and sometimes I think the body just switches off when it can't cope. I'll be fine now.' She gave him a wan smile, a ghost of the one she had flashed him earlier.

Still muttering self-admonishments he headed for the door, closely followed by Maxine.

'She'll be fine,' Maxine reassured him, 'I'll get her to bed. If she's no brighter this afternoon I'll get my doctor out to her.'

'May I call later and see how she is? I feel so responsible.'

'Yes, we'll speak to you later.' Maxine smiled.

As she returned to the living room, Pippa asked,

'Mum can I stay, for a while?'

'Of course Darling, you know you're always welcome,' Maxine got to her feet, 'I'll open the radiator, and make up the bed for you.'

'Leave the bed for now, Mum,' Pippa remained seated. 'When I told the Inspector that I'd been ill I was sort of telling the truth. The reason Dad couldn't get hold of me was because I've been in hospital,' her eyes filled with tears.

'I've lost the baby, Mum. When I came out Dad's message was waiting for me, so I phoned you straight away.'

'But why didn't Clyde...?' Maxine began, wondering why he had not relayed the message to her the previous day.

'Clyde's gone, Mum. When I was told I could come home I phoned him, but he didn't pick up, so I got a taxi, and a lot of his stuff had gone, clothes and stuff.

'Oh Pippa. I'm so sorry. How do you feel about that?' Maxine was gentle. Pippa considered. She could think of it now, not without sadness, but without her emotions escaping aloud.

'I'm not sure to be honest. At the moment I'm very emotional, so I'm not really thinking straight. I'm hoping I'll come to see it as a blessing, the miscarriage I mean, and that Clyde will come back. Maybe it was just fatherhood that scared him. Oh I don't know.' She shook her head, 'Our disappointment in each other was pretty much mutual recently.'

'Of course you can stay here, as long as you like. But I insist that we make the bed up now, open the radiator to warm that bedroom through, and that you go up for a lie down. You're only just out of hospital, and you've had a real shock this morning. Now, up you go, no arguing.' Maxine was firm.

Pippa slept through till nearly four in the afternoon. Maxine returned from taking the dogs around the block to hear her on the phone.

'Of course, of course and if we can do anything – anything at all. Give our love to Giles. Tell him we're thinking about him, about all of you. What time will Matt arrive? No, good, good, I'll speak to you tomorrow.'

She hung up, and Maxine noticed that there was a little more colour in her cheeks.

'Harriet.' Her explanation was superfluous.

'Thank you, Darling, I wouldn't have known what to say to her. Imagine me finding the body – seeing Susannah like that.'

She paused, 'I'll phone her tomorrow, shall I?'

Pippa's reply was interrupted by her phone ringing again. It was evidently Clyde calling, and Maxine went into the kitchen, discreetly closing the door behind her. After a few moments Pippa went through to the kitchen, gathering up keys and bag en route.

'Clyde wants to talk, Mum. He's just got back to the flat. I'm going to go up and see him. I owe him that.'

Maxine privately thought that she owed Clyde nothing, but remained noncommittal. She was aware that, as Clyde had gone, so he might come back, in which case anything negative she said would be wrong in the context of their future relationship. In view of her just having come out of hospital she merely said,

'I think you'd be more sensible to leave it until tomorrow, but if you're determined to go now, then please go carefully, and ring me if you need anything, or better still, ring your dad – he's nearer.'

* * *

DI Timothy pulled up at the gate as Maxine waved Pippa off.

'You can't give children your experiences,' she said as he followed her into the house, 'They have to learn by their own mistakes. Wasn't that a famous quote from someone?'

'I think it was Oscar Wilde,' he said. 'Pippa told me a little of her recent troubles, yesterday.'

Maxine was surprised that Pippa, usually quite a private person, should confide in a complete stranger. She said as much to him, but the Detective Inspector thought otherwise.

'But maybe strangers are the best people to confide in. They have no hidden agenda, and are often ships that pass in the night. Sounding boards who can be objective.'

He told Maxine that they had spoken to the owners of Murphy the Labrador, who confirmed that they had walked in a totally different direction because of the wet ground, and had seen nothing untoward.

It was gone midnight when Maxine heard the front door close. The dogs raised their heads, and tails wagged as Pippa came in. She was crushed, devastated. Over cups of hot chocolate in front of the fire, she told Maxine about it. Clyde was so relieved that they had lost the baby, but said that they would carry on as before, as long as she would promise not to get pregnant again.

All sorts of unkind things were said on both sides, and she had told him that she thought they should separate, at least for a while, so they could get their feelings sorted out. She asked where he had been staying, and he flew into a rage. She wasn't his keeper, he could stay where he wanted to, and so on. She said she thought that he had better leave, and he was delighted. He told her he was going to pull some bird who wouldn't saddle him with a kid at the first opportunity. But then he said he loved her, and refused to leave.

'Then he threw a plate at me. I was really quite scared, and just left him there. What a fool I've been, Mum. Thank goodness I didn't end up having his baby. He's been violent before, but this... I could hear him breaking stuff as I left. I'll have to go back tomorrow, if only to get the rest of my stuff but...' She broke down in tears.

'I tell you what might be better,' Maxine suggested, handing her the tissues and stroking her hair. 'Call your Dad tomorrow morning, he's on the spot – tell him to get the locks changed as soon as possible. If there's any argument from a locksmith, I'm sure a call to that detective at Merrial Street would be permission enough. Then you can go up, and see what's what when you're ready.'

Pippa hesitated. 'I don't want dad to know what a mess I'm making of my life.'

'Your dad is in no position to criticise anyone's lifestyle. Come to that, nobody should criticise your lifestyle. If you are happy, that's all that matters, and you won't be happy till you get this sorted.' Maxine was brisk. 'Phone your dad tomorrow.'

*   *   *

Maxine let Pippa sleep in next morning. She had heard her daughter moving around in the early hours, and then all had gone quiet shortly before dawn. When Pippa emerged in the kitchen, it was nearly eleven o'clock.

'You should have woken me, mum, I need to call dad.' Pippa grabbed at the kettle and put bread in the toaster.

'I phoned him,' said Maxine apologetically, 'I know it's not my business, but you needed your sleep. He called back about half an hour ago. He got a locksmith out first thing, and has the new keys for you at his house. He'll meet you there at one o'clock, and you can go to the flat together.'

'Of course it's your business, Mum. Haven't I just landed on your doorstep? Thanks,' Pippa buttered toast, 'Did you...did he?' she stopped.

'I just said there had been a bit of a disagreement, no details. How much you share with your dad is up to you.'

*   *   *

Pippa drove to her father's to collect the new keys, and then on to her flat to collect the rest of her things. Richard offered to accompany her but she declined.

'It's a mess, my love,' he persisted,

'Clyde must have been back before you asked me to change the locks. There have been some breakages.' It was a mastery of understatement.

'No dad, thanks but I want to go on my own.'

As soon as she opened the door she faced the turmoil, and was grateful that her father had been persuaded not to come with her. It seemed right that having got herself into this mess, it should be up to her to deal with the fallout.

Every breakable item in the kitchen had been thrown on the floor. Books had been ripped and soaked in a bath half-filled apparently for just this purpose. She could not believe the vindictiveness with which the attack had been carried out. Her clothes were shredded in the wardrobes, left shoes were soaking and ruined in the bath, the right one of each pair uselessly safe in the cupboard.

In the living room she stared amazed. Nothing was touched or damaged in here except for the Magic Decorations, the box of which had been removed from its place of safety in the small bedroom.

Each piece had been individually unwrapped and smashed. There were fragments of coloured glass and metal pulverised into the carpet, as if the heel of a boot had deliberately been used to grind them in. Suddenly under the corner of the sofa, something caught Pippa's eye, it was one decoration that must have rolled to safety.

Unwrapping the bauble, she found it was the one bought when she was tiny. *Baby's First Christmas,* very faded now, was etched across its surface. It was too much for Pippa, and she sat and sobbed.

Eventually she pulled herself together and was

looking through the Yellow Pages for someone to clear away the shambles when the phone rang. Richard.

'Are you okay, my love?'

'Yes Dad, I'll be fine. I'm just relieved that I've got out of this relationship now. He's one very sick man.'

'What are you going to do? I can come over right now, and help if you like – I don't want to interfere, but it might be easier. I'd like to help.'

'Oh, yes please, Dad. I'm feeling a bit fragile and this has knocked me for six. I'm going to give up the lease on the flat and get this lot cleared. I'll be staying with Mum for the moment.'

When they had finished packing up what was essential, including the treasured Christmas bauble, Richard looked around the devastation.

'Do you want me to deal with this lot for you? I will, you know. It's easier for me being on the spot than you hiking up and down the motorway.'

Her father could be remarkably perspicacious.

'That way you needn't come back to the flat if you don't want to. I can parcel up anything retrievable, and send it on or bring it down to you.'

Suddenly chilled by the unpleasantness of the situation, Pippa told him that she'd be grateful. She would load her car with what was essential, and he could send on anything else.

'I don't want to come back to the flat if I can avoid it. I want to draw a line under all this, and move on with my life.'

She had been relieved that Richard had never been told about the baby, she had felt it would have diminished her in his eyes.

Chapter 21

The police had known almost at once who the woman was. The Dolce and Gabbana coat, mouldy now and starting to rot, and all the jewellery, still intact, was highly distinctive. Detective Inspector Timothy stood watching the retrieval operation. The smell was strong now and unique to death. The body, twice disturbed, once by the torrent of water now filling the ditch, and then by the inquisitive dog, billowed and eddied, as it was buffeted against a tree stump fallen across the ditch, each movement causing a grotesque hand to wave upwards from the water.

The body moved like a live thing, but there was no life here. As the water pushed at the head, it turned as if in greeting, but the orbs of eyes were empty and the flesh was blackened and partly fallen away, subject to the gnawing and pecking of hungry predators. Chunks of hair had come away from the scalp, and drifted down on the current as a cloying miasma rose with every movement.

*　*　*

It fell to the Inspector to deliver the news to Giles. Harriet answered the door to him, and his expression told her that this was the news they had been dreading.

For days the police presence and questioning at Scot Hay increased massively, and Angela was kept busy providing them with tea and coffee; cleaning and laundry for Giles and his son, who flew in from America.

The police dismantled and took away the surveillance van, and moved the incident room back to Merrial Street – there would be no ransom demand now.

Harriet was a daily visitor, returning home each night, and the whole household was in mourning. Giles was challenged about his knowledge of Angela, and her history was again checked. Had Harriet been at the house during this discussion she may have raised her concerns with DI Timothy, but she had gone to spend a few hours at her Alderley Edge shop, and to collect more clothes from home.

Angela was unaware of all this, and her annoyance was focused on the fact that Susannah had been wearing that particular top when she died. It was one she herself would have liked, and the stupid woman had gone and ruined it. The thought led her once again to the principal bedroom, where she earmarked several items she planned to take, when the opportunity arose.

*   *   *

The day before the funeral Giles told Harriet that she should start to take out furniture and things that she wanted from the house. He would speak to Matt as well that evening and tell him the same. Once the funeral was over he would be putting the house on the market. He raised his hand gently to stop her speaking.

'I know what you're going to say Harriet, that I shouldn't rush into any decisions hastily, that this house has been our family home, my family home with Mummy as well as with Susannah, but I can't bear it here. I can't bring myself to even go into our bedroom. It's too redolent of everything that was Susannah.

'Matthew and you are both secure with your own homes, and it is my intention to move somewhere smaller, more manageable, and with no memories. Why on earth do I want seven bedrooms for heaven's sake? I won't be entertaining now.'

'Okay, Daddy. It sounds as if you're very sure. We just don't want you making irrevocable decisions that you may regret later.'

Giles rubbed her back, 'You're a good girl. I don't know what I'd have done these last weeks without your help, but I just can't go on living here. I should go mad.'

Later, as Matt took Giles into the office for an hour, Harriet went upstairs to the main bedroom. She looked at the mass of part-used cosmetics and lotions on the dressing table; the comb still with Susannah's hairs attached; the tissues and wipes. Hastily, before she could think too deeply, she swept the detritus of Susannah's life into a black bin bag. In the bathroom she did the same with a ruthless cull of shampoos and bath lotions, half burned candles, toothbrushes and paste. Reluctant to let Angela into this sanctum, she fetched cloths and polish and cleaned out the cupboards and drawers she had cleared.

Tackling the wardrobes would be a daunting task, not one she could face just now, but she could deal with returning the new items Susannah had bought immediately prior to her disappearance. Each bag and box still contained its relevant receipt, but there was one item she was unable to find.

Harriet turned her attention to the dressing table drawers. This was a beautiful piece of furniture, but would look too big and out of place in her own modern bedroom. She supposed her father would sell it, although if television programmes were to be believed, there was no market these days for brown furniture. Maybe whoever bought the house would want some of it.

She pulled open the left hand drawer and gasped in surprise. The drawer was filled with letters, notes, birthday and valentine cards, all in her father's hand. The romantic Susannah must have kept nearly everything he ever wrote to her. She felt like a voyeur, as she piled them all onto the bed. Beneath, was a stack of pocket diaries, again going back to the year Susannah and Giles had met.

Securing these together with an elastic band, she placed the letters and cards in an empty shoebox, and moved tentatively on to the other drawer. This was filled with personal underwear – frilly and bedecked with ribbons and lace, mainly in black and red. Harriet closed the drawer sharply, then took a deep breath and, reopening it, tipped the contents into another bin bag. She could not suffer her father to sort through these evocative fripperies.

The idea of Angela pawing these intimate items was repellent. Harriet went down to the kitchen drawer where Susannah had kept odds and ends; paperclips and rubber bands, batteries, biros and various keys. Taking all the keys back upstairs, she found one that fitted the bedroom lock. A spray of WD40 eased the long-disused mechanism until the key turned smoothly. After making sure that none of the other keys fitted the same lock, she tucked that one into her purse and returned the rest to the drawer.

She suddenly felt sickened by what she was doing – perhaps after all she should have just left it to Angela, and told her to empty the room of Susannah's things. To clear her head for a while, she went up to the top floor and took a few moments to open the window in the gold bedroom, where she gazed at the view.

The sky was clear in the way Harriet felt was unique to this part of the country. She looked across the Maer hills to the Welsh mountains in the distance, the horizon like a drawn pencil line across the sky. Unconsciously fiddling with her earrings, she followed the panoramic view, the rooftops of Keele University to the south, and, swinging around to the North West she could see the castle at Peckforton, and the ruins of Beeston. Turning further still she could just make out the top of the larger telescope at Jodrell Bank.

She had always loved the views from this window, and had stood for hours as a child with her own mother, making pictures out of the clouds, and building stories of long-ago princesses who lived in those two castles.

At length, beginning to feel chilled, she closed the window and turned into the room. Noticing that the bedcover was ruffled she went to straighten it, stubbing her foot as she did so on something under the bed. Kneeling down, she extracted several carrier bags full of wrapped Christmas presents. Pulling out a box wrapped in gold paper and garnished with red ribbon and a bow, she reached for the label.

To Mummy with love at Christmas from

Susannah and Giles.

Harriet sat back on her heels, her hands up to her face. Even though she had found the present for Angela and passed it on, she had never given a thought to any other presents Susannah may have bought. She had disappeared on the Saturday before Christmas. She was far too organised a person to have left her shopping until the last minute. All her presents must already have been bought.

Harriet decided against upsetting her father by taking her finds downstairs. She went through each of the parcels. There was something for herself, for friends and neighbours, clearly labelled envelopes for window cleaner and the gardener. One, clearly bottle-shaped, was labelled

A little extra present for my darling Giles from your Susannah xx

There was nothing for Matt, but his present had probably been sent to New Hampshire well in advance. That would be typical of Susannah.

Clearly the bottle was something for Giles to open on Christmas morning; perhaps his main present was something less tangible, but there was no indication of what it might be. Tearfully putting the goods back in their bags she went down to find Matt. He was in the process of finding Susannah's car documentation in the office. Giles had asked him to sell it back to the dealership now that the forensic team had finished with it. Matt confirmed that his Christmas present, a Boss cashmere sweater and toning casual shirt had been received at home ten days before Christmas.

Talk of a cashmere sweater reminded Harriet of Susannah's recent purchases, and the missing blue jacket, but Matt was unaware of any items being taken by the police as evidence. When the opportunity arose later she told Giles about the locked door.

'I've locked the main bedroom door Daddy, I've started going through Susannah's things as you asked, I can't tell you how awful a job it is, but I don't want them disturbed at all – I know where I'm up to. Is that okay?

'Of course, sweetheart. Thank you.' He reached for her hand and brushed his lips against it.

'I didn't even know it locked. There's probably another key in the safe. Susannah went through them all once and tagged all the duplicates together so we could always find them in an emergency.'

She went on tentatively to ask about Susannah's Christmas present to him. He shook his head. He had no idea what Susannah had planned. Matt took the initiative and told him about the bottle Harriet had found, which was obviously a supplementary present.

'I don't know,' said Giles, 'I really don't know what she was planning to give me.' Matt pressed perhaps more forcefully than Harriet would have done.

'Dad,' he said, taking Giles's arm, 'Think. Was there anything you said you wanted? Anything she may have picked up on. You have to see that, as we haven't found it, it may be significant?'

In characteristic gesture Giles ran his fingers

through his hair. 'I'll think. I really will think, but none of this will bring her back.'

Later, as the three of them picked at dinner Harriet asked Giles,

'Daddy, did Susannah show you a midnight blue evening jacket she bought just before...Christmas?' her voice faltered and her hands fluttered around her throat.

'No,' he smiled, remembering, 'but she told me about something special she had bought, said she was going to make me so proud of her when we went out over Christmas.' His voice cracked. 'Why?'

'It's not there,' Harriet was concerned, 'She wouldn't have worn it that Saturday night, and anyway if she had, it would have been found.'

'Perhaps she changed her mind and took it back to the shop.' Matthew suggested.

'I'm sure not,' Harriet shook her head as she stacked the plates, 'I went with her to get it, it was a beautiful fit, and there were several outfits she could wear it with. Anyway, she would have said.'

'Perhaps she didn't get chance to tell you.'

Harriet was thoughtful. She raised the matter again as she and Matthew loaded the dishwasher.

'I'll call Danielle from the shop, I've got her home number, I'm sure she won't mind. It's worrying me, and I can hardly speak to her about it on the day of the funeral.'

A call to Danielle later that evening confirmed that the jacket had not been returned. She happened to be working through December's invoices to complete her VAT return at home, and she had the relevant invoice there to hand. She explained the system she had whereby this invoice would have been attached to a returns docket had the garment come back into the shop.

Harriet was at a loss to know what to do next. She felt sure that Angela had taken the jacket, but there was no way she could prove any of it. Deeply troubled, she left the other items in the locked room, to be returned after the funeral, and then phoned Maxine.

'You sound cheerful,' she said, as Maxine answered the phone.

'I am. I've at last finished the translation of that series of children's books. French, Spanish and Portuguese – quite a big job to get out of the way. I can start on that bid for the European Parliament job now.' She went on to ask how Giles was coping.

'Oh, it's hard to say, he just looks so shocked.' Harriet flopped down into the sofa for a chat, inevitably fiddling with her earring. 'He's looking at moving – as soon as possible he says. I've tried to suggest he waits for a while to make sure it's the right way to go. I'm really worried about him – I can't tell you.'

Maxine surprised her. 'I can understand how he feels. In a happy marriage the fabric of the building you share becomes a part of the relationship. I know it's very different but that was one of the hardest things about separating from Richard.

'For your Dad it's worse – he's got good memories from there, both with your mother and with Susannah, but there's been a lot of sadness there too since before Christmas. A new environment that won't constantly remind him may help him to cope.'

Harriet could see the sense in this. 'That's why I've persuaded him to go back to Dubai. I'm hoping he'll do it soon, or he'll never do it at all. But that's not primarily why I rang you. I want to know if I'm paranoid about Angela. I need to talk to someone.

*   *   *

DS Talbot wandered into the Inspector's office, reading from a sheaf of papers and munching on an apple. He waved the papers at the Inspector.

'What's that?' Christopher Timothy rubbed his hands over his face. He was tired, dog-tired.

'Preliminary PM.' DS Talbot sat down and lobbed the apple core into the waste bin.

'What have we got?' The sergeant wiped his hands on a handkerchief, then took up the papers again from the edge of the Inspector's desk. He cherry-picked the relevant information.

'Gist. She wasn't killed there, but moved post mortem, possibly by car, most likely very soon after death.' he paused, 'You couldn't get a car up there though sir, the gates at each end of that bridle path are kept padlocked. I'll get onto the council, but I'm sure they'd have let us know if a padlock had needed replacing.'

The Detective Inspector hardly seemed to be listening, but sergeant Talbot's next remark got through to him.

'But what I have done already is to have the desk sergeant go through theft reports for the few days after she went missing, just for anything unusual. There's a guy with an allotment in Silvcrdale, reported a spade and a wheelbarrow gone missing on the Sunday morning before Christmas.'

'That's how he did it, sergeant. That's how he

moved her from the car park, down that bridle path and into the woods. In a wheelbarrow.' He thought a moment, then, 'Let's hear the rest.'

The sergeant cast his eyes back to the printout. 'Time of death approximately six weeks before she was found.'

'That means she was killed either as or soon after she went missing. What about cause of death?'

'Two contemporaneous injuries. A severe blow to the front of the temple, with the ubiquitous blunt instrument. Broken bone had punctured the brain.' He grinned and looked up, but catching the Inspector's severe expression, he straightened his face and looked down again to the document.

'And a broken neck, vertebrae C2 and C3. Suggests she was hit, maybe by a hammer or similar from the front, then there's bruising so probably she fell, possibly down steps or against a hard floor, and her neck broke in the fall. That was what killed her, but if it hadn't, the likelihood is she would have died of the head wound. There was massive interval trauma.'

'Would there have been extensive bleeding?'

'Apparently not, hard to say now, of course, but the injury suggests that the pressure would have been mostly internal. Possible bleeding from nose and ears, but it would have stopped very quickly as the two injuries occurred probably within seconds of each other.'

'Could a woman have done it?'

'Yes, if she was strong. The initial blow used plenty of force, but it would have needed only one swing, then gravity did the rest.'

'So she could have died at Scot Hay, in spite

of us finding no evidence there. If only that flaming cleaner wasn't so thorough. They weren't missing a hammer or any other tools?'

'Nothing that they could identify. That place is so huge they probably don't even know half the stuff they've got.'

The Inspector rubbed his chin, he needed a shave. 'Have we checked the women in this case thoroughly enough?'

The sergeant put down the notes and thought.

'Angela Davies; her alibi is sound, neighbours, people passing with dogs and so on. Harriet Scott-Ryder was in London. There wasn't time to get to Scot Hay and back again without being noticed, and no trains. She had left her car at home. Her neighbours confirm that. Her brother incidentally, was definitely at home in the States at the time.'

'Is there any connection with the Miner's Cottage burglary? Both burglaries carried out the same way.'

'Yes, but why target two such different properties? Harriet Scott-Ryder's place in Nantwich is much more similar to Miner's Cottage, she was away in London. The place was empty, wouldn't it have been more logical to go there?'

Chapter 22

Privately Angela was proud of the way she comported herself. Three weeks after the post mortem, with the police having apparently made little progress, Giles was told that Susannah's funeral could take place.

Angela had hoped that this may be an opportunity to make herself indispensable. After all, Giles was an eligible widower now, his family would go back to their own lives soon, and she would begin to carve for herself a bigger part in his life.

She cleaned the house more thoroughly than ever before, whilst the family sat in the drawing room planning the funeral service and receiving the inevitable stream of visitors. The house seemed to be full of flowers, and the constantly muted conversations began to depress Angela. She was finding it quite a strain to remember to be solemn and subdued, when she really wanted to sing.

When she was a child, a widowed gentleman down the road from her house had made a big impression on her. He was a military man – retired army she thought, and something above the usual rank and file. The house was substantial and he had lived there all his married life, but then his wife had died.

He took on a live-in housekeeper, a Mrs Jackson, who had a daughter of Angela's age. She was a real enigma to Angela – as a servant's daughter she should have been on a par, they could have been friends, but this girl gave herself airs, and clearly she and her mother were used to a much smarter way of life than Angela had ever known.

Eventually Mrs Jackson had regularised the arrangement by marrying her widowed employer, but Angela had always wondered why her own mother spoke almost reverently of the couple, whereas anyone else living together without benefit of clergy was soundly castigated.

Angela cast herself in Mrs Jackson's role now – moving smoothly and competently into Giles's life until he could see that she was indispensable. She wished now that she had long ago given herself the courtesy title Mrs, like a Victorian cook, it would have lent her more gravitas.

*   *   *

The weather had turned unseasonably mild. The funeral would have been an ideal outing for the Gucci sandals and the dark blue jacket, which was now stowed carefully in her own wardrobe, but even Angela could see that this would not be possible, and she spent a considerable amount of time scouring the Newcastle and Hanley charity shops for something suitable to wear. Eventually she found it – a tailored navy dress trimmed with white, which she felt was sufficiently sombre, but which she could wear again.

She was horrified to learn on the day that the funeral details were announced in the press, that far from attending the church, the family wanted her to remain at the house whilst the service took place.

'You see,' explained Giles, 'the service has been announced in the Times and in the Sentinel today, so people will know that during that time the house will be empty.' He stopped and his eyes filled with tears. 'The police inspector said that it would be wise as so many people will have been following the story.'

Harriet continued gently, 'After all, this started with a burglary that went wrong, or so the police believe. We don't want to invite another burglary.' She moved round the room, reluctant to get too close to Angela.

Giles gave a stifled groan, and dropped his head into his hands. Angela put her hand out to him, impervious to his flinch.

'Oh, of course Giles,' she gushed, ignoring Harriet completely, 'anything I can do to help. Now or at any time in the future.' She patted his shoulder affectionately.

Harriet felt a need to assert herself. 'Oh, and before you go today, could you please make up the bed in the top floor front room. It's possible that Susannah's mother may want to stay over after the funeral. The bedding is in the airing cupboard, and the fresh towels are there for the bathroom, the cream towels, please. Two bath and two hand.'

Angela was immune to Harriet's negativity. She heartily disliked the woman, although her attitude seemed unreasonably at odds with her having invited Angela to a party during the previous summer. However she attributed that to the arrogance of wealth, and refused to concern herself with it.

What Angela did, she did for Giles.

*   *   *

There was a spring in Angela's step next

morning, as she went to get her bicycle from the shed to go to work. The weather matched her mood. If it continued fine for the funeral next week, perhaps they would eat outside afterwards.

It would be like a garden party. Susannah had never liked al fresco dining, but Angela had always loved a picnic, perhaps she could suggest it to Giles this morning. Make a start at getting things done her way.

Arriving at the Scot Hay farmhouse, she found the door locked as usual, but unusually for the last few days and weeks, the burglar alarm was set. It looked as if she would have the place to herself again.

With no-one from the family at home, Angela determined to take the opportunity to do the downstairs rooms thoroughly this week, and she started with enthusiasm in the drawing room and had moved onto the kitchen by eleven o'clock. She stopped to make herself coffee, and took the mug upstairs. Trying the bedroom door, it took a moment for her to realise why it would not open.

In disappointment she rested her head against the wood for a moment. Why had Giles locked the door? Perhaps the poor man was suffering more than she had noticed, and would not even enter the room that had been Susannah's. The sooner he had a new partner the better.

It was time she made things happen. Going back downstairs, she caught a glimpse of her reflection in the mirror on the ornate staircase. Not too bad, she looked happier lately, but with Giles and all this soon to be in her grasp that was hardly surprising. The hairdresser had re-coloured her hair – a success she thought, this vibrant red – youthful looking.

Back in the kitchen she finished the coffee before checking in the drawer for a key, but all were obviously impossibly small for that door.

Angela had to content herself with the top floor. Of Susannah's clothes upstairs, there was nothing that she felt she would wear. However, there were some curtains in the third bedroom. Draped over the bed in a dry cleaners' transparent wrapping, they would not have been Angela's ideal choice of colour, but they were certainly better than those up at her own windows at the moment.

A floral Sanderson print in shades of cream and duck-egg blue, they were fully lined with French pleats, self-coloured button detail and tie-backs.

They would do her temporarily until such time as she could move in here. She doubted that Giles was even aware of their existence, but still she waited until it was time to leave before she took them downstairs, secreted them in a black bin bag, and put them in her basket to take them home. They were heavy and it would be difficult to steer, but it was worth it.

Passing through the kitchen on her way to load her bicycle, she grabbed another bottle of Giles's wine, white this time for a change. She felt in the mood for a little celebrating.

*   *   *

The story, which had long since disappeared off the front of the Sentinel, sparked into new life. It had, as a missing person enquiry, fizzled out as such stories must, first relegated to an occasional paragraph inside and then, after a few days, nothing. Gary was beginning to breathe normally again. (The newspaper articles about the disappearance of someone called Susannah had puzzled him. Who was Susannah, and why was there no word about Angela?) He fretted about this, but there was no one he could ask. He had convinced himself that this story bore no connection to him.

He could no longer ignore it however, when he passed a Sentinel placard in Knutton emblazoned 'Woman's body found in Bateswood.'

With shaking hands he bought a paper, but was unable to follow the extensive story. It seems to be saying that the body he had buried at Christmas, was not called Angela at all, but some woman called Susannah Scott-Ryder. Gary's head ached as he tried to decipher the print.

Simon telephoned him within minutes of the Sentinel hitting the shops, and told him to be in The Railway at nine. Gary wandered through the pub to find Simon drinking alone in the beer garden. He zipped up his coat. How could Simon bear to wear open-necked jackets all year round?

'What's it say, Si?' Gary tried to sound disinterested.

Simon read from the paper,

'*The badly-decomposed body found yesterday morning in Bateswood Nature Reserve has been identified as Mrs Susannah Scott-Ryder, who has been missing from Scot Hay since before Christmas. Mrs Scott-Ryder's car was found at Manchester Airport three weeks ago. The police are appealing for information.*

'Tell me again what happened,' he said,

before Gary had chance to say anything. He took a deep draught of his pint, keeping his eyes steadily on Gary's face, and spinning his glasses between his fingers.

Gary had his story honed and ready.

'I told you, I got there at about two o'clock on the Sunday morning, and the place was crawling with police. I didn't even slow down. I just drove straight past, turned round in the next gateway, and drove home.' Gary tried to pick up his drink, but his hands were slick with sweat and he was afraid of dropping the glass. He had slightly more success lighting a cigarette, turning his back to Simon in the doorway, which hid the shaking of his hands.

Simon drummed his fingers on the table slowly. 'And you are quite sure there's nothing that can link you with that woman?'

Gary inhaled deeply and, thinking of the jewellery and the phone in his wardrobe, blew out a stream of smoke before saying with false assurance,

'Nothing; everything's fine.'

Simon was approaching the bar, having left his mobile phone on the table, when it rang. Making use of the skills remembered from Dave's class, Gary retrieved the number linked to Emma's name showing on the display panel. With no particular motivation, he memorized the number. He returned to the pub doorway and lit another cigarette.

Later, both Clyde and Emma joined them and the drink flowed freely. Gary was getting concerned, he was running out of money.

'Where's Janice tonight?' Clyde asked, returning with his second round of the evening.

'Should be bloody here. Her's always late.'

Gary fiddled with his glass.

Gary watched Simon over his pint glass, as he waited with growing annoyance for Janice to join them. Simon's arm draped over Emma's shoulder, his fingers playing casually against her breast as she leaned across him, laughing raucously with Clyde, who was showing her something on his phone.

Janice was late, very late even for her. By the time she arrived Gary was feeling embarrassed at the open display of affection opposite, and humiliated that he was necessarily excluded from sharing in the seemingly endless stream of text jokes Clyde was displaying. He was a little alarmed to see that Janice was wearing the pendant he had given her – they were after all sitting in a pub not very far from Miner's Cottage. It made him nervous.

While he was at the bar, Janice subtly moved her stool away from his own and nearer to Emma. As Gary returned to the table having dug into his fast diminishing resources, she and Emma began a conversation about a celebrity they both admired. Gary grew more and more angry, feeling sure that Janice was deliberately distancing herself. The anger grew in him as he downed his fifth pint of the evening.

'Come on, Janice,' he said, banging the glass on the table, 'drink up. Things to do.'

Janice looked at him steadily, the proximity of her friends giving her courage.

'Just a minute, Gary,' she said sharply, 'Emma and me, we're talking. I can't drink as quick as you.'

Gary slammed the flat of his hand on the table, making Janice jump and earning himself a glare from the barman. 'You can't drink at all if you're gabbing. Now drink up will you.'

Casting her eyes upwards, Janice emptied her glass and stood up.

'Yes Boss,' she said sarcastically. Gary caught the conspiratorial glance between Clyde and Simon, and Emma's slight smile. Without a word he left the pub, and waited outside for Janice to join him.

Gary wanted to go straight home to bed but Janice tried to divert him. He had become increasingly aggressive during sex on the last few occasions, with Janice being left bruised and sore. And now something had occurred that was making her rethink her future. Her period was late, one – and now two months.

Janice was distraught. Ken had been away for four months, there was no way that any child born to Gary could be passed off as his. She decided that, whatever she was faced to deal with, she would stop seeing Gary after tonight and undergo an abortion before Ken's return.

*   *   *

The call came through to Merrial Street police station from the hospital at two thirty in the morning. A young woman had been brought in after being badly beaten up by her boyfriend.

Her nose had been broken by his fist, and she had three cracked ribs. She told the uniformed constable who interviewed her that she had finished with her boyfriend, resulting in this beating. She seemed relieved rather than upset at the loss of her unborn child, and was adamant that she did not want to press charges.

So DI Timothy learned nothing of the attack, and if he had, would not have known to make any connection with his current case.

* * *

Janice now had a second reason to dispose of the pendant. She neither wanted Ken to see it and start asking questions, nor did she want such a tangible reminder of the interlude with Gary. She decided to advertise it on the internet. That way, she could get a wider audience than with just a small ad in the Sentinel.

Discharged from the hospital but still not back at work, Janice wrote Ken a long letter about the attack she had sustained, omitting to mention that her assailant was known to her, indeed had been her lover for several months.

A generous-hearted girl, she was actually quite grateful to Gary in that she had miscarried the baby, and now Ken need be none the wiser. She would have no cause to find money for an abortion, and according to hospital staff no permanent damage had been done.

She re-read Ken's last letter, in which he hoped that they would get engaged on his next leave, if she wouldn't find it to dull to be married to him. Looking at her bruised face in the mirror, Janice decided that it was time she settled for dullness.

She would sell Gary's pendant, with that and the money she had mentally set aside for an abortion in the bank, it would be nice to have a little nest egg put away for Ken's return.

*　　*　　*

Sitting in front of her laptop a few evenings later, a glass of red wine to hand, Pippa opened the shopping site and looked again at the photograph of the pendant she had found the previous evening. Harriet had told her about Maxine's stolen pendant, and she decided that she would replace it.

She would just do it without saying anything, and give it to her Mum for her birthday. It seemed fitting that as she had bought the original, so she would buy another. She hadn't been able to find anything exactly like it in the shops or on-line, but there was a similar item available on e-bay.

She enlarged the picture on the screen and looked more closely at the detail. There was an opal, which was supported on two short gold bars, each an inch in length, with another smaller opal at the top of each. The filigree was similar to the stolen pearl pendant, and it was all linked on a sixteen-inch chain. She decided what she wanted to spend, and made her bid.

Chapter 23

Giles had wanted the funeral to take place in St. John's, the pretty 1911 church perched on the bank above Halmer End. He and Susannah had been fairly regular, if not frequent attendees; Harriet and Matthew had been Christened there, and it seemed an appropriate way to close the circle of Susannah's life.

However, such was the level of public interest in this local tragedy, that he was prevailed upon to shun the tiny pretty church in favour of St. James's in Audley, altogether a larger, colder and gloomier place, set amidst glowering trees; the final resting place of John Wedgwood, of the great pottery dynasty.

*   *   *

On the Saturday morning, DC Himsworth did his usual stroll around the stalls on the market in Leek, and the second hand and antique shops. Interested in model making himself, and a keen member of the local modelling club based in the Moorlands, he stopped at *Models and Medals* for a chat.

'Anything new?'

'Not really. Could have done with you here last Saturday though. Had a guy here effing and blinding because I wouldn't buy his medals. Some relative's, he said they were but they were an interesting combination. Unusual, you know. I got talking – you know me,' he smiled an apology and broke off to serve a customer. The constable lingered, looking at boxed kits, until the stallholder came back to him.

'An interesting combination?' he prompted.

'Oh, yes,' the stallholder's memory was jogged. 'Naval medals. World War Two – but with both the Africa Star and the Atlantic Star – quite unusual that. 'Scuse me.'

Again he turned to a customer, this time less successfully. His smile when he returned was rueful.

DC Himsworth had taken the opportunity to make a quick telephone call, and was cutting the connection as the stallholder approached him. At once he was businesslike.

'What exactly did he say? I'd like to hear some more about these medals he was offering.'

The stallholder glanced at his watch. 'I finish for dinner in five minutes. I can talk to you easier then.'

Ten minutes later, the two sat in a cafe in Getliffe's Yard, a sandwich in front of each of them.

'Can you describe this chap?'

'I've been thinking about that since you said you was interested.' He took a huge bite of the sandwich, spurting mayonnaise down his chin and onto his hand. Wiping both with a grubby-looking handkerchief he continued, open-mouthed, 'He was young, about eighteen or twenty.' He splattered food crumbs across the table. DC Himsworth pulled back his chair surreptitiously on the pretext of reaching into his coat pocket for his notebook, which he flipped open.

'Young and dark, like foreign dark but I don't think he was. Foreign I mean – he was just dark.' He watched the constable write.

DC Himsworth remained quiet whilst the stallholder masticated energetically.

'His hair was long – down on the collar of his coat at the back but real long, and he could hardly see his way it was so long at the front. All swept to one side like a girl.' He demonstrated the sweep of hair. 'And he had a grey hat on, sort of knitted.'

The ensuing pause brought another bite of the sandwich. Prudently DC Himsworth waited till it was swallowed, before asking his next question.

'Tall? Short? Fat? Thin?'

The answer was immediate.

'Tall, and very thin, dark eyes.'

'Clothes?'

A shake of the head indicated a lack of information.

'Dunno.' His face screwed up in disappointment that he could give no more help, 'Just the usual. Dark jacket and jeans, I think. Sorry.'

'S'okay. What about accent?'

'Local,' he said immediately, 'Stoke. He asked did I buy medals. I asked him what he'd got, and he showed me. He'd got a long service medal in its case, and a set of four in their original box. I was just chatting while he tipped them out, whose they were and so on.' He paused to allow the constable to catch up in his note taking.

'I could see he didn't like it, the questions. He waffled a bit, said they were his uncle's, then he said his great-uncle's, who'd died. Didn't know much about them, not even that they were naval medals. The reason I really remembered him was two things. First, it was that interesting combination, not many people got both Atlantic and Africa Stars; that and how spooked he was. He kept pushing me for a price. How much? How much? I stalled – told him I needed to know whose they were to be able to buy them. I took the box off him 'cos it was all complete with OHMS Official Paid stamp, and would have been sent through the post. So I would know whose they had been from the name and address.' He stopped speaking, took the last of the sandwich and burped unpleasantly.

'What happened?' the constable prompted.

'He grabbed them all back, cursed like crazy and legged it,' he supplied, again plying the handkerchief and looking at his watch. Plonking both hands down on his ample knees he stood up and finished with, 'That was about dinnertime Saturday. I didn't think it was worth calling you lot.'

'No, I suppose not, and you didn't get a glimpse of the name on the box?'

The stallholder's face screwed up again, as if in agony. 'Sorry, no. Now I must get back to the stall. You know where I am if you need to talk to me again.'

As he left DC Himsworth was again reaching for his phone.

Chapter 24

It seems right that funeral days should be dull and sinister, with weather bleak enough to match the mood. The morning of Susannah's funeral dawned dry and bright, with a haze promising a sunny if cold day to come. It was the Tuesday after Easter weekend, and the church was still dressed in its jubilant triumphalism of white and gold, with lilies vying for centre stage on the altar with seasonal narcissus and early tulips. The air was heavy with the perfume of flowers.

Maxine attended the service, accompanied by Pippa. Neither had known Susannah, but the connection with Harriet was a close one, and it seemed right to support the family. As they left the church after an emotional service, Detective Inspector Timothy came up behind them.

'Ladies,' he said quietly, 'are you going on to Bradwell?'

'No,' said Maxine hurriedly, it's just family and close friends at the crematorium. We don't want to intrude.'

'Then may I buy you a coffee?' Taking them each by the arm, he escorted them across the road to the Peak Pursuits cafe. They sat and watched youngsters, freed from the shackles of school for the Easter holidays, enjoying themselves on the climbing wall.

'It's good to hear children's laughter,' Pippa said, as he brought over the tray. Maxine looked at her sharply but, detecting no sign of distress on her daughter's face, agreed with her.

The Detective Inspector took his time about placing their coffees, and milk, and then sugaring and stirring his own. Once seated, he addressed Maxine,

'Mrs Chapman, we have some news about your father's medals.'

Maxine nearly choked. 'You have? But that's wonderful.'

He put up his hand to stop her getting too excited, and quickly went on, 'We don't actually have the medals, but we believe that they were offered to a market trader in Leek ten days ago. He very correctly refused to buy them without provenance, and spoke to us. We are very lucky here ladies, the police force has an excellent relationship with the traders.'

Maxine was downcast. 'I wish you'd stop calling us ladies,' she said, 'It makes me think of a comedy duo off the television. I'm Maxine, and my daughter is Pippa.'

He smiled at her over the rim of his cup. 'Then you must call me Christopher, or Chris if you prefer. Unless I come to arrest you, of course,' he laughed, 'in which case we would have to put things back on a formal level.'

'So what does this tell us with regard to the burglary?' Pippa asked.

'It suggests that the burglar is likely to be local or fairly local. He didn't go far away to try and sell the goods, but he didn't know the man he approached wouldn't touch stuff like that, so I think he's more an opportunist than a professional. As you said the medals aren't really unusual, but it's too much of a coincidence to think it's unconnected. Tell me a little more about them in case they surface again.'

So Maxine explained: the long service medal in its blue mock-leather case, not named but dated 1947; then the group of four medals - some of them, three she thought, star-shaped, these together in a small brown cardboard box that had been posted to her father. She gave him the name and address that was handwritten on the box.

'We've made sure descriptions of all the goods have been disseminated to local forces. We've got an image of the William Russell Flint picture, so they have that too. It's a limited edition print. Do you happen to know its issue number, by the way? It may help.'

Maxine laughed, and Pippa smiled with her,

'Oh yes,' she said. 'It's number 195 of a limited edition of 750. I'm quite sure,' she confirmed, looking at his quizzical expression.

Maxine leant across the table, 'I use the first four digits for my burglar alarm,' she whispered, but don't tell anyone.'

Chris smiled at them both. They were very engaging, these ladies.

'It's a horrible feeling,' said Pippa, 'knowing that he is still around, whoever he is.'

'If any of this stuff emerges any time soon, we will get him. I don't think you need to be concerned, Pippa,' Christopher smiled at her. 'He wasn't interrupted at your mother's house, so he has cleared out what he went for. He won't be back.'

'That makes sense,' said Pippa, as Maxine got up to return the tray of pots to the counter, 'and Mum has changed the locks and got new chains on the front and back. The problem is of course, if we make it too much like Fort Knox, we may not be able to get out if there's a fire.'

'We?' he questioned, 'Are you still staying with your mother?'

'More living with,' explained Pippa. 'I've had to give up my flat, so for the moment I've moved back in with Mum. It's a bit of a commute to Manchester, but if I decide to stay round here long term I can get a transfer.'

'That's good,' he said ambiguously, 'Now, I must get back to work.' And he left them as they headed home to the two restless dogs anxious for a walk.

*   *   *

Angela took advantage of the funeral day to scour the Scot Hay house with new eyes. She reviewed the small sitting room, not as her place of employment, but as a potential home. She would get rid, she decided, of the delicate gold black and white striped wallpaper, and emulsion the walls in her favourite bright sunshine yellow. The gold edged mirror over the original fireplace could go, although she like the white wood-burning stove, flanked always by a pile of neatly chopped logs and pine cone kindling.

The kitchen had been newly refurbished and painted in subtle Farrow and Ball colours. She loved the central island with its sink and ceramic hob, but was rather intimidated by the Aga and felt that she would have that removed, along with the ancient bread oven at its side – useless thing.

The sofa under the kitchen window seemed

unnecessary – with so many downstairs rooms to choose from, who would sit in the kitchen for goodness' sake? Her contemplation was brought to an abrupt end by a knock at the kitchen door. It was the gardener.

Sitting him down at the kitchen table with a cup of coffee, Angela explained that the family were all at the funeral and had left her in charge.

'Actually, we shall need more logs cutting for the drawing room for when they return,' she said imperiously, glaring as he piled sugar into his mug and lit a cigarette, 'and perhaps you could collect pine cones from by the tennis courts. Then I think it will be best if you continue to do whatever you had planned for today.

'Actually, by next week the household will be back to normal, and I shall be able to tell you exactly what we want doing.'

Angela smirked to herself. She liked giving orders – she could really get used to this.

He eyed her narrowly through a stream of smoke.

'You will, will you? I think I'll call when Giles is around and find out what *he* wants doing if you don't mind. Talk to the engine driver, you know.' He took his mug and headed for the garden shed.

Angela was livid. How dare he talk to her like that? Like they were equal. For goodness' sake, he was only a casual worker one day a week, whereas she was almost family. Watching through the window as he went into the woodshed, she turned the key in the back door and went into the dining room. Let him ring the doorbell when he was ready to bring the logs in. She would make him wait for her convenience.

She liked the oak suite in here; that could stay, although she may get rid of some of the side tables and ornaments lying around. That silver should go in the bank – nasty stuff to clean. And the rugs, which Susannah had once told her were Kazan – whatever that meant. She had gone on to say, 'Please take extra special care of the rugs Angela, they belonged to Harriet's mother's family, and are rather old and quite delicate – perhaps the carpet sweeper would be more gentle than the vacuum cleaner.'

'Of course,' Angela had said, determined to use the vacuum cleaner on them whenever Susannah was not around. Well it no longer mattered. She would throw all these old rugs away, and get wall to wall carpet fitted, perhaps something in yellow.

She wondered how much it would cost to hire a skip.

As she reflected, the grandfather clock boomed out the hour in sonorous tones. That would have to go, she couldn't abide that clanking and chiming every fifteen minutes.

Angela moved her attention to the drawing room, filled as it was with tastefully arranged ornaments, and what Angela thought of as nick-nacks. The grand piano took up only a tiny corner and was covered in family photographs. She had no interest in those.

She studied the various ornamental pieces; none of the ubiquitous Jasperware for Susannah, but silver snuff boxes, and pieces of carved ivory; Hammersley, Minton and Spode china; and other makes she could not identify.

From her daily television diet of antiques

programmes, she recognised caddy spoons and candlesticks, mentally rejecting those that were merely silver-plated. She smiled as she imagined the reaction in the charity shop where she currently bought so many of her clothes, if she went in and gave them a box of rejected silver plate.

Moving from room to room, she found it all terribly old-fashioned. The television in the small sitting room had not been on since Susannah had disappeared, and she missed her usual morning quizzes, home improvement and collectables programmes. She put the television on now, and sat down before it with a cup of coffee. Of course, when she took up her position here, there would be a problem with Susannah's clothes and personal possessions that she had taken. She would have to dispose of the things she had stolen from Susannah's room. It was a shame, but once again the charity shop could benefit, or perhaps nearer the time, she could sell them on the internet.

She went up the grand staircase to the first floor and paused outside the still-locked master bedroom, or should it be mistress bedroom, for she had assured herself that Giles seldom slept there. That would all change of course. She would get rid of that hideous sculpted bed with its dust-gathering drapes, and the walnut inlaid dressing table, buy a modern divan and dress it in modern beige and brown poly-cotton. Not this Egyptian pure cotton rubbish that was the very devil to iron.

Not that that would be her problem anymore. Of course, she would have a cleaner to deal with all that. What fun it would be to interview someone and check their credentials. She remembered her own interview with Susannah, who had been so desperate for someone that she had asked for no references, not even where Angela lived. She had handed over keys and the alarm code apparently without a second thought.

'It's a good job I'm honest,' said Angela aloud to herself, with no sense of irony.

The en-suite bathroom she thoroughly approved of. The large white bath and Jacuzzi shower were almost new and exactly to her taste, although she would exchange the spotless white towels, luxurious as they were, for something in her favourite yellow.

Outside the main bedroom the floor was stacked with shoe and boot boxes, no doubt the product of Harriet's rummaging. Most of these bore designer names and all now looking for a new owner. Angela had just tried on a pair of suede boots when the doorbell rang.

Guiltily, she ripped them off and dashed downstairs to find the gardener leaning on the back doorbell. He scrutinized her face.

'What you been up to, duck?' he asked, 'You look dead guilty.'

'Don't be ridiculous,' she said haughtily, 'I work hard while I'm here, that's why I'm so warm. Actually I'm going to turn down the heating. It's a ridiculous waste of Giles's money the way Susannah had it on so high all the time.'

He raised his eyebrows at her, but before he could speak, Giles's car swept round the circle of the driveway, followed by Matthew's hire car. Without a word, Angela charged upstairs to put away the boots, slamming the box lid shut as Harriet called out to her,

'Angela, we're back.'

Angela splashed her face with cold water, then arranged her features into suitable solemnity. She went down the stairs carrying dusters and polish, and immediately put her arms around Harriet, ignoring the stiffening of her shoulders that she felt.

'How was it?' she said in sepulchral tones. 'It must have been a real ordeal for all of you.'

For once Harriet was at a loss for words, and Giles put his hand on Angela's shoulder.

'It was really grim. Somehow knowing how many people cared about Susannah made it harder. Poor Susannah's mother was taken ill during the service. Her sister and brother-in-law took her straight home from the church.' He turned to his daughter, 'We should phone and see how she is.'

Angela looked suitably pained. 'What can I get you? A drink? Giles? Matthew?'

'No thanks, Angela,' Matthew spoke curtly, as if she had no right to offer, 'Dad, I'll phone and see how Susannah's mother is.'

'I'll do it, Matt,' Harriet interrupted, 'She knows me better than you.' She was glad to get away from Angela.

They were getting on with what needed to be done. The cleaner stood useless on the sidelines of the family.

'Nothing for me either thank you, Angela,' said Giles, eventually, as if just noticing that she was still there. 'We've delayed you quite long enough today. You get off home now, and thank you for all you have done,'

It was very polite, but it was a dismissal. Matthew was edging her towards the door, handing her the carrier bag she always brought. She gave in with good grace, after all it was Giles's wife's funeral day. There would be plenty of time, Angela thought as she said her goodbyes.

Chapter 25

The station had long gone from Station Road, lost with the closure of the local pit. Social housing replaced the station buildings and yard, and opposite these with their pretty gardens, was a mismatched row of old cottages. Of the row, all but one were well-tended, painted and cared for.

The middle terrace however, of the block of five, looked more down at heel. It still had the original wooden-framed windows and these, along with the door and weatherboard, were badly in need of painting. Several roof slates had slipped, giving a somewhat inebriated look, more pronounced as the lower ones had knocked the downspout aside where it hung at a drunken angle.

The gap in the gutter spewed water down the wall when it rained, blackening the render, and weeping green slime onto the crumbling concrete path. The garden was a mean rectangle which had once been of grass, but the whole was overrun with dandelion and nettle, and was reached through a rusting metal gate.

It was this house where Angela had lived alone since the death of her mother nearly twenty years earlier, and in that time nothing had been done in the way of improvements.

The clutter on the mismatched units in the kitchen bore testimony to the fact that Angela cleaned for money, and not for the enjoyment or satisfaction to be derived from it.

Cobwebs clung to long-unused cake boxes, mixers and other paraphernalia that reflected the late

Mrs Davies' culinary skills, but not Angela's. The surfaces sported vintage breadcrumbs, and spilt milk on the draining board had congealed into a pile of used teabags.

The smell was of sour food and dirty dishcloths, stale milk and possibly mice. The windows, now in such bad condition that they could not be opened, added to the sense of mustiness and the sunlight that filtered through the small windows was thick with dust motes. The same curtains had hung at the windows as long as Angela could remember, and these were now lace-thin and trimmed with a border of dead flies.

It was the only house Angela had ever lived in, and now she dreamed of an escape from its squalor. Her mother had used up on the house the little money left on her father's death, making changes he would not have deemed necessary.

The removal of the septic tank and connection to the mains water supply took up most of the available money, with a large portion of the remainder spent on rewiring and installing central heating.

It was now nearly thirty years since all this work had been done. The place needed reroofing and new windows. The shower had stopped working long ago, but the shower curtain still hung around the bath, its bottom edge soiled like a petticoat in mud. Fingers of mould crept up the cracked tiles, and the hot tap dripped relentlessly.

There was no way Angela could afford to deal with any of it. There was a small pension from her father's firm, made insignificant now by inflation, and whatever Angela could earn.

Arriving home from Scot Hay in the middle of the afternoon when the funeral party returned from the crematorium, Angela went straight for the kettle to make herself a mug of tea. She could not understand how she had got things so wrong.

In her mind's eye she had been at Giles's side, grieving with him and supporting him so that he started to see her not as an employee, but as a woman. Initially having agreed to stay at the house rather than attend the service, Angela had seen a way to turn this to her advantage.

'Of course, you'll need drinks when you get back. I'll put out the best tea service shall I? Or will that be enough cups and saucers - how many people do you think will be coming back? You don't want all and sundry traipsing in. Shall I do sandwiches, I could make some cakes.'

Resisting the temptation to say that this wasn't a party, Giles put out his hand to stop her, 'No, no, Angela. Thank you. Everyone's being so kind, but that won't be necessary. If you could just come along and be here, don't bother about any food or about any cleaning. We just don't want the house left empty.

'After the service, some of the ladies from the Women's Institute have offered to do tea and biscuits in the church hall. So many people want to come and do their bit you see. Susannah was loved by everyone.'

Angela knew for a fact that was not true, she had no love for Susannah – not even a liking for her, but to say so would hardly endear her to Giles, and that was increasingly becoming her focus. She rallied,

'Giles, you will need something hot when you

get back. Why don't I...?'

Giles rubbed his hand over his eyes, and Harriet stepped in quickly.

'Angela. Thank you so much, but Daddy, Matthew and I will go out for a meal when we have finished at the church hall. If you wouldn't mind just hanging on until we get back that would be most helpful. I can't tell you. We'll pay you for your time of course.'

'It's not about the payment,' muttered Angela like a mutinous child, although it was partly. 'I would have liked to pay my respects.' Her eyes followed Giles hungrily as he got up and left the room.

For a moment Harriet wondered if she had misjudged Angela.

'Oh I'm sorry, of course,' she had crossed to the mantelpiece, and retrieved a small white business card from a pile. This she handed to Angela.

'The funeral directors,' she said, 'Susannah will be in their chapel of rest until Tuesday morning. You can go and see her at any time. They are open all over the Bank Holiday weekend.' She glanced at Angela's face as she left the room, and could see from the tight, pleated mouth and hardening of the cold eyes, that her sympathy for Angela had been misplaced.

* * *

'Daddy, I think that once the funeral is over you should go away for a while – perhaps back to Dubai? It's such a big part of your life going there. Going again soon will get it over with, if you see what I mean, the first visit. Once you've done it,

221

future visits and returns home will be easier.'

Angela came in and caught the end of what Harriet was saying. Initially annoyed that this would mean Giles would be temporarily beyond her reach, she realised that this would give her a great opportunity to have the house to herself. She could begin to make some changes, in Giles's interest of course, the better to help him forget Susannah, but Harriet's next words brought her up short.

'It would let Angela have a few days off too', Harriet smiled at her, 'she's done so much extra this last few weeks.'

'Oh, no,' blustered Angela, hand creeping to her mouth, ', it was nothing,'

'Of course.' Giles agreed, 'You must take some time off if I go away. I will pay you, of course.'

A frown of impatience flashed briefly across Angela's face. Why did these people think that money would solve everything? Suddenly she felt weary. She would leave arguing about this for now. Giles would be more pliable when Harriet was out of the way. And she had her door key, she could always let herself in at anytime and go through Susannah's things.

She sat in front of the computer that evening wondering what she could write to Kevin. Since this business with Susannah she had rather cooled to the idea of Kevin, but it would help to pass the time.

She wrote inconsequential things; a bit of car trouble, some shopping she had done, and a planned holiday. She asked whether he had taken the break he had spoken about previously and general chit chat.

For once there was so much going on in real life, that her world of make-believe held little attraction, and she soon logged off in favour of the television.

* * *

After the funeral, Matthew only just returned to New Hampshire in time.

After an unseasonably mild spell, the weather changed the following day, as it is prone to do in March, with hail and snow falling overnight.

Travel at Manchester and Birmingham airports was suspended temporarily, and local roads were beset by myriads of minor weather-related traffic accidents. The ground was frozen, the Moorlands were snowed in for several days, and the Macclesfield to Buxton road closed for nearly a fortnight.

Harriet telephoned her father that as long as he was all right she would not risk coming over from Nantwich. She had gone back to work, and was one assistant down. There were problems with the new manager at the Alderley Edge shop, and she had much to do.

* * *

Giles was not expecting Angela, the weather was far too bad to cycle across the hills of north Staffordshire. However, just a few minutes later than usual, he heard a vehicle in the drive and, looking out from the bedroom window, saw a taxi at the front of the house. Angela immediately sought him out, and found him in the main bedroom going through items Harriet had put aside.

'Daddy you really will have to look through some of these, and decide what's to be done with them.' Harriet had said, 'Some are far too personal for me to do, and some of this stuff is too good just to throw away. If you'd rather I boxed them all up and put them in storage then I will, but I need to know.'

When Angela entered the bedroom, Giles had sorted three bin bags of assorted clothes, shoes and bags. There was a pile of belts on the bed, and two hats, obviously worn at weddings, hanging on the back of the chair. The bed was spread with papers, letters, and what looked like notebooks.

'Oh Giles, I would have helped with this. If there's anything you want to go the charity shop I can take it, Susannah may have told you I work there some afternoons.'

'What? Oh yes, she may have mentioned it.' Giles recalled Harriet's doubts about Angela, and hesitated, 'I need to speak to Harriet about some of it. I'll let you know.'

Speaking to Harriet later that evening, he related the story of Angela's altruism. Harriet was sceptical.

'I can't see that woman doing anything for nothing, Daddy. Please don't let her take any of Susannah's stuff. I'll sort out a few things to keep her quiet.'

Despite the weather, Harriet battled through to Scot Hay on the Sunday. Angela would be at work the following day, and she wanted to try something. Giles was hunched over the table looking intently at two sets of property details.

'Hello, Daddy.'

'Hello, darling, I didn't hear your car. You

shouldn't have bothered in this awful weather, but I'm glad to see you. I'd like you to cast your eye over these, although I think I've decided.'

Tossing her keys and bag on the table, Harriet joined him and perused the papers, massaging her earring as she read. The details pertained to two flats – quite different.

One in the conversion of a huge Victorian house, almost a stately home, with traditional features and marvellous views; the other brand-new in a select riverside gated block. She tried to second guess her father.

'The Victorian one would suit the style of your furniture, and look at the view from that drawing room,' she mused, 'but the other is better placed for your journey to the office. What is included in the service package?'

He referred again to the details, 'Communal areas, window cleaning and grounds for both. The modern block also has an optional cleaning service.' He glanced up at her, his lips raised in a smile, 'and no, I'm not considering that one just so that I can get away from Angela.'

He pulled that set of details towards him again, 'but I must admit that she has made me nervous about taking anyone on at face value again. At least this way, I'd have some reassurance if they were centrally employed.'

Harriet nodded, 'It may not have the views, but it's by the river and a lovely area. A bit far from here though, where you've lived for so long.' She played devil's advocate, but Giles was shaking his head.

'That doesn't worry me at all. It's a little

nearer to you,' he said, getting up, 'and people around here are very awkward – they don't know how to talk to me. That Julia Corner actually crossed the road to avoid me when I went to the post office yesterday.'

Harriet smiled, 'But her friendship is no loss, Daddy. She never got over having to have her fingerprints taken when Susannah's car was found. It was only for elimination purposes from all those in the car, but you would have thought she was being accused. I can't tell you.' She fiddled with her earring, turning the stud on its butterfly fastening.

'For the most part I think people are just embarrassed, they are anyway when someone dies, and it's worse when it happens like this, people don't know what to say. That's exactly why it will be easier to move away.'

He combed his fingers through his hair then stood up and kissed her hair, 'Right, decision made. I'm going to phone the agents today, I'd like to get it signed up before I go to Dubai.'

*   *   *

Harriet went upstairs to the main bedroom. She selected a number of items from the pile of boxes and put them into a large carrier bag. She had pulled out the taupe cashmere sweater, a powder-blue spangled scarf, and a Miu Miu handbag, plus some unopened tights, and a pink slip from Susannah's cupboard. She left the bag in a prominent position in the kitchen with a note on the table – *Angela, the bag is stuff for the charity shop, thank you. I'm sure there will be more things later.*

But first Miss Davies, she thought to herself,

let's just see whether these goods ever get to the shop. I wouldn't put money on it.

Before she left she spoke to Giles. 'Now Daddy, when Angela comes tomorrow, please make sure she takes that bag, and if you can, find out which charity shop it is she works at. It may be too far for her to take them by bike, in which case tell her I can drop them off in the car one afternoon when she's on duty.'

*   *   *

Angela could hardly contain her delight when Giles gave her the carrier bag. Carefully keeping her face sombre she thanked him, saying that she was sure the manager would be very grateful.

Trying to hide her excitement, she even added for good measure that they were always able to sell quality items such as Susannah's, and that the manager was keen to get as much for them as possible. The hospice was such a good cause, wasn't it? Of course she could manage on her bike – she would not dream of him having to go through the distressing job of bringing stuff down to the shop, and it was only in the High Street.

She would take it that very afternoon, when she went to do her couple of hours at the till. If there was anything else, as Harriet had suggested, she would be more than happy.

*   *   *

She tried on the sweater as soon as she got home. Not really her colour, but it would do for cleaning in. One plain sweater was much like another, it would not be recognised. It occurred to her that Giles had probably never even seen it, so once Harriet had gone back to Nantwich, she could wear it any time.

The scarf was different – too distinctive, but with its designer label still attached it should fetch a bit on the internet. She had no need for a silly little bag like that, but again it carried a label and was obviously brand new, so she might get a few quid for it on-line. The tights and underwear she would keep for herself.

When she had checked all the items, she felt a little deflated. Not much for her own use really, but at least she might get some cash back for this stuff – she began to think of it as *this first batch* - and that was probably safer than wearing it. She was revived by the thought of Harriet's note – clearly she was expecting there to be more stuff that could be handed over.

The following morning, knowing that Angela would be at work at her father's, Harriet went straight to the charity shop in the High Street, where a quick look around the shop established that Susannah's items were not on display.

The manager arrived a few minutes after Harriet, and was able to confirm that, not only had no such items been brought in yesterday afternoon, but there was, and never had been, an employee or volunteer called Angela Davies. They had never heard of her.

Thanking the manager profusely and promising that when her stepmother's effects had been sorted she would come back with a donation,

Harriet made her way home.

Angela arrived at work with a number of carrier bags folded into her bicycle basket. If Giles was clearing Susannah's stuff, this was a positive sign of his moving forwards. She was surprised to find that once again both Giles and Harriet were sitting in the kitchen drinking coffee.

'Oh, here she is now.' Harriet had clearly been talking about her.

'Goodness Harriet, I hope you have good staff at that business of yours. The amount of time you are spending here.' She tinkled a feeble laugh to take away the sting, but avoided Harriet's eye.

'My business is fine thank you, Angela,' said Harriet coldly. 'I think Daddy needs my attention more just at the moment. No, don't get the cleaning things out yet please, fetch a mug and come and have some coffee.'

Once she was seated, Harriet continued, fiddling with her earring as she spoke. It made Angela feel slightly sick and she looked away. She picked at the cuticle of her thumb.

'As you know, we have discussed Daddy having a little time away from here, and he's decided to go back to Dubai for three weeks from Friday.' She picked up a cheque from the table and passed it over.

'This is for three weeks' money, and a bonus for all that you have done over the past few months.'

She raised her hand as Angela started to protest. 'Daddy would like you to take three weeks' holiday at the same time. You don't, of course, have a contract, and would be quite free during that time to look for another employer if you wish, but Daddy will be needing some help on his return, although of course things will be very different.'

She smiled at her father and covered his hand with her own. Angela looked at her blankly. Did the stupid woman really think she was likely to leave Giles at this stage, just when things were beginning to look hopeful?

'This week, if you would please dust and vacuum through, and do all the bathrooms and the kitchen. Then get the laundry up to date, the bedding and towels, as well as Daddy's clothes. Then perhaps on Thursday you could empty and clean out the fridge, and make sure that all the bins are taken out to the gate.

'Does that seem in order, Angela? It's not asking too much of four mornings? Whilst Daddy is away, I shall be popping in from time to time to make sure all is well. Please set the burglar alarm when you leave on Thursday.'

Angela drained the coffee mug and stood up. A waft of body odour assaulted Harriet's nose. 'That will be fine. I'll sort everything out for you, Giles, don't you worry.'

Angela made a decision. There was one more item she had taken from the house, and she had been wondering how she would get a chance to use it. Giles's trip had just given her the opportunity.

*　*　*

Opening the envelope at home, Angela had at first been disappointed. It appeared to contain merely a few sheets of paper, but closer examination of these showed them to be a collection of vouchers, three in all, with a covering Christmas card. As she , she gnawed on the skin at the side of her thumbnail.

The first voucher did not impress. A flying lesson in a Tiger Moth, whatever that was, at the Imperial War Museum at Duxford. She had never heard of Duxford, and had no idea where it was.

The other two though, were more interesting, and she decided in a fit of recklessness that she would make use of them as carefully she replaced them all in their original envelope.

This was Angela's third mistake.

*   *   *

Having been told that Giles was leaving on Friday, Angela decided to take one more journey to the Scot Hay house on the day after he left, to see if that bedroom door was once again open. She was destined to be disappointed. As she approached the drive and dismounted her bicycle – cycling over that gravel was so difficult – she could see two white vans parked in front of the house, and behind them was Harriet's car.

Nobody seemed to be about and leaving her bike at the side of the shrubbery, she peeped out silently. Picking at the cuticle of her thumb she smiled to herself, realising what a figure of fun she would be thought, were anyone to see her.

It was easy to see what was happening, as both vans were clearly marked with the same colourful logo. A smiling man in red overalls, wielding a paintbrush dripping with red paint, and the details also in red, *Peter Meredith, Superior Decorators, Indoor and Outdoor*, annexed with a local telephone number.

Retrieving her bicycle Angela cycled home. Bloody Harriet! No doubt that bedroom was unlocked today, and she was beginning the process of eradicating Susannah's memory for Giles in his absence, but Angela would have preferred this left until she was more involved in his life. She would have liked some say in what that bedroom looked like for the future.

*   *   *

And so it was with mixed feelings that Angela set off for Cambridge that afternoon. She saw no irony in exchanging watching television in her solitary living room, for doing the same in a distant hotel bedroom.

There had been some initial confusion, as it was a double room that had been booked, but thinking on her feet she said that at the last minute her partner had been unable to come. The hotel receptionist was at pains to stress that no refund could be made on the unused part of the deal, and Angela waved her away lightly saying that the money was of no importance.

She was having second thoughts about the flying lesson, and again took out the voucher and examined it. Perhaps it would be a talking point with Giles – something his toffee-nosed daughter could not share. If this was an interest of his, it may be to her advantage. She chewed on her finger as she thought. She would go to the museum, and make a judgement when she got there.

*   *   *

Angela returned from her holiday refreshed. She had taken in her share of culture and knowledge, with which she planned to impress Giles. She had visited the Fitzwilliam Museum, and King's College. She had taken in the Botanical Gardens, and walked along the river to take tea at the Orchard in Grantchester.

On the return walk she had stopped to watch the various college eights pounding up and down the river, and had chanted over and over to herself, *and is there honey still for tea?* the only line from Brooke's poem that she could remember.

She had marvelled at the number of bicycles one city could contain.

She had used the other voucher in the package with enthusiasm and delight, dinner at a high class restaurant the like of which she had never before visited.

She reckoned that Giles would be familiar with the kinds of menu on offer, with little bits of tasters between the many courses, and a wine waiter eager to advise, and even allow her to sample the wines beforehand. She laughed aloud at one of the courses, a quail egg served in a rosti basket.

She felt that with her freshly retouched hair and wearing the dress planned for the funeral, along with Susannah's blue jacket and the Gucci sandals, she looked the part of a lady. The waiter kindly took a photograph of her sitting in front of her dessert course, an impressive strawberry and champagne confection, steaming with dry ice.

It was a far cry from her previous holidays. When she was a child, she and her parents had visited Blackpool for a week each August, staying in a boarding house where children were expected to keep quiet, and where guests were expected to be absent between ten in the morning and teatime. Her abiding holiday memories were of irritating sand in her shoes, rain, and the smell of boiled cabbage.

She had decided against taking up the flying lesson. At first she had thought that perhaps she should go, maybe even learn to fly a plane. That would impress Giles and give them something to talk about, but no. Susannah may have intimated what his Christmas present was to be – it would be wiser to use this time taking in the culture of the city, and learning at the hotel how things were done. Then she would be the equal of anyone. If that Susannah who used to iron shirts, could get a catch like Giles, then so could she. She would sell that voucher on the internet; it was not fixed to a particular date. That way she should be able to recoup her holiday money.

She went as far as visiting the museum at Duxford to see what was there. Mostly planes, she discovered. All sizes and types of planes. She recognised the Concord, and walked through its fuselage, surprised at how small it seemed, but the only other name with any familiarity to her was the Spitfire – she knew a little of that, coming as she did from the Potteries, and she had once been to the DIY place on Reginald Mitchell Way, when a neighbour had offered her a lift to collect something now long-forgotten.

She stood for some time in the museum, chewing on her fingers and reading up information, determined that she would impart her knowledge to Giles when the opportunity arose.

Yes she had enjoyed her holiday. She would

have fun telling Kevin about it when she next wrote, and next year of course, it would no doubt be Dubai.

She could see now why people took holidays. She had been able to relax, and had given a good deal of thought to how she would now tackle Giles. She had even spent the second week of her holidays slapping a bit of bright yellow emulsion on the sitting room walls at home.

She hung the curtains she had taken from Susannah's and reckoned it was a serious improvement. Her buoyancy was to be short-lived however. Rain fell at the weekend, and she could see the damp patch already begin to reappear beneath her front window.

*   *   *

All her positive thoughts were about to be blown out of the water.

During the third week of Giles's absence, she was again at a loose end. With all her bonus spent on the trip and the decorating, she longed to get back to work. Deciding that with two vans' worth of decorators on the job, the rebirth of Susannah's bedroom must long be completed, she set off a week earlier than expected for Scot Hay.

The driveway was deserted. Angela had her excuse ready should Harriet or Giles put in an appearance. She had heard in the village that the decorators had been in, and decided to throw open a few windows to release the smell of paint.

She was congratulating herself on her ingenuity as she approached the back door, and stopped dead. The door was newly painted, but more significant were the two shiny new escutcheons it sported, neither of which, very evidently, was going to accommodate her key. Angela was stunned. In all her daydreams this was something that had not crossed her horizon of possibilities.

She went round to the front door, but was already aware that it would be useless. She had never had keys to the front door, and she could see from a distance that here too the fittings had been changed.

She took some comfort from this as she cycled emptily home; at least it was not just her they were trying to keep out.

Chapter 26

The first thing Angela noticed when she turned into the drive at the Scot Hay house the following Monday, was that the fountain was working. Susannah had usually turned it on for a few hours each day, but it had not played since her death, and Angela took this as a positive sign about Giles's recovery.

The second thing she noticed was Harriet's car, the blasted woman was here again – had she no home to go to?

Leaning her bicycle under the wood-store as usual, Angela passed across the side elevation of the house to reach the back door and here she noticed the third thing, which completely stunned her. The local estate agent's representative was hammering a distinctive yellow and black For Sale sign into one of the flowerbeds beside the front door.

He raised his hand in salute to Angela,

'Morning, Duck,' which she ignored.

The back door was unlocked, and Harriet and Giles were in the small sitting room. Angela took in Giles's appearance before they noticed her. He really was a handsome man, although desperately thin now. He seemed to have lost more weight than ever in the three weeks since she saw him, but was looking tanned and attractive. He was talking earnestly.

'Here's Angela.' Harriet put out her hand to her father, and stopped him mid-sentence. Giles changed the subject.

'Hello, Angela, I hope you enjoyed your

holiday?'

'I did.' She said, picking at one forefinger with the other. 'You've put the house up for sale.'

'Yes,' Harriet laughed slightly, 'Daddy doesn't waste time when he's made a decision.'

She saw the look of shock on Angela's face and said hurriedly, 'Oh, but don't worry. Really, it will probably take ages for this place to sell, I can't tell you. Years possibly.'

Angela could not bring herself to speak. She stared open-mouthed at Giles.

'I have a new key for you, Angela. The police suggested we change the locks in case additional keys have been cut during that break-in. With one thing and another it took a while to get around to it.'

Angela sighed with relief, so she had been right, the added security was not on her account. She noticed her finger was bleeding where she had been picking, and wiped it on her leggings. Harriet suppressed a shudder.

'With these locks extra keys can only be ordered by Daddy, so no-one can get extra ones made.' Harriet found it unnerving the way that even when she spoke directly to Angela, her reply was always to Giles.

'I'll take good care of it, Giles,' she said now, adding the key to her key ring.

'Some things have already been packed, Angela, and that process is continuing,' Harriet continued. 'Please do Daddy's bedding each Monday and his other laundry as usual. Other than that it's a matter of dusting and vacuuming – keeping everywhere presentable for viewings.

'You will be paid your usual rate, but don't

feel that you have to stay here for the full four hours. Once the work is done you can leave, just make sure you lock up and set the alarm.'

'Actually, I could help show people round, Giles, if that would help.' Angela sounded keen.

'Oh, thank you Angela, but that won't be necessary. The agent will deal with all that.' Giles was firm. 'I shall be working in the office this morning. Perhaps you could leave in there today. There's plenty else to do. As Harriet said, I am not anticipating a quick sale under all the circumstances, so I very much look to you to keep things ticking over.' As he left the room, Angela looked uncomprehendingly at Harriet.

'You see, Angela,' Harriet ran one pearly pink fingernail down the side of her cheek, 'the police think Susannah may have died here, then been moved, which may rather put off prospective purchasers.'

Good! thought Angela. Hopefully this place will never sell, and we can get back to normal. Harriet's next statement gladdened Angela's heart.

'Daddy seems to be much more ...' she hesitated, 'happy's the wrong word, but resigned I suppose, coming to terms with things. A move away from here will do him good. I'm finishing some packing up today, but I shall keep out of your way, then from tomorrow, I shall be back at work as usual, so Daddy is very much relying on you.'

With that, Harriet took herself off to the drawing room, closing the door behind her.

Angela went first into the laundry room, where she busied herself for an hour or more. Then she made coffee for the three of them, taking

Harriet's through to the drawing room first.

Warned about the packing, she was still surprised at the amount that been done. The grand piano, normally awash with family photographs, was clear, as were most of the surfaces.

There were four packing crates – tea chests she supposed they were – with their lids already nailed down. Another crate was still open, and Harriet was in the process of wrapping porcelain with a huge roll of blue padded paper, and a similar roll of bubble wrap.

'Angela, how thoughtful. I seem to have done nothing but pack for days. But where's yours? Please, join me. Give me an excuse to stop.'

'Actually it's in the kitchen, I'll just...'

'You sit down, I'll get it,' said Harriet.

What on earth was the blasted woman being so nice for? Angela had planned to take her own coffee into the office with Giles's so that he would have to talk to her. Still, Harriet would not be here after today.

Angela allowed herself to be waited on. She stood looking out at the manicured lawns and tennis court beyond, chewing at a fingernail. Thank goodness she had not invested in tennis lessons if Giles was moving away. She was still smiling at the thought as she turned to see Harriet coming back.

Good Lord, thought Harriet, the woman could look almost human when she smiled, but she kept her eyes averted from Angela's chewed hands, which made her feel slightly nauseous.

'Sorry,' she said, 'I took Daddy's in first. He's up to his ears in paperwork. It's too awful. Thankfully Matt sold Susannah's car before he went home. He got a pittance for it naturally, it puts people off you know. The dealership said they may move it to Scotland or London for sale, somewhere people don't know its story. Anyway, what have you been doing whilst we've been busy here?'

Angela told her briefly about the trip to Cambridge, but kept the details to herself. She would share those with Giles when she got the chance – *the engine driver not the oily rag* – she thought to herself and smiled again. Harriet caught the look and smiled back at her. She drained her mug and put it on the side table.

'Well,' she said, 'we'd better get on. There's a lot to do today. Have you been upstairs, Angela? Seen the decorating? You must see what you think.'

The decorators, Angela saw, had done wonders in Susannah's room. The swags and drapes had gone, and the room was emptied of most of its clutter. The dressing table had been cleared of everything except two stylish Victorian scent bottles in crystal and silver.

The ornate wooden bed was still there, although turned through ninety degrees, and dressed now in exactly the kind of modern bedding of Angela's daydreams. Both chests of drawers had been cleared and polished, and the only other decoration was an ornamental bucket of gold and yellow chrysanthemums in the corner. The wardrobes and drawers were empty. The en suite sported more of the chrysanthemums, and matching towels in gold and yellow were highlighted by just three bottles of toiletries in the same shades.

Angela took the vacuum cleaner to the top of the house, and saw that a similar transformation had occurred here. Harriet must have spent hours doing all this. The clothes rail and its contents had gone, and each room was dressed simply and attractively with no clutter. Plying her duster, Angela thought that she would not give Harriet the satisfaction of asking where Susannah's clothes and things had gone.

In any event, she saw this clearing out as a good thing. Although there was little scope for her to help herself to things now, at least Giles's life was being wiped clean of Susannah, without apparently giving him any distress. He would soon be over her completely. She would, though, have to focus her attention on snaring him before this house business got too far. Pity she couldn't be involved in showing people around, she could made sure that nobody ever bought the house.

* * *

I've decided to move house, she wrote to Kevin that evening. Actually the house is far too big for me really, and although I entertain a fair bit, I really don't need seven bedrooms and am so often away. I am just back from a holiday in Cambridge, and have spent the last few days packing away all my valuables for storage until the move takes place. She elaborated with a few details about the trip, but her heart was not really engaged and she soon logged off.

* * *

Simon immediately trawled the internet for homes for sale, Scot Hay area, with seven bedrooms. There was just one, and it definitely matched

Angela's earlier descriptions. Gnawing at him still, was the puzzle of who was this other woman who had gone missing at Christmas and then turned up dead? He decided to go and find out.

Chapter 27

Angela was bored. There was little to do save a bit of dusting and vacuuming. Giles seemed to be living in the kitchen, one bedroom and the bathroom. The drawing room and small sitting room were virtually closed up. Each morning she opened the windows to air the rooms, and did jobs that had no real need of doing in the hope that Giles would return during the morning. On Tuesday the doorbell rang mid-morning, and although it clearly was not Giles, who would have just let himself in, Angela was glad of the diversion.

At the door stood a smartly dressed young man, short and stocky, with thin gingery hair and heavy-framed glasses.

'Hullo,' he said with a cheerful smile, 'I know this is a bit naughty, but I just passed the For Sale sign at the end of the lane. I'm sure I should go to the agents or whatever, but I'm just passing through and haven't really got the time. My parents are looking for a house like this.' He smiled again.

'I wondered,' he put his head on one side, 'whether I could have a quick look round? If it's not what they want I needn't waste any more of your time, but if they may be interested I can send the details through to them in Scotland and they can do it all properly with the agents.' He smiled again, and raised his eyebrows. Sensing her hesitation he thrust out a hand. 'I'm David, David Grant.'

'The master isn't home just now, but I could give you a quick tour round if you like. I can spare you twenty minutes.'

Here's one prospective purchaser, she thought, who can be told the tale and put off buying.

As she led him upstairs she said, 'Funnily enough, I think the master would be glad to sell to someone from out of town, too many people locally are put off by what happened.' She threw out the bait, and the young man gobbled it down.

'What happened!' he repeated, 'Why, what has happened?'

'Oh, sir,' she said, warming to the role, 'the mistress was killed, sir. Actually, here in the house the police think, during a burglary, although they don't know for sure. It happened the Saturday before Christmas, but they didn't actually find her till February. This is the main bedroom, sir,' She hurried him through the upper rooms.

'Found her in woodland they did actually, about three miles away. Heavy rain had washed her out of a sort of drain or ditch or some such I understand. Then her car, sir,' she paused, turning to look up at him as they made their way back downstairs, 'Funnily enough, they found that at Manchester Airport. This is the drawing room, sir.'

She led the way through into the small storeroom, where the subterranean safe could be accessed.

'Here's where he got in actually, sir, whoever did it.' The young man seemed reluctant to enter the small room.

'He'd criss-crossed sticky tape across that window, and smashed it, so the police said. The bars weren't there then, of course.'

As they returned to the kitchen he was very

quiet.

'I'll just get you the agent's details.' She found a copy of the double A4 sheet on the counter, as the back door opened and the gardener came in.

'Is there any coffee yet, Angela? It's gone eleven.'

'Angela?' the young man repeated.

'Yes. Angela Davies, Actually, I'm the housekeeper.' She cast a look at the gardener, who smirked but said nothing.

As she showed the young man out, she saw that her deterrent tactics had worked. He wouldn't be sharing any information with his parents. He was as white as a sheet.

*　　*　　*

Simon barely made it down the drive, to where his car was parked out of sight of the house. He banged his hands on the steering wheel, and opened the roof. He felt stifled.

Housekeeper! Angela Davies was the bloody housekeeper – probably not even that, probably just the bloody cleaner. The bitch – she'd conned him, and that bloody pea-brain Lewis had killed the woman that had lived there. Thoughts raced through his mind, as he sat in the stationary cabriolet. She would not recognise his car, but still he had to move it from the drive, and he had to know where the woman really lived.

Parking up in the same lay-by Gary had used on that fateful December night, he scanned every vehicle as it passed. He had no idea what she drove, no cars had been visible at the front of the Scot Hay house. The place was isolated; the gardener too must have transport, so there had to be parking space around the back. The description of the car she had given him online was clearly her employer's car, the one found at the airport. Again he banged his hands on the steering wheel in frustration.

As it was, he nearly missed her. He had not been looking for a bicycle. Fortunately that bright crimson hair was very distinctive, and he spotted her just in time to duck down before she passed him. It was easy to follow her down the hill, and he cruised along Station Road watching, and noting the gateway she entered.

Now to tackle Gary.

*   *   *

Simon pounding on the door at two in the morning, awakened Gary and brought his elderly neighbour to her window.

'Fuck off,' he shouted at her, and hastily she drew back. She was reluctant to get involved. He continued to batter on the door until Gary, bleary eyed, opened it, wearing just a pair of grubby boxer shorts. Simon pushed past him, slamming the door against the wall so hard that a dusting of plaster fell from the ceiling, and the light fitting swayed.

'Now, here's the deal, pea-brain,' Simon started, without preamble, brandishing his glasses at Gary. 'I'm in the shit, but you are in it three, no four, times deeper. I've been to that house in Scot Hay where Mrs Scott-Ryder lived,' he paused, 'until you bloody killed her.'

Gary turned grey. He staggered through to the

living room like an old man, and collapsed unseeing onto the sofa. As the colour returned to his face, his spirit revived.

'Now just a bloody minute, Si.' He shook his long hair out of his eyes, 'You said she was away, you said it was safe to go. You,' he pointed a finger at Simon, 'are supposed to do the planning, right, mate? I just do the bloody execution.' The word seemed to resonate in its own meaning.

Not on strong ground, Simon mustered his indignation.

'The situation now is this, pea-brain. I could be going down for a stretch, but only for aiding and abetting I reckon, maybe receiving stolen goods, probably a suspended sentence. But you, old thing? You're going down for life. Mandatory sentence for murder that is. Unless I help you.'

'It weren't murder, I just pushed past her on the stairs and she fell. When I looked, she'd hit her head and her neck was all twisted like. It weren't murder, honest, mate.' He stopped a while, breathing hard and then, 'Unless you help me, how?'

'As I see it, I'm the only one who knows about this, so if I keep quiet, no-one will ever know, but you have got to do something for me to make it happen, and this time I don't want it screwed up.'

Gary was fully awake now. 'What? What have I got to do for you?'

'For us, Gary,' Simon was relaxing now the younger man seemed more cooperative.

'This Angela woman, the housekeeper at the Scott-Ryder house, she's got stuff on me on her computer that could put us both inside.' He raised his hand as Gary started to speak, 'You don't need to know what. You need to get into her house, and get that computer. Hopefully it'll be a laptop, but whatever it is, you need to get it to me.'

'No problem, Si, when? Tonight?'

'No, we don't know who else lives there. There could be a houseful. Best would be tomorrow morning. She works at Scot Hay nine till one. Get there after nine o'clock.'

'Can't do it tomorrow, Mate, gotta sign on.' Gary was worried as Simon considered.

'Okay,' he relented, 'she doesn't know the information she's got is important, so she's not going to do anything with it, but it will have to be Thursday – no question, she doesn't work Friday or weekends. Don't let me down.' The threat was clear.

Chapter 28

The rest of the week had passed without incident. As well as the For Sale sign on the house, Angela noticed that there was also one at the end of the lane, the one the young man had seen.

She supposed this was to alert passing traffic. Neither Giles nor Harriet was in evidence, although on Thursday morning, there was a note from Giles that the florist would be delivering. Would she please put the flowers in the buckets that were ready in the utility room? Harriet would be coming for dinner, and would arrange them then.

Angela wondered idly whether she should take a flower arranging course, then she could dazzle Giles with her skills. Funnily enough, she enjoyed learning things. She had after all taken that technology course the previous autumn. Her plan for Giles was taking far too long. She sighed – she would start to make things happen the very next time she saw him.

* * *

Her opportunity came the following week. Giles was emerging from the office when she arrived, his arms full of papers, which he began feeding into a shredding machine on the table.

'Can I help, Giles?'

'Not with this, thank you, but a coffee wouldn't go amiss. Get yourself one too, before you start.'

He had not really expected Angela to sit down opposite him at the table with the two mugs between them, but, as he had agreed with Harriet, they would keep Angela on for the moment. She was good at what she did and the end was in sight. He switched off the shredder.

'Did you get a holiday whilst I was away?'

Clearly Harriet had not shared the information Angela had given her. She launched into her tale, saying she and a woman friend had gone to Cambridge, and telling where they had stayed and visited. Giles watched her closely as she spoke, not saying anything until she told him about the meal, when he said, 'I know that restaurant. But surely you didn't just get a table there by turning up. People have to book weeks, sometimes months in advance.'

Angela was slow to dissemble, and turned quite pink.

'Oh! I don't know. My friend had organised all that.'

'Well,' said Giles, bringing the conversation to an abrupt close, 'I'm glad you enjoyed it. Now I must get on.' And he disappeared into the office, only to reappear almost immediately with his briefcase. He said a brisk goodbye to her, and went out to his car.

Work done for the morning, Angela made herself another drink and thought about what had been said. Definitely progress she thought. Giles had sat and talked to her for a while anyway. Actually, perhaps it had been a bad move to mention that restaurant. Maybe he'd been there with Susannah and they had had a row or something. Still, it was definitely progress.

Chapter 29

'Forgive me, Harriet.' Giles was contrite. 'When you said you thought Angela was stealing from me I didn't think you could be right, but it was when she talked about eating at that same restaurant. It's so good and so popular she would have had to have pre-booked, yet she said that going to Cambridge was a last minute thing.' He paused and took a large gulp of wine.

'I wonder if that hotel and restaurant were already booked. You see, the Wednesday of that week she was away would have been our wedding anniversary.'

'I know,' Harriet smiled at him across the table. They were eating in the kitchen; there was no point in opening up the dining room just for the two of them. 'That's the reason I wanted you to be away from here just then.'

'I wonder if that may have been Susannah's Christmas present to me, you know, the one we couldn't find. She may well have booked for that night deliberately. It was a special place for us.' He pushed his plate away, and fiddled with the wine glass, remembering, 'It was before Susannah and I married. We went to stay in Cambridge for a week.'

'Oh, but that's...' Harriet started to interrupt but Giles raised his hand to stop her.

'I'd booked it ages beforehand. The hotel and the restaurant on the banks of the Cam. It was idyllic. Lovely food – two Michelin stars as I recall. We ate in a sort of conservatory affair, and it was there I proposed to Susannah and she accepted me.'

'I remember you coming back and telling me,' said Harriet smiling, 'and then you phoned Matthew.'

'That's right,' he said, and went on more soberly, 'Earlier this year Susannah asked me, apropos of something we were watching on the television I think, if I could go back in time, when would I go back to, and I said, There. Then. Cambridge on that night at the Midsummer House Restaurant, to have all my time with her over again.' He smiled at Harriet fondly.

'She'd laughed and said she wasn't sure she could manage the time travel, but certainly we could go back to the city and to the restaurant some time.

Now, if she'd gone ahead and booked something like that, it would have been by computer or by phone so there'd be no paper record of it, unless she printed a copy out. It would all be on her laptop, and of course we don't have that.' He paused and laid his hand over Harriet's where it lay on the table. She clasped him tightly.

'I may be wrong,' he raked fingers through his hair 'and I couldn't think of a reason for asking what night she went there. I couldn't think of a reason to ask Angela anything at all.'

Harriet emptied the remains of the wine into their glasses.

'I think the time for us asking question has passed, Daddy. I think it's up to the police now.'

'Oh, I know Darling, but that's such a big step. After all, I'll have moved within a fortnight. Thank God I don't have to wait until this place is sold. The carpets will be fitted in the flat on Friday, did I tell you? So I plan to move in about ten days.'

'That's really good news Daddy but I still think the police should know. She shouldn't get away with it. May I talk to Maxine, and see what she thinks we should do? She and Pippa have become quite friendly with that nice Inspector.

In the meantime, perhaps it's better to carry on as usual with Angela, if you can bear it. Don't alert her to what we suspect.'

Chapter 30

Angela woke early. After an unsettled night, she was prepared to believe that her dream was significant. A celibate spinster, she had dreamed of Giles circling her in his arms and her body had responded alarmingly. Letting herself into the Scot Hay house just before nine o'clock, she blushed to find him clearing cupboards in the utility room.

'How many vases does one house need, Angela? I can't believe that we have ever had occasion to use all these at once, and I don't know which to keep.' He sat back on his heels, 'Where is Harriet when I need her?'

'Shall I make some coffee then we can decide together?' she suggested, 'Actually, possibly get rid of any cracked or chipped ones, and see what we're left with?'

'Yup,' he smiled, 'A strategist worthy of Napoleon,' and he jumped up, dusting off the knees of his jeans and following her into the kitchen. As she made coffee, he unloaded the dishwasher.

We work well as a team, she thought, wishing she had the confidence to say it aloud. She set two mugs on the table, disappointed when he took his back towards the utility room.

'I'd better get on, there's a lot to get finished this week.'

Angela could not understand the imperative.

'Surely, as Harriet said, it could take some time to sell the house?'

'Oh yes,' he responded innocently, 'but I have to sort all the stuff that I'm going to need at the flat from next week.' He had again turned his attention to the utility room cupboards, and failed to see her expression. She had to put down her coffee cup, her hands were trembling so much. She followed him out of the doorway.

'Next week?' she said quietly.

'Monday,' Giles confirmed, unaware of the affect his words were having, 'I'm taking possession of a new flat on Monday. I hope to move in by the weekend. It's time to move on.'

'Oh, but I hoped....' Angela was frantically picking at her fingers, 'Actually, I hoped...'

'Don't worry.' Giles was oblivious, 'I shall need you to come here, unless you're ready to find somewhere else that is. Just say the word – I'll give a reference, of course.' He worried a bit about this, given Harriet's reservations.

'But I thought you needed me.' Angela had drawn blood now, and the mess of her hands revolted Giles, who had to look away.

'I do,' he said patiently, as if to a child, 'I need you to clean here for me until the house is sold.'

'No, I thought...' she took a deep breath; there was nothing to lose now,

'I thought we were getting on so well now that Susannah's not...' she paused, *in the way* was clearly not the right thing to say, 'dead,' she finished, blushing. Giles turned round to face her, as if in slow motion.

When he , his tone was icy, 'What exactly did you think Angela?'

'Doesn't matter,' she back-tracked, her face nearly as red as her hair. Giles grabbed her wrist and grasped it tightly.

'It matters a great deal. What exactly did you think, Angela?'

Trapped now, Angela blurted out,

'I thought perhaps you could get fond of me. I know your ways so well. I know your family, and the way you like your home run. Your daughter invited me to her birthday party in the summer. I thought that, after a while. After a while...' she faltered. Giles was still holding her wrist.

'You thought that after a while, what? We might live together? Get married?' His tone was incredulous. He was gazing in distaste at the gnawed and broken skin around her stubs of fingernails.

'Whatever did I do or say to make you think all of this? I have never given you any indication,' the revulsion in his tone was transparent. 'Angela, you are my cleaner; our cleaner – I barely even spoke to you when Susannah was alive. I had to ask Harriet what your name was. Whatever did you think had changed?'

Giles's confusion and disgust was mortifying, as was his horrified expression. Dropping her hand as if it was red hot, he had moved away from her to the far side of the room.

'This puts a very different complexion on things,' he said. 'Under the circumstances, I think it is inappropriate..... I have to think.'

He shut himself in the office, and moments later Angela heard him talking on the telephone. She could not make out the words, but could hear the incredulity in his tone. No doubt he had rung that bloody Harriet. She could imagine the sneer in her voice, *Oh Daddy darling how awful. What could the dreadful woman be thinking?*

Suddenly it was all too much for Angela. Unable to bear Giles's presence any longer, she ran out of the house and went home.

*   *   *

Harriet rang Maxine immediately, after telling Giles to do nothing more for the moment.

'May I come round later? I don't know whether to report all this stuff about Angela or not. I want to know what you and Pippa think.'

'Mmm,' Maxine spoke, her mouth full of rice she was preparing, 'Of course, Pippa will be here about seven, and Chris may drop in later if he has time.'

Curled on Maxine's sofa next to Pippa later that evening, with a chilled glass of Pinot Grigio in her hand and a retriever whiffling quietly against her shoe, Harriet began to relax.

'Maxine, I thought he must be joking! The poor woman. I don't like her or what she's done, but this is the limit. It's only four weeks since the funeral and she's busy planning her future with Daddy, maybe even marrying Daddy! It beggars belief.

*   *   *

'Sir. A Ms Chapman on the phone for you? Says she has some information.'

He lifted the phone,

'Pippa?'

There was a slight pause, then,

'It's Maxine, Chris. I'm at home and Harriet Scott-Ryder's here. There's something we think you should know. Shall we come in to Merrial Street?'

He glanced at his watch.

'No, I'll come to you. I was planning to come over later anyway.'

Chris Timothy was at Scot Hay within the hour, listening with grim countenance to Maxine's tale.

'I'm sorry to drag you out Chris, I know how busy you are, and this may be a storm in a teacup.'

He had never seen Maxine look so confused.

'But we must tell you about this.'

She looked at Harriet, who told him firstly about Angela propositioning her father.

Maxine rose and went to the sideboard, where she poured large glasses of Pinot Grigio, two of which she handed to Harriet and Pippa. She proffered the bottle to the Inspector, who caught her eye and indicated that a small measure would be acceptable.

He listened patiently whilst they told the story of Angela's thefts, the sandals and jacket, Harriet's deliberate ploy to catch her out, and her conversation with the charity shop manager. Harriet even told her about the chrysanthemums and the quails' eggs – even though she couldn't see any commercial rationale for taking these.

She told him too, about Angela's changed attitude to her father, and the trip to Cambridge and the award-winning restaurant.

Chapter 31

Could anything more go wrong?

After the humiliating set-to with Giles, which would have to be sorted out, she had left the washing machine fully loaded with towels, some of her own and some brought from Scot Hay, overnight, and got up this morning to a disaster.

The contrary machine had danced its way enthusiastically into the middle of the kitchen floor, dragging after it the outlet hose usually draped over the sink. This had consequently disgorged gallons of water across the floor and these had been sufficient to seep under the living room door and into the carpet. As the machine doubled as a much-needed worktop space, a small pile of plates and bowls had crashed behind it, and smashed on the quarry tiles.

Angela had spent most of the following morning cleaning up the mess in her dressing gown and slippers. She made toast, the crumbs showering ignored onto the damp floor, as she shook the kettle to check the water level. Waiting for it to boil, she picked listlessly at the tattered edge of one of the plastic mats she used in a vain attempt to protect the surfaces of the various cupboards in the kitchen.

She wondered whether the time had come to look for another job. She would feel awkward now with Giles, and it might be better. If he was moving out next week, at least she wouldn't keep bumping into him. Everything had gone horribly wrong, and it would be embarrassing.

On the other hand, he may even at this minute be thinking over what they had discussed. Perhaps it had just been a shock to him initially, and he would warm to the idea. She had invested so much effort into this, and now the future was uncertain. She nibbled and nibbled at her fingernails.

If she stopped going, would he still give her a reference? And, if she stopped going it meant that her income would stop immediately. God, she would have to go and sign on or something. It didn't bear thinking about. She would have to go back. If she left, should she return his key, or throw it away? He had no idea where she lived, so he had no way of coming to collect it.

Perhaps the house would sell quickly, and the new people would keep her on. She should keep the key.

This needed some thought. The first thing to do was to sell all this stuff she had taken from Susannah's, that way she would have some money to tide her over. She would do it today.

As usual on the first Thursday of the month, she had stripped her bed and now she fed the bedclothes into the washing machine, once more reinstated into its usual place and with its hose tucked carefully over the sink.

She was just settling down in front of the television to begin her belated breakfast, when the doorbell rang.

'Damn.' She switched the television off and, pulling her dressing gown protectively across her concave chest, tightened the belt. DI Timothy was framed in the doorway, flanked by two constables, one in uniform, the other she had seen with him before at Scot Hay. The uniformed officer wrinkled her nose in distaste.

The Inspector was impatient. He felt almost sure that this was just petty theft, but this stuff had been taken from the home of a murder victim. He had to deal with it promptly, and get back to the matter in hand.

'Miss Davies, I have a warrant to search these premises for property we believe to be stolen from the house of Mr Scott-Ryder, your employer in Scot Hay.'

He continued to speak, but she could not focus on his words. The room swam in front of her eyes, and she held onto the door frame for support. She was stunned that Giles had gone to the police, told them all this, just because she had misunderstood him. As she recovered, she heard him ask if she understood.

Her fingers went up to her mouth, and she inclined her head slowly,

'Actually Inspector, I...'

'Please sit down, Miss, and let us get on with what we have to do. Do you understand what you have been told?'

Angela drew herself up, trying to retrieve what dignity she had left.

'Of course I understand, Inspector, I'm not stupid.' she said in a small voice 'Carry on, get it over with. Although I assure you this is all a matter of....'
He raised his hand.

'It may be better if you say nothing for the moment, Miss Davies.'

She flopped back into the chair, unable to summon the strength to stand. Her mind raced, but none of her thoughts made any sense, and she sat submissively, shaking and white, as the two constables moved to search the house. It took just minutes for them to find what they expected; the evening jacket, the sandals, handbag, and the goods Harriet had used to lure her into this trap. Angela watched as one of the constables placed each item in an evidence bag and labelled them.

'Please get dressed, Miss Davies,'

He indicated PC Thomas, the only female officer on the team.

'This officer will accompany you.'

As she came back into the room, having been allowed to get dressed, and now in her customary sweater and leggings, DI Timothy was apparently looking out of the window. He turned his steely expression onto her,

'Pretty curtains, Miss Davies. Are they new?'

Angela had decided that her only option was to bluff it out. She sat in the easy chair.

'Susannah gave me those curtains – they were old ones she had lying around upstairs. And the jacket and sweater actually, and you can't prove otherwise. Surely the police have better things to do than to worry about a few flowers, and half a dozen eggs.'

The inspector wavered, but had worked long enough with DS Talbot to recognise the subdued excitement in his voice as he called from upstairs.

'Something here Inspector.'

The Inspector went upstairs, and Angela commended herself on her management of the situation. That had told him, he would know better than to mess with her. She pulled at loose skin on her thumbs. After a few moments, the inspector came back into the room and sat in the chair opposite. He smiled.

'I believe you've been away recently, Miss Davies. Somewhere nice?'

'I went to Cambridge actually, if it's any business of yours.' No longer so worried, Angela was inclined to be over-confident. 'I really think you are wasting your time Inspector, you should be concentrating on serious crime. I've a good mind to make a complaint...' The cuticles were receiving severe punishment now.

The young constable found it hard to contain his excitement, as he brought two more evidence bags down the stairs. DI Timothy laid them on the table, and then took them up in turn. The first contained an envelope addressed *to my darling Giles* and a voucher for a flying lesson at the Museum at Duxford.

'Where were these, Constable?'

'Tucked in the inside pocket of a suitcase, sir, underneath the bed.'

The inspector looked at Angela, who refused to meet his eyes. The colour drained from her face as she focused on ripping at a snag of skin by her thumbnail. Pulling it loose finally, she popped it into her mouth in an unconscious gesture, and moved onto another finger. The constable turned away in disgust.

DI Timothy turned his attention to the second bag. A Christmas card opened to show the inscription:

a chance to revisit perfect times darling, the hotel and restaurant booked to coincide with our wedding anniversary. Yours always, Susannah

Christopher Timothy sat and waited, this tied in only too clearly to what he had heard at Maxine's the previous evening.

Angela burst into tears.

'I need you to accompany me to Merrial Street to answer further questions,' he told her,

'I am also impounding your laptop computer, your camera, and your mobile phone. We will give you a receipt for them.

Angela was undone as much by his coldness as by his words.

'I made you biscuits,' she muttered irrelevantly, as she made her way slowly towards the stairs, 'and this is how you pay me back.' She looked suddenly like an old woman.

*   *   *

It was apparent on arriving back at the police station that Angela had considered her story, and it seemed likely that some of it at least was the truth. The interview room was stark but warm, and DS Talbot had provided coffee and a plate of moth-eaten biscuits that Angela ignored.

'Actually, I was given that stuff, Inspector. By that...by Harriet.'

'Some of it, yes, for a charity shop that you...' ostentatiously he looked at his notes, 'work for in the afternoons.' He paused, and then went on, 'and which has never heard of you, Miss Davies.' The atmosphere was becoming increasingly unpleasant. Angela had not bothered to wash before dressing, and the room was very warm.

'And what about the curtains, the sandals and

the blue jacket? You weren't given those.' The Inspector soldiered on. Angela gulped, and bit at one of her nails. They seemed to know everything. Eventually she looked at the Inspector again.

'Nobody needed that stuff, Inspector. The woman was dead.'

'And were you already aware of that, Miss Davies when you took these items? Did you know before Christmas that she was dead?'

'Actually, no,' she whispered, her voice hoarse, 'but it must have been something like that. I decided that I would take stuff – new stuff, and stuff that wouldn't be missed, or so I thought, then I would keep it here. If she came back I would return it, if not I would sell it. I didn't try to sell anything until after I knew she was dead.' She had pulled skin off her fingers, so that three of them were bleeding now. The detective silently watched her.

'New stuff, and stuff that wouldn't be missed,' repeated the Inspector after a pause, 'and the wine, Miss Davies, the bottles of wine, and the quails' eggs?'

The constable by the interview room door struggled to keep a straight face.

'What wine?' she was indignant. 'Funnily enough, at Christmastime I like to treat myself to good wine and to quails' eggs as a treat. I go to the supermarket, Inspector, I can buy wine like anyone else.'

'Of course,' he agreed pleasantly, then his eyes hardened, 'so I won't find Giles Scott-Ryder's fingerprints on any of those empty wine bottles we found in your shed? Nor Susannah Scott-Ryder's fingerprints on the egg box from the fridge?'

His hand moved from one of the evidence bags to another as Angela watched open-mouthed, then again started to cry. Silently, DS Talbot pushed a box of tissues towards her.

'Tell me about the chrysanthemums.' The Inspector seemed impervious.

'That was silly,' Angela snuffled into a tissue and lowered her eyes, 'but she'd actually ordered a dozen chrysanthemums just for the bathroom. The bathroom! I can't afford flowers for my living room, never mind the bathroom. It seemed so unfair, and actually, the house was in such turmoil I decided they wouldn't miss them. I could always say that the order was wrong. It would have been my word against the florist's; and I can't afford wine. He buys it by the box – sometimes five or six boxes at a time.

'I thought with her not there, he couldn't possibly drink all that. There were other people in and out of the house all the time, I planned to deny it if he said anything, but no-one even mentioned it.' She looked down at her fingers again, and dabbed at them with a balled tissue now flecked with blood.

'Not to you, perhaps.' DI Timothy smiled encouragingly at her, 'and the Christmas present?' he prompted.

'I'd opened it. Actually it wasn't sealed, just tucked in, so I opened it for a read.' She spoke defensively, as if the fact that she had not broken a seal on the envelope, made what she had done acceptable.

'I knew he wouldn't use it. It was for their wedding anniversary – he wouldn't want to be celebrating, when she was missing. Actually, I didn't know when the anniversary was, so I phoned the restaurant, said I had mislaid the details, and could they confirm the date. They were ever so helpful.' She smiled in reminiscence, then sighed.

'He wouldn't have used it anyway – actually, the money spent would have been wasted if I hadn't gone.' Her warped logic made DI Timothy feel suddenly very weary.

'And the quails' eggs?' he asked.

'She used to have them for breakfast, Lady Susannah.' Her voice dripped vitriol now. 'I'd never actually seen a quail's egg before, never mind eaten them. The silly thing was, I took them just before Christmas and they're still there – in my fridge, well they were until your people found them.' She glared at the constable seated by the door.'

I didn't know what to do with them – how to cook them, and then they went out of date, and I just wanted to keep them for a while - something so posh. I've eaten them now, though, had them at that posh restaurant.' She nodded, 'very nice.'

The Inspector continued to question her for a further half hour, going over and over the jewellery Susannah had, and Angela's movements on the weekend before Christmas. But of the pendant she appeared to know nothing despite his probing, and DI Timothy was drawing the interview to a close when DS Talbot called him out of the interview room.

The sergeant had a particular interest in the technology that rather intimidated the inspector. He had been trawling Angela's computer, phone and camera for evidence, and liaising with the police force in Cambridge. Hc had printed off a photograph taken by the waiter at the Cambridge restaurant, and confirmed with the hotel that the booking had been made for that specific Wednesday evening by a Mrs Scott-Ryder some weeks before Christmas. Her debit card number had been given and used to pay for the meal. Nothing else on the laptop seemed at first look to be significant, but he determined to carry out a more thorough search of this and the phone.

Chapter 32

Gary phoned Simon on his mobile.

'It's not here.'

'It must be. Look again. She used it the night before last.'

'There is no computer here. She must use somewhere else, or she's taken it to work with her.'

'Christ,' Simon thought hard. 'Okay, get out of there and meet me at the pub at twelve. I've got to think.'

Gary relocked the back door. It had only taken a pair of pliers to turn the key from the outside to let himself in. Now he went out of the front, pulling it shut behind him. He had just reached the gate when a voice from the other side of the hedge made him jump.

'Is it a parcel?' A small wizened face appeared over the gate, 'only she's not in. If it's a parcel, I could take it.' The face looked hopeful.

'Signature,' said Gary, shaking his head. 'Gone to work has she?'

'Oh, no,' the neighbour was eager to talk, 'The police took her this morning. Two cars came. Three officers there were. Took some stuff out, too. Wondered if you were something to do with them?'

'No, no,' Gary was blindly closing the gate behind him, his mind racing, 'No I just need a signature.'

Simon would kill him. If the police had talked to her. Maybe she'd hidden the computer. He hadn't been up in the loft. He hadn't pulled up carpets.

What had the police wanted her for? Couldn't be to do with this business – she didn't know anything about it. What the hell was he going to tell Simon? If necessary, he decided, he would turn his mobile off, and lie low for a while.

* * *

Simon was at the pub at noon as arranged. He had softened sufficiently to buy a pack of cigarettes for Gary, and took his preferred table by the door. By twenty past he was concerned and by twelve thirty he was sure that Gary would not show.

Simon was desperate. He could not go to Station Road. Angela had seen him now, shown him around the Scott-Ryder house. Still searching for an idea he failed at first to notice Clyde, until a fresh pint was placed in front of him.

'You look like you've got worries, mate?' Clyde raised an eyebrow over his glass.

'Cheers, Clyde.' Simon raised his pint, then: 'Clyde, I've got a little job I need doing. How are you fixed?'

Clyde smiled widely at him, and listened.

'I'll deal with it, mate. I won't let you down'

* * *

Gary had thought it funny at the time he left the parental home, that his mother had moved to the other Newcastle in the north east; but the joke had soon worn thin and now, when he needed a bolt hole he had not the means of getting to Tyneside.

He had not even the means of getting his own

pack of cigarettes.

He considered his meagre list of friends. Obviously he had to avoid Janice. Clyde could not be relied upon not to talk to Simon. He wondered awhile about Emma.

She would probably keep his whereabouts a secret from Simon if he asked her, and her brother may come up with somewhere for him to stay, but he had heard Clyde's conversation about rent and deposits and knew he could never go down that route.

Suddenly it came to him what a sad life he led and he wallowed briefly in self-pity. He could sell the van, but it was old, and with no MOT and a history so confused and suspect that no-one would touch it. He could not even recall where its original registration plates had been stashed.

He would have to go thieving, and live rough for a while. He thought of his recent successes such as Miner's Cottage, but that row of dwellings was fairly basic, not likely to yield rich pickings, unlike the Scott-Ryder's, but he still had the bits and pieces he had creamed off those burglaries before everything had gone so horribly wrong.

Then an idea came to him.

*   *   *

Angela was home from the police station by three o'clock in the afternoon. The incident had shaken her badly. On the way in, she had managed to avoid her neighbour who was hovering, clearly wanted to know what was going on, and she decided that to calm her nerves she would spend the rest of the afternoon enjoying her favourite pastime, sitting on the sofa with a large bar of chocolate as she watched daytime television.

She was under no illusion that this matter was over. The Inspector had told her not to go near Scot Hay, to make sure she slept at her own home every night – as if she had anywhere else to sleep for goodness' sake - and to be prepared to go in and answer more questions.

They had kept her laptop and her phone, as well as all the other things they had taken from her house. Well, she hoped the quails' eggs broke and stank out the police station. That would serve them right.

*　　*　　*

The sound of the door knocker she was tempted to ignore, but it might be something important. It might be the police back again. Turning down the volume fractionally, she opened the door to a young man with a clipboard. He had his jacket collar turned up and his shoulders hunched against the rain.

'Water.' he said confidently, and moved to enter the house. Angela stayed exactly where she was, barring entrance, and she wondered fleetingly whether she should have a chain fitted to the door. Too late now.

'What about it?'

'Water inspection, duck. Oh, don't tell me you're another one that's not had the letter. I don't know what they do in that office all day, honestly. If you knew how much time I've wasted today, instead of just in and out, a two minute job. Can I talk to you inside, duck? I'm getting soaked.'

A moment's hesitation, then she stood back and with a quick glance over his shoulder, he stepped smartly into the living room, wrinkling his nose a little at the unsavoury smell.

'I need to check the kitchen taps first, could you go upstairs, and when I shout could you flush the loo?'

Angela hurried up the stairs. After a few minutes, the young man called up and she flushed the lavatory as requested. As she came down he was jotting details on his clip charts.

'That seems all right, Miss....er,' he hesitated, referring to his paperwork, 'Miss Davies. I just need to check upstairs, if you could turn the kitchen taps on full.'

One eye on the television screen, she left the room.

'I hope this won't take long. Actually, I've got a busy afternoon.'

'Five minutes duck, no more.'

In fact, it was nearer ten minutes before the young man was bidding her goodbye on the doorstep.

Angela went straight back to the television. Had she gone to the window, she would have seen the young man screw up the notes he had made, and impatiently toss them into the rubbish bin by her gate. He reached for his phone.

Chapter 33

DI Timothy decided to call it a night and to write up his findings. Competently typing up his reports, with only occasional reference to his notebook, the task was coming to an end, and he was turning his mind to the plan for the following morning.

Along the corridor in the general office the sergeant spent the last hour of the working day trawling through Angela's laptop for anything he may have missed, before handing it over to the IT team who would find the subliminal as well as the obvious. Primarily he was checking what other goods may have been sold on e-bay that may implicate her in the burglary at Miner's Cottage.

As he scanned the emails he almost missed the photographs.

Scrolling back he recognised pictures of Angela's employers' house; Susannah's car and a picture of Susannah herself. These had been sent as an attachment to someone called Kevin, purporting to live in Thunder Bay in Canada. Why would she be sending a picture of the murdered woman and her belongings to Canada?

Keen to impress the Inspector, before saying anything about his find he checked with the chat-room provider. Taking his contact details they were happy to phone him back with the information, and he discovered that Kevin's internet address in fact belonged to Simon Napier.

'Bingo!' DS Talbot gathered up the various

printouts and headed for the Inspector's office.

* * *

'Sir,' he showed DI Timothy the printouts he had made, along with the response from the *findyourmates.com* accounts management department and the electoral register for Audley.

Christopher Timothy rubbed his hand across tired eyes and tried to make sense of it.

'We've spoken to the neighbours in Audley already sir. It was them who told us Simon had not been around all evening.

Apparently his father, Kevin Napier died close on four years ago. Simon Napier now lives there on his own. They confirmed his description, ginger hair, glasses, not very tall. This account purporting to be in his Dad's name was set up in....' he referred to the details, 'June last year, nearly three years after his dad died.'

Immediately the DI sat up. 'Was it now?' He scanned again the documents. 'I think we need another chat with Angela Davies, see what she has to say about this. We'll have her in again tomorrow morning.'

* * *

'I was in the pub,' Simon said when DS Talbot challenged him for an alibi for the night when Miner's Cottage was burgled. He pushed his glasses up his nose.

'Girlfriend, Emma Francis,' he displayed Emma's photograph on his phone, gave it a smile and replaced the phone on the table. 'Right little raver. We were in the pub till it closed, then went on to Liquid in Hanley. There were about eight of us, we go a lot, ask for Pete on the bar – he might remember. We were there till about three – probably half past by the time we'd finished nattering, then Em and I went back to hers. It must have been getting on for four o'clock by then. A guy in one of the other flats saw us come in. He was getting up for work! Gets up at five – he's on the earlies at a distribution centre on Lyme Park, and he goes down there on his bike. He saw us.'

He was so confident in his replies, that DS Talbot was sure that this was the truth.

'Thank you, Mr Napier, now if we could move on to the Saturday night. Could you tell me where you were?'

'Of course, went clubbing with another guy – name of Clyde. Went to Lace in Newcastle. I was loaded, fell over coming out and had to go to hospital, I'm sure I broke my wrist,' he held it up to show them, 'here, but they x-rayed it, and said not. There for bloody ages. Clyde slept on my floor. He'll tell you. He rents a room off Em's brother now, but he was living in Manchester then.

He read out Emma's and Clyde's mobile numbers from his phone.

*   *   *

Emma Francis was quite excited at vicarious involvement in a crime.

She happily let the police into the cosy bed-sitting room she had created in her brother's house, and let them talk her through the evenings and nights they were interested in. She was able to confirm Simon's story for the night of the Miner's Cottage burglary, even calling in the chap who had seen them early that morning and who, amongst a great deal of grumbling about being disturbed and young people today, confirmed their arrival time. He too, was intrigued about the police interest, entering the room excitedly, shaking hands with both officers as if it was a social occasion, much to their private amusement.

As DS Talbot spoke to Emma, the detective inspector wandered over to admire a picture over the fireplace. It depicted three scantily-dressed beauties, all dark-haired, and dressed in Spanish style peasant dress, a pleasing image.

After taking their leave, Christopher Timothy went straight back to his office and Maxine's statement about the burglary, notably the description of the missing William Russell Flint print. Noting the issue number of the limited edition, he smiled to himself.

Things were falling into place.

After the police had gone, Emma stood and admired the picture. It was a lovely image, the girl on the right looked a little like herself she fancied – perhaps that was why Simon had liked it.

*   *   *

When asked, Clyde said that he had just moved from Manchester to Fenton, and offered to come to the police station at Newcastle rather than, as he put it *Having the filth here in my gaffe, don't want the landlord thinking he was mixed up in something.*

Unknown to him, DS Talbot, who took his statement, had twenty minutes before been talking with Pippa Chapman, his former partner.

Clyde was quite willing to alibi Simon for the night of Susannah's murder. He was also able to provide details of other people at the club. Clyde and Simon would be remembered as they had eventually been refused any more alcohol; Simon was becoming belligerent and aggressive.

On leaving the club when it closed, Simon had tripped over the kerb edge and, convinced that he had broken his wrist, insisted on Clyde taking him to the University Hospital where, having been logged in at 3.35am they waited several hours before he was x-rayed and discharged, along with his sprained wrist. By the time both arrived home, Emma was there, summoned to look after Simon, and the three remained in the flat until late on the Sunday evening, when Clyde returned to Manchester.

DI Timothy reluctantly concluded that there was no way in which either Simon or Clyde could have killed Susannah. There must be someone else.

Chapter 34

The following Saturday was Maxine's birthday. She had phoned to suggest that Harriet may like to try and get back to normality as much as was possible, and they arranged to meet for lunch.

Arriving at noon at the Dorothy Clive Gardens, Harriet suggested that it was too early for lunch, and that they should walk through the gardens first, before heading for the cafe. As they entered the scree garden from the car park, Maxine gasped at the wonderful view across the pool.

'This place never ceases to delight me,' she said, 'I know the daffs will be over, but let's head up to the Azalea and Daffodil walks. The views of the Maer Hills, and over to Wales are spectacular.' Giving all their energy to the climb, they were silent until they reached the green sward of the north perimeter. Pausing at the gazebo to enjoy the view, Maxine said,

'Do you know there are over twenty thousand Jack Snipe narcissi in this garden? Pity the azaleas aren't quite out, but you get an idea of what it will be like in a couple of weeks.' She stopped, aware that Harriet's attention was elsewhere.

'Okay, Harry,' she reverted to the schoolgirl nickname, 'What's eating you? You've hardly said a word.'

Harriet sighed, and linking Maxine's arm as they walked back past the waterfall and through the Quarry Garden, she told her friend about Angela and the charity shop. Maxine hugged her friend. Always very slim, she had not until now noticed how thin Harriet had become. As she talked, Maxine could feel her shaking.

'Now I know she's stealing from Daddy. Stealing poor dead Susannah's things, and the Christmas present seems to be the worst of all. It's too awful – I can't tell you, and I don't know what to do.'

'Let's go and get some lunch,' suggested Maxine, 'and see what options there are.' Settling at a corner table, Maxine sat opposite her friend, and took off her scarf.

Harriet finished her conversation with the lady on the till, ordering their food and drinks. She turned back to face Maxine across the table, and flicked a lock of hair behind her ear in a subconscious gesture.

'I had a lovely evening yesterday,' Maxine began, 'Pippa and I went to... Harriet, whatever is it?'

Harriet was sitting stock still, staring at Maxine's throat. She was very pale and breathing heavily.

'Maxine,' she said slowly, 'where did you get that pendant?'

'Harriet, you're so intense. Whatever's the matter?'

'Humour me, Maxine. Where did you get the pendant?'

'Pippa bought it me as part of my birthday present. You told her the original one was stolen, remember? I told her all about it the day after I found.... after Susannah was found. I think she got it off the internet. It was you that recommended I replace it, remember?'

Harriet continued to stare, she covered Maxine's hand with her own, and Maxine noticed that she was shaking.

'When, when did she buy it?' she asked, 'and who from? Was it someone local?' Maxine laughed weakly, and put her hand up to her throat.

'I don't know, she didn't say. Why? Harriet, you're scaring me now. What's all this about.'

Harriet moved her cutlery to one side, and leaned across the table, taking Maxine's hand.

'Maxine,' she said cautiously, 'I'm sure I've seen that pendant before, or one very like it. Susannah had one.'

'Susannah? Oh my God, do you think this could be anything to do with her disappearance? What do you think we should do?' asked Maxine, 'Do you think we should tell the police? Or go to Giles? See if he recognises it.'

'I don't know. I really don't know. It's too awful. We can't go to Daddy – what would we say? – 'Sorry, Daddy but I think my friend may have bought a pendant stolen from your murdered wife?' She caught the waiter's eye, and paused as he set down their plates.

'The police would know what was taken. We'd better tell them.'

'I'm not even sure, Maxine, that the police would know about it. Daddy said he didn't really know what was missing. Most of her good stuff was either in the bank or in their safe. Apparently she kept trinkets and costume jewellery in a box in the bedroom drawer, and that was what was taken.'

Maxine was unsurprised that Harriet's smart young stepmother had regarded this pendant as a trinket not worthy of particular security, but nevertheless it was a pretty piece, and she fingered it gently as they spoke.

'I know,' said Harriet suddenly, 'I could check and see whether she's on any of the photographs. Her pendant may prove to be quite different. I may have totally misremembered it.' She clutched at straws.

'Photographs?' Maxine was amazed, 'You have photos of it?'

Harriet gave a nervous laugh, her glass poised at her lips.

'It's really rather embarrassing. I was having a party for a few friends on my birthday in the summer. You were away at the time, otherwise you would have been there too.'

Maxine nodded, trying to lighten the mood. 'I remember, my first holiday for ages, and you plan a party.'

Harriet ignored the interruption, 'Susannah and Daddy came, of course. Susannah's cleaner Angela, came too.' Seeing Maxine's puzzled expression, Harriet sat back in her chair.

'Let me tell you about it.' Harriet paused whilst Maxine topped up their glasses with water, then took a large gulp before continuing.

'I was round at Scot Hay for a coffee, and you know what I'm like Maxine, I have these brilliant ideas like a party for my birthday, then I have a struggle to cope with it all, I'm really not a natural hostess, not like Susannah.

'Anyway, Angela was at Susannah's, and we were all three chatting. I was talking about the party and saying how stressed I was about it, and how disorganised, and I asked her if she would come along. I meant would she come to help, you know – clear tables, stack the dishwasher, go round with nibbles, and so on. She asked what time because she had something on in the afternoon, and I said something like 'Well, I've invited people for eight o'clock, so come along whenever you can.'

'I was a bit miffed to be honest.' She smiled vaguely at the waiter as he asked if everything was all right for them.

'The first guests were early, Barbara and James – wouldn't you know it. Anyway, I had expected her well before that. She was the next person to arrive, but done up to the nines and with a present for me. I can't tell you. I couldn't have been more shocked. I felt really embarrassed, but she didn't seem to notice, and everyone else thought it was funny.

She had a long skirt on, and quite a low blouse – not a good look I can tell you. At least she'd had a wash. But worst of all, she brought a camera and kept going up to people saying *May I?* and then snapping them. She had got this thing for her own birthday a few days before apparently. *My birthday present to myself* she kept telling everyone.

I was mortified, it was too awful, but people just took her as some eccentric friend I had invited.' Harriet dabbed at her lips with a napkin.

'Susannah was wearing a new shot silk dress, beautiful. I'd suggested that she wear the pendant when she was deciding what to wear. I said the opals picked up the lustre in the fabric.'

Harriet raised her eyes to meet Maxine's, 'and she wore it.'

She looked again at Maxine's throat.

'That pendant.'

As they returned to Harriet's in her car, she elaborated.

'Susannah, typically thought it was just hysterical, she went on about *fraternizing with the plebs*, thankfully not in Angela's hearing.' Harriet paused as she negotiated a roundabout, smiling at the memory.

'A couple of weeks afterwards, I got a note thanking me for my hospitality, hoping we could get together soon, and enclosing a complete set of the photographs! I'm sure there'll be some of Susannah amongst them. We'll have a look when we get home.'

Susannah was indeed in three of Angela's photographs. One was a three-quarters view of her, partly hidden behind someone's shoulder, and the second was a back-view, but the third clearly showed Susannah face-on, and the pendant around her neck.

Silently Maxine took her own pendant off and laid it beside its photographic facsimile.

She looked bleakly up at Harriet, and then reached for the phone.

*   *   *

Chris's eyes clouded as he heard about the pendant, bought on the internet, and the apparent likelihood that Angela had stolen that too, and sold it on, which may implicate her in Susannah's murder. It took DS Talbot mere minutes to go through Pippa's computer and find the details of her purchase of the pendant that Harriet had recognised.

Janice Jones of Keele had sold that pendant,

and the sale had been perfectly legitimate. E-bay had been keen to co-operate, and had provided all the details. She had apparently bought and sold goods on an occasional basis over the past three years, and there was nothing to suggest that she was either a professional dealer, nor that any of the goods were the subject of criminal activity.

He had trawled the records for Ms Jones. She had no criminal record, but something had rung a bell with him, either about the name or the address – he could not be sure which.

Questions around uniform branch had proved his hunch to be correct. Janice Jones had been admitted to the University Hospital of North Staffordshire a few weeks earlier. She had been the victim of a serious assault by a boyfriend she had dumped. Broken ribs, broken nose, and she had lost the baby she had been carrying. PC Hughes had taken her statement at the time.

'She was frightened,' he confided when DS Talbot tracked him down in the canteen. She had not been prepared to say whether her assailant was the father of the child, and had seemed relieved rather than distressed about the miscarriage – she was more concerned about the visual effect of the broken nose. She had refused to press charges.

Leaving PC Hughes to finish his bagel in peace, the detective sergeant flourished a document in front of the Inspector, giving Ms Jones's address in Keele. DI Timothy listened carefully, then once again the two headed out of the building, this time towards Keele.

Chapter 35

The police arrived at Janice Jones's early in the evening. She had just served out her meal, and continued to fork it into her mouth as she spoke.

'Sorry,' she said, 'need to get this while it's hot.' She sat upright on the sofa, the loaded and steaming plate perched precariously on her knees. The spicy aroma reminded DS Talbot that it was a long time since lunch, and his stomach growled noisily.

'S'cuse me,' he whispered, opening his notebook.

'Now, Ms Jones,' DI Timothy began with a smile, 'an item has come into our possession that I believe once belonged to you. We need you to help us, okay?'

'Sure,' said Janice, safe in the knowledge that boyfriend Ken would be away for some weeks yet, and need know nothing of all this. As long as he never learned about the pregnancy, she was happy to share information with the police, and then to draw a line under the whole business.

'What do you need to know?'

DI Timothy showed her photographs of the opal pendant that had been taken from Scot Hay before Christmas.

'Yeah,' she said, looking at the pictures, 'Yeah, I sold it on e-bay. Someone in Manchester bought it. I sent it through the post. She got it all right 'cos she left feedback. Why?'

Ignoring her question, the detective continued,

'Where did you acquire the pendant?'

'Ah,' she looked at him steadily as she scooped up the last forkful of pilau rice, using her finger to make sure she missed none. DS Talbot's stomach grumbled again, causing Janice to flash him a quick smile. She tucked her feet underneath her, and took time to gather her thoughts while she set the plate down on the floor.

After a moment, she settled herself back into the sofa, pulling a cushion round to her lap where she hugged it.

'A friend gave it to me as a present. He was just a ship that passed in the night, no-one special.' She paused, her fingers plucking nervously at the cushion's piping. The Inspector knew when to give a witness thinking time. The sergeant hoped his alimentary system would not punctuate the silence.

'Okay,' she said, suddenly reaching a decision, 'This was someone I knew slightly at school,' and she gave an abridged version of her relationship with Gary, leaving out the violent aspects of their dealings.

The Inspector remained quiet, then said,

'We will need his name.'

Janice blanched, and he recognised her fear. She bit her lip, and subconsciously rubbed her ribs with her left hand.

'I'm not sure,' she hesitated, 'I know his name of course but he wasn't very nice when I finished with him.'

The Inspector stepped in before she could give herself any more reasons for not cooperating, saying sternly,

'Then we shall have to charge you with

wasting police time, a serious offence Ms Jones.' He let her digest this then went on more gently, 'We can of course check every male you were at school with, but that will take time, and with this man, frankly, we don't have that luxury. Now, we need his name.'

He waited, staring at her solidly. Eventually she sighed and stood up, throwing the cushion down on the sofa behind her.

'Inspector, his name is Gary Lewis. He lives in Knutton.' She put her hand up to her forehead.

'I can't remember the exact address, I'm sorry,'

'That's all right, Miss, what does he look like?'

'He's late teens, very thin and about six foot one or two. He stoops a bit, deep voice, His hair he wears very long at the front, and sort of sweeps it across one eye.' She looked out of the window a moment, making unfavourable mental comparisons with Ken. 'His hair is very shiny; he could do shampoo adverts you know; and his,' she fingered her throat, 'his Adam's apple sticks out.'

'Thank you, miss, that's a very clear description.'

She raised her eyes to his and held his gaze steadily, 'I can tell you one thing more about him. He's a sadistic bastard.'

Chapter 36

By Monday, Gary was desperate. He needed someone who knew more about computers. He had to sell some of the jewellery and stuff he had nicked. Again he thought of Emma. He planned what he was going to say, then keyed into Susannah Scott-Ryder's phone, the number he had memorised in the pub.

'Emma? Gary. Look is Simon there? No? Are you seeing him later? No, that's okay, it's you I want really. I'm having some problems with my computer, could you help? Yes, yes. Great – shall I come to you or...okay. Yes, I know the address. About eight o'clock then? See ya.'

Gary arrived promptly at eight, having had just enough time to tidy up a bit, and call at the off licence for a bottle of wine. To his embarrassment, he had to change his initial choice for a cheaper one, as he had insufficient cash. It did nothing to improve his mood.

'I thought Janice would have helped you with this,' Emma began as he took of his jacket. He glanced across at her, noticing once again her voluptuous figure.

'I've not seen Janice for a while,' Gary was nonchalant. 'We're not joined at the hip you know.'

Emma drank half the glass of wine in one go, and dropped the stone in the pool.

'I wondered if perhaps she was busy with her preparations,' but Gary was too intent on fishing in his pocket for the watch he had brought, to notice the ripples. The watch had fallen through a hole in the lining and he had to empty out several other items of jewellery to be able to get at it. He placed the laptop from Scot Hay impatiently on the desk beside her, as he struggled.

'What is it you want doing?'

She drained the glass and leaned forward, showing a vast amount of bosom as she plugged in and flicked on the computer. Typing swiftly on the key pad she said,

'You should protect this with a password. I can't find anything wrong here, Gary, what exactly were you trying to do?'

Gary had planned his story. He reckoned that if he could persuade Emma to demonstrate how to sell this one item of jewellery, he could use the same description over and over for the other pieces. That, and a photo of each, which she could show him how to upload, should be good enough.

He produced the watch, and explained what he wanted. But Emma was only half listening, she was rapidly pressing buttons so that different screens appeared, and she was reading what was written on the various documents and emails. Turning her back to him, she asked,

'Whose is this computer, Gary? Where did you get it from?'

'It was my Aunty Angela's,' Gary thought on his feet, 'She changed it at Christmas, and gave me her old one.'

Emma turned to face him. It was just feasible.

'Okay, Gary, pour me another drink then, and we'll get this sold for you.' As he poured she said in a playful voice, a smile on her lips.

'I just wondered about Janice you know,

because she'll have things to do, with Ken coming home in a few weeks, and planning for the wedding and all.'

'Ken?' He paused, 'Who's Ken? What wedding?' Gary felt the colour drain from his face. He stood very still.

'Her boyfriend, well fiancé really, they'll be getting married soon. She told me last time I saw her. Have you not met Ken? He's in the army. I wondered if you knew them both, as a couple like?'

She drained her glass and held it out to him again, watching his face with her mischievous smile, but he said nothing.

Turning back to the computer, she started to type, speaking aloud as she did so.

'Okay, let's see what we've got. Gents' watch, gold bracelet, black face. Pass the phone will you, with the photo you took of it.'

Taking the phone from him, she accessed its photo memory. There were several photos flanking the one of the watch, each of a different item of jewellery.

'Whose was the watch Gary, it's not yours is it? She glanced at his wrist, where he already wore a watch; then her smile faded as she continued looking through the phone – calls made; calls received; texts inbox.

Gary was like a coiled spring. The air was heavy with tension. Slowly she looked up at him.

'This stuff is stolen isn't it?' she challenged him, narrowing her eyes. He remained silent, staring at her.

'Gary,' she said very quietly, 'Who is Susannah?'

Chapter 37

The first blow caught her totally unawares. Gary's fist slammed into her face, banging her head back against the door jamb. Thankfully, she lost consciousness almost immediately and slid into oblivion onto the floor, into the pools of blood pouring from her nose and the wound in her head.

She didn't feel the computer slammed down onto her shoulder, nor did she hear the bone break. But Gary was not finished yet. He picked up a chair and smashed it down over Emma's legs, then pummelled and kicked her as she lay unaware.

That's for you, cow,' he muttered over and over through gritted teeth, then, energy spent for the moment, he looked down at her, breathing hard.

'And you won't be flashing those tits around anymore.' Gary took up a pair of scissors from the desk.

*   *   *

As he left and slammed the door hard enough for the house to shake, the next door neighbour peered out from behind her net curtains. She was talking into the phone.

'Yes, ambulance, quick as you can. I can't do anything – I'm eighty-two but there's been such a fight next door. Oh, there's someone coming out. Oh no, I don't know him. It's a young girl lives there, in the flat next to my house. He's wearing dark jeans and a zipped jacket. Long hair, very long at the front, and a hat, sort of grey or dark blue. He's getting into a car. I can't see the number but it's blue, he's turning towards Newcastle at the end of the road.

'I don't know his name. I've never seen him before.' She replaced the phone and remained at her vantage point, too timid to come out, but not wanting to miss out on any excitement. As she stood awaiting the ambulance, she saw Clyde arrive home and told him what had happened. He dashed up to find Emma semi-conscious. She was just able to say a few words before she lapsed again into blessed oblivion.

*   *   *

Despatched to collect the print from Emma's, PC Thomas arrived ahead of the ambulance and hard on the heels of Clyde, who had arrived to pay Emma's brother his owed rent. Clyde took one look inside the room, and, once assured that the ambulance was on its way, he thought it expedient to leave.

In the following weeks, Emma's neighbour would tell everyone she met that the police were marvellous – they had arrived within seconds of her putting the phone down.

After a hurried conversation with the paramedics, in which she learned of a vicious attack on the young woman that had left her unconscious, the young PC rang into the station. She then secured the flat and awaited the arrival of CID, before going on to the hospital. The call had been taken by DS Talbot, who immediately relayed the information to the inspector.

'Sir, Simon Napier's girlfriend has been badly beaten up in her flat. Emma Francis. Paramedics say she's critical sir. They've taken her to North Staffs Hospital. She's not going to be talking to anyone for a while. I've sent PC Thomas to wait for her to regain consciousness. A neighbour has contacted the girl's brother. He's on his way.

Arriving at the flat, the two detectives took in the scene as they donned protective gloves.

'It looks like Emma's implicated in the burglaries too, sir.' The constable was bagging the medals stolen from Maxine's cottage. Jewellery from both crimes was still spread over the bed, where Gary had tipped it as he searched for the watch.

Not so sure about this, DI Timothy moved to look at Susannah's laptop, which was still open where it had crashed to the floor, displaying a page on e-bay, with an offer of a watch for sale part-completed.

If Emma were implicated, why was she so relaxed whilst he had been scrutinising the William Russell Flint print on his previous visit?

They bagged and removed all these small items, as well as the print, having established with some satisfaction that the edition number matched the one stolen from Miner's Cottage.

Chapter 38

Simon had been trying to phone Emma since eight o'clock, but still he was just getting the answering service. 'For God's sake, Emma old thing, what are you up to? Answer the bloody phone. Look, have you seen Gary this evening? I need to talk to him. I'll wait in the pub ten more minutes, then I'm going home. Call me.'

*   *   *

Gary had fled from Emma's in a blind panic. How he got away without crashing the van he would never know. Think, think.

Once again his memory served him well. The Scot Hay house was in darkness as before, but this time instead of approaching it directly, he skirted round by the tennis courts to the outbuildings. Here he got a shock. Even by torchlight he could see that the ramshackle doors and fastenings had been repaired and painted, now carrying substantial padlocks.

Prowling around the buildings, he found one door which could be opened, being secured only on a latch. He entered the building, and found it contained a sink and a pile of large flattened cardboard boxes, and a few gardening tools on a shelf. Cursing himself for not calling at home to collect a sleeping bag, he settled down on the boxes and tried to sleep.

*   *   *

Christopher Timothy stopped off at the hospital on his way into work next morning. Emma Francis was still in a critical state and would not be talking for some time. She was being prepared for surgery and would be in theatre for most of the day.

As the inspector arrived at Merrial Street the desk sergeant was on the phone. He excused himself and covered the mouthpiece.

'Sir, you may want to take this. It's the estate agent who's handling the Scott-Ryder house.'

Reaching his office the DI picked up the phone.

'I'm sorry to trouble you,' the caller began, 'but of course we are all familiar with the situation that the Scott-Ryder family have endured, and I was concerned. I am the estate agent handling the sale of the house.

'I went early this morning to Scot Hay with a gentleman who is interested in the property, and as I was waiting for him to look around I happened to be looking out of the window of one of the top floor bedrooms. That particular window overlooks the old stable block and the dairy, and I saw someone come out of the dairy and hurry round the back of the building out of sight.'

'Description?' Inspector Timothy pulled a pad towards him and uncapped his pen, repeating the description as he wrote it down: 'Late teens, early twenties. Tall, yes, dark and thin. Long shiny hair, swept to the side, and a woollen hat?' He paused, 'And what time did you say this was? Thank you sir, thank you very much. Yes, I'll send someone down to take a statement.'

DS Talbot knocked on the door and came into

the office with the usual morning cups of coffee and teacakes.

'Where have we heard lately about a tall, thin, very dark young man, late-teens, who wears his hair long at the front, swept to one side, and with a woolly hat?'

'Witness who lives next door to Emma Francis in Fenton. Simon Napier's girlfriend who has attacked last night. She's still unconscious by the way.' Talbot responded, taking his teacake, 'At least,' he referred to his notebook, 'she's in an induced coma. Apparently that means she's being kept unconscious so that her brain has time to recover from the pressure caused by the injuries. Poor kid.

'Erm, Janice Jones's attacker.'

'And....' he broke off, his mouth full of toasted teacake, and leafed his way through the piles of papers pertaining to the murder enquiry and to the burglaries,

'Yes, here we are.' He handed the paper across the desk, 'It also fits the description of the guy who tried to sell Ms Chapman's medals on Leek Market.' He wiped butter off his mouth.

'The medals we found at Emma's flat. Gary Lewis. He's the missing link. Finish your teacake sergeant, we're going to Scot Hay. We'll need backup. I'll fill you in on the way.' ·

Arriving at the Scot Hay farmhouse, they saw the gardener's van pulled up at the back of the yard. The door to the dairy was open.

The inevitable cigarette hanging from his mouth he said,

'Someone's been using my old jacket. I leave it hung on the back of the door here,' he thrust a hand into the pocket, 'and they've pinched me bloody fags.'

'Have a look around, is anything else missing?' The detectives looked at the rough bed made out of cardboard boxes.

'Hard to say. Giles left some tools in here for me to get at, everything else being locked up.' He was about to finger the trowel and spade but the DS told him not to touch anything. A phone call to Giles Scott-Ryder established that as well as the trowel and spade there had been garden scissors, not very sharp, and a garden fork. Nothing more.

* * *

Gary had been sleeping rough since Friday and was dirty, cold and hungry. He was also desperate for a cigarette. Over a wakeful Friday night he had smoked all the cigarettes he had found in the foul-smelling waterproof jacket, and had used it as a makeshift blanket.

* * *

The young man spent a few moments looking at Emma from the foot of her bed in the Intensive Care Unit. She was attached to machines and her face and head were heavily bandaged. Some sort of cage was keeping the bedclothes off her legs. Under the developing bruises, her face was ghostly pale. Nurses bustled around the machines. She had recovered consciousness briefly, but was now in a state of induced coma to aid her recovery. Her brother had spent hours at her bedside, and had now gone home to rest, leaving behind the Sentinel he had been reading.

After a few moments, a white-coated doctor, who looked very young, entered the room. He went first to the monitoring panel on the machine. Only when he had referred to the chart hooked over the base of the bed, and consulted with the attendant nurse, did he turn his attention to Emma's visitor.

'Relative?' he was brusque, allowing no nonsense.

'Er, no, just a… er….friend.'

'You'll have to wait outside. Waiting room on the left at the end of the corridor.'

Thus dismissed and with the newspaper thrust into his hand, the young man paced up and down the waiting room. He sat for a while, trying to concentrate on what he was reading then, flinging open the double doors, he crashed down the stairs and out to the car park. Slamming the car into gear, he accelerated away towards Audley.

*   *   *

Returning to the station with Gary Lewis, who had been detained in Madeley, DS Talbot took the call that came through from forensics. Two sets of fingerprints in addition to Emma's, were identifiable on the William Flint print; those of Maxine and a very clear set of prints belonging to Simon Napier.

PC Thomas, having been relieved of observation duty at the hospital, had been sent to bring Angela Davies in for further questioning.

The sample of Gary Lewis's DNA collected from his room, proved a match with unidentified hairs found in Susannah Scott-Ryder's car.

Clyde went to the hospital trying to find Simon, but Emma's brother was alone in the family room, sitting with his head in his hands.

'I thought Simon might be here. I brought him this, it was on the floor in her room.'

He took out the phone he had picked up from Emma's floor before he fled.

'Maybe you should have it.' He handed it over.

'What happened?'

I went home and Emma's door was open. I stuck my head in and found her like this. I didn't hang around I can tell you. Just grabbed her phone and ran.'

'Did she tell you who did it?'

'Yeah, she was just about conscious for long enough to name Gary Lewis.'

Emma's brother was looking at the phone.

'This isn't Emma's. I'm going to the police.'

*   *   *

The ten o'clock news had just finished when there was a knock at the door again. Angela was once again sitting watching the television in the grubby dressing gown, having been brought home by police car. Probably that nosey neighbour, she thought, unable to contain herself any longer, coming round to see what was going on. Angela had spotted her peering through the curtains when the distinctive panda car drew up, and had hurried up the path to avoid conversation.

Now Angela flung open the door furiously, 'What the hell do you want?' Then she stopped, gazing open-mouthed at the young man before her.

'Hello Angela, I think we need a little talk. I have a proposition to put to you.'

*   *   *

At first it looked as if the victim was simply sitting on the floor, head slumped to one side, ignoring them, but why would anyone sit on the floor in a cupboard under the stairs? As they moved the body gently to get a better look, they could see that there were a number of gaping wounds clearly visible through the open clothing, and the blood – copious amounts of blood, that had seeped into the surrounding floorboards, and had pooled on the lino.

*   *   *

This time one look at that distinctive hair and they knew at once the identity of the victim.

Chapter 39

The arrangement was to meet at the Moat House at Acton Trussell for lunch. It would be a chance to clarify what had happened. It was too soon for a celebration, but Chris Timothy had only one more job to do at the station this afternoon, before he could consider this case closed.

Chris and Pippa arrived first and sat outside, awaiting their companions. The detectives had been up all night and the sergeant had been sent home for some sleep, but Chris felt that these three women needed a full explanation from him, before they read the details in the Sentinel. The lunch was by way of a celebration, albeit muted, that the investigation was now all but over. Pippa was eager for information.

'I know you said you wanted to talk to us all together, but what I can't understand is Angela's role. I know she didn't intend it, but is there nothing other than the thefts she can be charged with? She was the catalyst for all this, after all.'

Chris put a restraining hand on Pippa's arm, as the two retrievers bounded over to them, and they looked up to see Harriet and Maxine approaching across the grass.

'Let me get you both a drink,' Chris stood up, 'then I can tell you all you want to know.'

It took some minutes for the drinks to come, and the dogs to finish their greetings. Jasper flopped under the table, whilst Hettie sat leaning on Harriet's leg, watching a pair of swans glide by.

'It all falls into place.' He took a sip of his drink and replaced the glass on the table. 'Simon

Napier had used the internet to set up burglaries. Not that he carried them out, of course – he hadn't the guts. He met Gary Lewis by accident. They got talking, and it transpired that Gary had been thieving on and off since his early teens. He was known to us, and had spent some time in Werrington YOI.

'Angela Davies was one of Napier's potential victims but, just as he abused the technology, so did she. She sent him all Susannah's details – like a fantasy life. She both despised and was fascinated by her employer. When Susannah went missing, Angela had no idea of her own involvement, she just transferred her obsession to Giles, seeing herself as taking Susannah's place.'

'It was surreal the way she stole Susannah's identity almost,' said Pippa, 'but how did she manage to post Dubai photos on the internet? She'd never stalked him there, surely?'

Chris shook his head.

'No, although she might have done if she'd had any money. She used his photo store. She was really quite knowledgeable about technology. She bought a camera on the internet last summer, not knowing that the seller was Gary Lewis. She found an IT class locally, and enrolled to learn how to use it, one of these subsidised classes that cater for our ever-growing collection of technology. Of course, the camera came with no instructions because Gary had stolen it.

'She had a real aptitude, and she was able to use Giles's computer at Scot Hay to upload his stored photographs - of the house, of Susannah and her car, and of Dubai. Gary had no idea how close he came to his intended victim. Having sold her a camera on-line, he subsequently enrolled in the same class himself after Christmas.'

He chose his words with care.

'Simon Napier of course believed that the photos were genuine, and that Gary Lewis had double-crossed him when he said that he hadn't been able to do the job. Then, as the details appeared in the Sentinel, he didn't know what to think, especially as Angela said nothing about it in her emails. When the car was found, and then Susannah's body,' he glanced at Maxine, 'he couldn't very well ask her.'

Chris ran his hand wearily over his eyes.

'Gary believed that Napier had set him up – the woman supposed to be in Dubai came home, and landed him in trouble. Then later poor Emma became involved in Gary's attempt to get back at Napier by using his girlfriend to help sell the goods.

'In Gary's eyes, keeping that stuff from the burglaries had been getting one over on Simon. Like Susannah, Emma genuinely was an innocent bystander. She's in a coma still. It's possible she may never recover.'

Pippa shuddered and cuddled more closely to the dog that was leaning against her leg. 'I'll feel better once that Gary Lewis is behind bars.'

Chris glanced at her affectionately.

'Gary Lewis has been charged with Susannah's murder, as well as other lesser crimes,' was all he was initially prepared to say.

'It isn't right that Angela and the other man should get off scot free.' Harriet was very upset. 'She's an evil woman, and he was the mastermind behind it all. If it wasn't for what they did Susannah would still be alive.' She twisted her earring abstractedly.

Chris looked at her levelly.

'Neither of them has got away with it, Harriet. All your father's goods that we have obtained from Angela's house will be returned to him - all the stolen goods in fact.' He looked again at Maxine and rubbed the side of his nose with a forefinger.

'Angela won't be prosecuted for her part in Susannah's death though, and neither will Napier.' He shifted his glass, making rings of condensation on the table top.

Maxine protested.

'It was all Angela's fault that Susannah died, and she's getting away with it, and him – the Napier person who planned it all. I know it wasn't his intention that Susannah would die, but it all came about through him. Why won't they be charged?'

For a minute Chris said nothing, continuing to make patterns with his glass. Then he took a deep breath, and continued as if she had not spoken.

'Simon Napier realised that correspondence he had had with Angela online incriminated him in the burglaries. By default he could therefore be implicated in Susannah's death.'

He went on quietly, 'He set up two failed attempts to retrieve Angela's laptop and the information it contained.

'Firstly, he sent Gary round to steal it, but she and the laptop were at Merrial Street. We had taken her in for questioning because of your reports of theft.'

He leaned over to pat one of the dogs, who responded by placing her chin on his knee. He continued as Harriet made to interrupt.

'Angela's next door neighbour has identified Gary. She saw him, and spoke to him as he left the house.' He paused and took a sip of his drink.

'The second attempt,' He gave a sidelong look at Pippa, and covered her hand with his own, 'was by Clyde, who posed as a water board official.'

He watched her face closely as Pippa closed her eyes, then he squeezed her hand gently and continued.

'By that time it was late afternoon, Angela had been released on bail, but we were still trawling through her laptop, so he didn't find it either. He reported back to Simon, who was beside himself with worry. He decided that he had to go himself.'

Chris paused to consider his words.

'Going back for a minute to Christmas-time. Gary had panicked when he realised that Susannah was dead. He had hit her with a torch, which we later found in his room. DNA tests showed a match with hair caught in the head of the torch. He had also left a cigarette stub in her car, and that contained a match to his DNA. He had used a wheelbarrow he stole in Silverdale to wheel her into Bateswood.

'We found him the morning after he attacked Emma. He had been hiding in the dairy at Scot Hay – of course your father had already moved out and the house was empty, but the estate agent saw him. By the time we got there he had gone, but he was picked up trying to steal some bread in Madeley.

'As DS Talbot brought Angela in for questioning that second time, so Gary Lewis was brought in by uniformed officers. They met on the police station steps, but neither knew the other, nor had any idea of how inextricably their fates had been linked.

Pippa and Maxine stared at him, amazed.

'Oh, my God,' said Maxine. 'But what about my picture? How did Emma come to have that?'

Chris smiled ruefully.

'She saw it in Simon's room, liked it and he gave it to her. We spotted it when we went to check on Simon's alibi, and realised that the edition number matched. Then, when we checked it for fingerprints there were Emma's, yours and Simon's.'

He took a deep breath, 'To answer your question of a few minutes ago, Maxine, Simon Napier was so terrified of being locked up that he went round to Angela's determined to steal her laptop and destroy the evidence. He went the next day and he challenged her. By that time we had had her back in for questioning again, because we had found the link to Susannah and the Kevin scam on her laptop, but we were confident that she wasn't implicated in stealing the pendant, or in Susannah's death, so she had once again been released.

'She had already seen Simon of course, posing as someone interested in purchasing the Scot Hay farmhouse.

'We don't exactly know yet the detail of what happened when he went and confronted her, except that she tried to bluff it out, and that he was found dead in the cupboard under her staircase the next morning.

'What tipped the balance was her rejection by Giles. Having spent months trying to inveigle herself into his world, she now had nothing to lose.'

There was a stunned silence.

Chapter 40

Sitting alone in his office at the end of that afternoon, DI Timothy read the pertinent part of Angela Davies' statement.

I opened the door and there was a young man I had met before. He had come to the house at Scot Hay and told me his name was David Grant.

This time he said that his real name was Simon Napier, and that he wanted my laptop. I decided to let him in and see what was going on. He eventually told me that he had pretended to be his father, who went to my school. I was very upset that he had lied to me, and cross that he kept asking for the laptop over and over. I didn't have the laptop because the police have it. I decided that I would get back at him. I didn't say that the police had my laptop but I told him that they hadn't been able to find it because I had hidden it.

I told him that there was a trapdoor in the cupboard under the stairs and it opened onto a space below the floorboards. This is true. I told him that the laptop was hidden in this space and he could get it if he wanted.

When he went into the kitchen I followed him, saying he'd need something to prise the floorboards up. I picked up some scissors from the counter. He opened the door to the cupboard and I could see he was frightened. I had noticed at Scot Hay that he was scared to go into a small enclosed room there.

I gave him a push and at the same time I stabbed at him with the scissors again and again. I heard him grunt, but I did not look to see where the scissors cut into him. I slammed and bolted the door and turned off the light. He called out for a bit and I could hear scratching, then it went quiet and I just went to bed.

In the morning I went to look at him and he was dead. He had tried to get out because there were scratch marks on the paintwork on the door, and his fingernails were all ripped. I took the scissors out of him and washed them up. Then I put them back in the drawer. I am not sorry for what I did. He deserved it for what he did to me.

Running fingers through his hair Chris said to himself,

'That was Angela's final mistake.' He pulled his jacket off the back of his chair, switched off the light and went home.

Chapter 41

The boxes were piled outside Miner's Cottage and Chris Timothy, sleeves literally and metaphorically rolled up, was hefting them into his car. As it was DS Talbot's day off, he too had been roped in to help.

'Stop moaning, Pete,' Chris told him as the junior officer staggered through the door, part-hidden under an armful of clothes, 'If you ever grow up enough to leave the nest, I'll give you a hand.'

'I beg your p....' the indignation died out of Pete Talbot's voice, 'Oh, very funny.'

'That's the lot.' Maxine appeared in the doorway, 'Cup of coffee before you go?'

'Tell you what, Maxine,' Pete moved into the planned manoeuvre, 'I'll take the first lot of these and start unloading at Chris's house, whilst you say your goodbyes.'

'He makes it sound like the two of you are going to be miles away, not just in the next village.' Maxine laughed as she led Chris back into the cottage.

'Pippa's just checking that she's not missed anything upstairs. She'll be down in a minute.'

She led Chris into the living room. 'I'd like you two to have this.' She withdrew the William Russell Flint print from behind the sofa, where it had been since the police returned it to her.

'I'm not sure I want it back on the wall in here, and I know Pip's always liked it.'

Chris put his arm lightly across her shoulder,

'That's lovely of you. I'm sure Pippa will like to have it. But what about your bare wall?'

'Oh, I've got a big job coming in at the beginning of next month, at least eighteen months' work, so I shall be able to treat myself to a replacement.'

Chris smiled at Pippa who had come into the room. 'I think we should take the dogs out for a walk, the three of us before we go over to Leycett,' he said, fondling Jasper's ears, 'I'm going to miss you guys.'

Hearing the magic 'w' word, both dogs were now dashing in giddy circles around the room.

'Come on,' he said getting up, 'get your leads.'

As they went along the bridle path, Pippa took Maxine's arm.

'Let's go down Narnia. It's time.'

So for the first time in nearly ten months, Maxine and the two dogs turned off the bridle path at the large patch of gorse and the picnic table, where they had waited for the police all those months ago.

The dogs seemed to recognize the significance of the moment, staying close to the two women and from time to time looking up at Maxine's face.

It was autumn now, and beginning to go dusk already. The shadowy birch trees were swaying in the wind, and Maxine could clearly hear the soft babble of water down the drainage ditches. She stopped awhile at the entrance to Narnia. Quietly she smiled to herself.

Chris took Pippa's hand. 'I thought it would be a good idea, to lay the ghosts.'

'That's what I thought I would be doing,' said Maxine, 'but there are no ghosts, just beautiful countryside as there always has been.' Pippa put her arms through her mother's.

Chris fell into step beside them, and they walked down the path past the pit memorial and back to Miner's Cottage.

21446129R00174

Printed in Great Britain
by Amazon